DUTY FROM ASHES
Honor and Duty
Book 2

Sam Schall

Hunter's Moon Press

2014

OTHER TITLES

Vengeance from Ashes
Honor from Ashes (coming Spring 2015)

DUTY FROM ASHES

Sam Schall

Hunter's Moon Press

ISBN-13: 978-0692455661
ISBN-10: 0692455663

Cover art: Space Pilot and Spaceship by Innovari
Cover design by Sarah A. Hoyt

If you enjoyed this novel, please check out http://nocturnal-lives.com for more titles.

Thank you for your support.

DEDICATION

To my son, who makes me proud every day of the week and who understands the true meaning of the words honor and duty.

DUTY FROM ASHES

HONOR AND DUTY
Book 2

Sam Schall

2014

GEAR UP!

CHAPTER ONE

SMOKE FILLED THE AIR AND THE GROUND SHOOK BENEATH HER boots as another explosion sounded. It was close this time. Too close. Cursing, she ducked behind the makeshift barricade she and her team had erected outside the school and tried to catch her breath. As she did, the tell-tales from her battle armor warned that her heart was racing and her breathing was labored, not that she needed the onboard computer to confirm what she already knew. This was her worst nightmare come to life and, just like the last time, there had been no way to avoid it.

But she'd be damned if it ended the same way as before.

Not this time.

Carefully, she inched forward until she could see around the edge of the barricade. As she did, dirt and rock kicked up just inches from where she knelt as yet another round of enemy fire filled the air. Even as her team returned fire, she scanned the area, flipping through the various screens of her HUD. Then her lips pulled back in an almost feral smile.

There!

Finally, she'd located the last of the areas where the enemy had dug in. Now it was time to show them just how foolish they'd been to think they could get the drop on her and her team.

"Boomer, two o'clock. The culvert near the edge of the first building." Once again, she cycled through the various filters on her HUD, taking careful note of what each told her. "Scans show six bogies. Looks like one SAM and three unknown heavy weapons. We'll give you cover fire so your team can move into position. Hold your fire until I give the order. We need to take those guns out before they decide to turn their attention to the school."

"Roger that, Angel."

"Hound, second target's yours. Same building. Four stories up. Third window from the corner. I spotted at least one sniper." She paused and scanned the area, looking for any indication the enemy had hostages with them. As much as she'd like to just level the building and be done with it, she couldn't. Not if there were civilians inside and, knowing the Callusians, there would be. One of the first lessons they'd learned in the last war was that the enemy never hesitated to hide behind innocents. "I'm not picking up any other life signs in the immediate area but that doesn't mean much. They could have hostages elsewhere in the building so remember your target zone." She waited for his response, knowing he was calculating the best way to carry out her orders.

"Got it, Angel. I'll be ready on your order."

Her heart beat a little slower. So far, so good. Her team still had a chance to get out of this alive and, with a little luck, they would manage to save those civilians sheltering in the school and elsewhere.

Knowing their next move could mean victory or defeat, she called up the last data they had received on the enemy's movements. As she studied it, her mind did the one thing she'd been fighting to avoid since the battle began. It went back to that terrible day more than two years earlier. She had been in this exact location, fighting this same battle. Only then she'd been given compromised intelligence. As a result, she and her squad, a different one from this time, had walked straight into a trap. So many had died. She and the six who had managed to make it back to the shuttle for extraction had been lucky to get out of there alive. At least that's what she'd told herself. Of course, that had been before they were arrested, brought up on bogus charges, court martialed and sent to the Tarsus military prison.

Damn it! She couldn't think about that. She couldn't let the past distract her from what was happening right now. Not if she wanted her team to survive.

"We're almost in position, Angel," a voice reported over her comm a few moments later. Master Gunnery Sergeant Kevin "Loco" Talbot. Another asset, an invaluable one, and one she hadn't had on that previous mission.

"Roger that, Loco. Let me know when you are."

She paused, waiting to hear from the final team she'd sent out. As the seconds drew out into minutes that seemed like hours, her concern grew. She'd been forced to split her forces before with disastrous results. Was history repeating itself?

She licked her lips and fought the urge to message the last team. It was difficult, but she didn't. Instead, she reminded herself that they needed to move slowly and carefully to avoid detection. At least she hadn't heard anything from the direction they'd taken that might indicate they'd been discovered. Surely that had to be a good sign.

Stop it!

She closed her eyes and breathed deeply. Her emotions and doubts were running too high. She had to get them under control. This was her command, her mission. If she couldn't hold it together, they would fail. But she couldn't think about that. She couldn't let herself be distracted by the dead, hers and the civilian lives that had been lost in that previous battle.

This wasn't the time to let distractions in.

Finally, just as she was about to give up and demand an update, her comm came to life.

"We're in position, Angel. We have four bogies and we're ready to paint them," Captain Lucinda Ortega reported.

"Hold position, Sorceress. I say again, hold position until we confirm air support."

"Roger that, Angel."

"Eagle, are you ready to paint your target?"

"Eagle is ready, Angel," the squad's sniper replied.

"Alpha Team, prepare to lay down cover fire. Boomer, the moment we do, you and your team haul ass and take out those heavy guns and that SAM."

"Roger that, Angel. Beta Team is ready."

She nodded, not that the demolitions expert could see her, and drew a deep, steadying breath. A quick check of her battle rifle and she was ready. It was now or never. With a glance at the four Marines crouching behind the barricade with her, she snugged the butt of the rifle against her shoulder.

"Now!"

She leaned around the corner of the barricade and opened fire. Instantly, the sounds of weapons — battle rifles, railguns and more — filled the air. Three of the four teams laid down heavy fire to cover the fourth team as it moved into position. On her HUD, three small green lights moved quickly toward the target zone. So far, so good.

"Almost there," Boomer's voice said in her ear.

"Keep it up, Devil Dogs. Don't give those bastards time to breathe, much less regroup."

"Fire in the hole!"

Boomer's shout was the only warning they'd get. Instantly, she set her visor to block the flash from the explosion even as she kept firing. At least this time when the ground shook, it would be working for them instead of against them.

"Keep firing!" she ordered. "Eagle, Sorceress, stand ready. I repeat, stand ready. Paint the targets on my signal. Once the air strike begins, we move in."

Without waiting for the teams to respond, she activated her 'link once again. "Angel to Kali, we are a go for the airstrike. I repeat, we are a go for the airstrike."

She waited, scanning the battlefield in front of her for any movement. Smoke and dust from the explosion filled the air. From the distance, she could hear the enemy. Some called for help. Some, those caught in the blast and not lucky enough to be granted a quick death, cried out for their mothers. A small part of her felt sorry for them. But another part, the soldier in her, knew it was either them or her and she much preferred living.

As she knelt there, ready to swing her rifle toward anyone who came her way, she imagined each member of her team wanting to look skyward, but keeping their eyes on the enemy locations, as they waited for the air support to come.

Air support that hadn't come that first time. Would it now?

"Angel, this is Kali. We are on approach. Paint the target. I say again, paint the target."

The voice coming over the battle-net was like an answer to her prayers. She relayed the message to the rest of her squad. As she did, she inched further around the edge of the barricade. Once in position, she raised one gloved fist, knowing the others were watching for her signal. Then she waited, knowing any number of things could still go horribly wrong and praying that they didn't.

Moments later, the sounds of the fighter wing racing in their direction filled the air. The target, six heavy ground transports that had been moving closer and closer to the Devil Dogs, exploded into a wall of flames as the fighters dropped their payloads. Instinct and training had the Marines diving for cover, any cover, as shrapnel from the transports flew through the air. Screams from the enemy soldiers unlucky enough to be caught in the open followed. Then, before the screams died out, she gave the order to move in.

"Take out those snipers!" she yelled as she sprinted across the clearing in the direction of the school.

Damn it, this time she would save those innocent bystanders huddling inside.

Hound, moving at a speed no human could without the assistance of powered battle armor, leapt from where he'd been taking cover. The moment he landed, he turned and leveled the grenade launcher that was currently his armor's primary weapon at the target. The building she had identified for him a few minutes earlier was soon missing part of its far side. Smoke billowed from the area where the sniper had been holed up. Someone would need a new office or apartment when this was all over. But, hopefully, they'd survived the fight and would be able to return home soon. Even as the thought came, she knew the truth could be far different. War was never clean, no matter what the politicians wanted. There was always the possibility of collateral damage, especially when the enemy had no compunctions about hiding behind a shield of innocents.

Ahead and to her left, a head popped up from the culvert. A split second later, it exploded. She smiled slightly as Eagle gave a war cry that almost split her skull. She'd remind him later about how that sort of thing sounded through the battle-net. Not that she blamed him. They had spent too much time hunkered down behind makeshift barricades and hiding in the shadows. It felt good to finally be on the move again. Now it was time to make the enemy pay for all they'd done.

"Angel, to your right!"

Loco's warning came at almost the same moment that her armor's sensors warned her of someone – or something – suddenly appearing and moving in her direction. She turned, bringing her combat rifle to bear. Her finger slipped behind the trigger guard and she felt her combat implants coming to life as she focused on the figure running hell bent for leather in her direction.

"Hold your fire!"

Without waiting for confirmation, she broke into a sprint, racing toward the small figure. The child couldn't be more than five or six. Where he had been hiding during the fighting she didn't know and, just then, she didn't care. Not when her armor's onboard computer was telling her that several of the enemy were bearing down on them.

She had to get to the child before he was hurt – or worse.

Without conscious thought, she switched out her battle rifle for her sidearm. Using the targeting system of her HUD, she laid down fire in the direction of the nearest enemy soldier. A scream of pain followed. Good. One down but who knew how many more to come.

Three more steps and she scooped the child up in her arms. He cried out as an enemy trooper appeared to the right and opened fire. Reacting on instinct, Angel shifted the child so he was shielded by her armor before returning fire. Then she pivoted, running in the direction of Loco and the rest of his team. They were laying down cover fire, forcing the enemy troopers to duck back down into the trench. At the same time, Sorceress was calling in air support. But that was all in the background as Angel focused on the child in her arms and the need to get him to safety.

"Down!"

Loco's shout was all the warning she needed. She dropped, sliding feet first toward the barricade. At the same time, Loco stepped forward, Tank and Hound on either side of him, and all hell seemed to break loose. As they opened fire with everything they had, so did the rest of the squad. If that wasn't enough, three Sabres, the newest and most deadly fighters the

Fuerconese Navy currently had in operation, screamed overhead and opened fire on the culvert.

The ground shook again and another explosion – no, a series of explosions – deafened her. Then there was silence, the kind of silence that really wasn't. Angel's pulse pounded and her breathing was ragged. The crackling of fire mixed with the heavy smoke that filled the air. She heard someone, one of her people, offering up a quick prayer of thanks. Someone else uttered a curse. For once, she agreed with both sentiments. Then she heard the boy whimper. Much as she wanted to reassure him, she couldn't. Not yet. She had to make sure the area was secure first.

Still cradling the child in her arms, Angel twisted around so she could look in the direction of the culvert. Nothing moved except for the smoke rising from it. Without warning, the silence was broken by a single shot to her left. Instantly, half a dozen battle rifles responded. Then nothing.

Barely daring to hope that it was over, Angel went to active scans. For several long moments, she studied the readouts on her HUD. The locations they had tagged as being held by the enemy were either showing red, indicating they were too hot for anyone – even armored – to survive or there were the tell tales of the dead and dying. Could it finally be over?

"Sound off!" she ordered as she carefully climbed to her feet.

As she did, the medic assigned to her squad hurried forward to take the child from her. Except the child had other ideas. He wrapped his arms and legs more firmly around her and burrowed in. with a jerk of her head, she motioned the medic off. She could spare the child a moment as she caught her breath and her people reported in.

One by one, each member of her team sounded off. A few sounded the worse for wear but she had lost no one that day. Thank God. The nightmare hadn't replayed in all its horror. It had come close, though, and she wanted to know why.

Relieved, she looked down into the child's face and the world came to a crashing halt. No! He couldn't be there. Damn it, he couldn't be there. As bad as that time had been, that would have made it worse, so much worse.

"End sim!" she ordered, ripping off her combat helmet. "I said to end the damned sim!"

CHAPTER TWO

EVERYTHING WENT DARK FOR A MOMENT. THEN THE LIGHTS CAME up and, with it, the return to reality. Gone was the battle torn landscape. Gone was the school building with the barricades before it. The smells of smoke and death lingered only in her memory. Instead of standing in the middle of a warzone, she stood in the center of a large room the size of a warehouse. Battle armor had been replaced by BDUs. Battle rifles and other arms had been replaced with training weapons. It hadn't been real.

Her team looked around for a moment, reorienting themselves, before moving in her direction. Despite the return to so-called normal conditions, nothing could hide the aftermath of what they'd been through. Each member of the squad looked as if they'd been through hell. Panting, sweating, exhausted from four hours of almost non-stop battle, it had been real for them.

Almost too real, at least for Major Ashlyn "Angel" Shaw.

"What the hell was that, Major?" Tank demanded as he turned to face her. "That wasn't what we were briefed on."

The others grumbled in response. At least they hadn't appreciated the change in mission parameters any more than had she.

"Quiet!" Ortega snapped, her eyes on their commanding

officer, her expression worried.

Ashlyn didn't respond. Instead, she closed her eyes and breathed deeply. She had to get control of her emotions before she said anything, even to her squad.

"Very good, Devil Dogs," a male voice said over a speaker hidden somewhere in the shadows. "You are dismissed. Debriefing for officers and senior NCOs in two hours. As a reminder, your squad is to report back here at 0800 hours tomorrow for your next training mission."

As if from a distance, Ashlyn heard her people grumbling in ill-temper. She knew it was a combination of frustration over the just completed *mission* as well as having to do it all over again come morning. Not that she blamed them, especially about the change in this particular *mission*. They had been given the parameters and had prepped accordingly. As their CO, she'd made sure of it, for all the good it had done them. Not a one of them, least of all her, had expected to find themselves suddenly on Arterus and in the middle of that thrice-damned firefight. The members of this particular squad might not have been on the original mission with her, but they had studied it. She'd insisted they be given access to her reports on what happened. But this, having them actually go through the scenario without at least giving her a heads up was too much. It was too close to being set up again and she wasn't going to stand for it.

And that didn't even begin to take into account her anger with whoever had the audacity to write her son into the sim. Someone had better have a damned good explanation for it or she wouldn't be responsible for what happened next.

"Major, did you know about this?" Sergeant Major MJ Adamson asked softly as she moved to Ashlyn's side.

"I did not." She forced herself not to turn and hit the wall – or the nearest person. "I have just one question for the rest of you. Did any of you know about this change in the mission parameters?" She waited, watching as they processed what she'd asked and knowing the answer before it came.

"Ma'am, no, ma'am!" each member of her team answered in unison.

She nodded, trying to rein in her anger. "Go hit the showers and then get some chow. Forget about the debriefing as well as the morning's mission until you hear from either Captain Ortega or myself." She held up a hand to ward of any argument. "And don't discuss what happened here with anyone, not even the other Devil Dogs. Not until you get the go ahead from me."

With that, she turned on her heel and moved toward the only entrance to the room. Her boot heels hitting the floor sounded loudly, a sure indication of just how angry she was. She didn't care. She wanted answers and they'd sure as hell better be good ones. Otherwise, she might just find herself back in the Tarsus military prison. At least if she did, she'd have earned the trip this time.

As she reached the door, she paused. A frown touched the corners of her mouth. For a moment, she looked at the three who had followed her and considered telling them to do as she'd ordered. Instead, she simply punched in the code to end the lockdown and stepped through the door as soon as it slid open. If the three meant to follow, they'd have to keep up.

Without a word, she moved through the corridor leading between the different simulation rooms toward the control room at the far end of the building. The few people they passed quickly made room for them. Whether they read the anger on her expression or it was just the sight of four members of the Fuerconese Marine Corps' best SpecOps battalion moving with undeniable purpose, she didn't know nor did she care.

The door to the control room slid open and she stepped inside. A split second later, silence filled the room as the junior officers and ratings manning the monitoring stations turned in her direction. Without a word, she glanced around, her anger rising. As if sensing it and knowing they didn't want her focus on them, everyone turned back to their stations and tried to look busier than they had been just a moment before. She knew what they were doing and didn't care. They weren't important, at least not just yet. Their only part in the sims was to monitor and record how the different groups reacted to the scenarios thrown at them. They had nothing to do with setting up the sims. That person was in the office beyond the control room, hiding, too much of a coward to come out to greet her.

"Major Shaw." A lieutenant with more guts than common sense hurried around his desk to intercept her before she could barge through the next door.

She stopped, the toes of her boots almost touching his, her hands fisting at her sides. "Lieutenant Young." She made a point of glancing down at his name tape since he hadn't identified himself, much less called the others to attention as senior officers entered the room. "Step aside."

"Ma'am, you know I can't do that."

She simply stared at him, her expression closed.

"What I know is that I outrank you, as well as everyone else in this room, by some magnitude, *Lieutenant*." A hand gently touched her arm and she turned, ready to tear into whoever had been foolish enough to interrupt her. Then, seeing her XO standing there, she nodded slightly. Something in Ortega's expression told her to let the other woman handle things, for the moment at least.

"Lieutenant Young, you happen to be the senior officer on duty, isn't that correct?" Ortega's voice was deceptively gentle but her eyes flashed dangerously. Recognizing it, Ashlyn closed her mouth and waited, wondering what her XO was up to.

"Yes, ma'am."

"As an officer, I assume you actually went to the Academy and passed your course work. Would that be a correct assumption?"

"Y-yes, ma'am." Sweat now beaded on his forehead and upper lip.

"And part of your time at the Academy was spent learning proper protocol when senior officers enter a room. Isn't that correct?"

A slight smile touched Ash's lips. Her XO – and one of her closest friends – was about to teach the poor lieutenant a lesson he wouldn't soon forget.

Young nodded.

"I'm sorry, Lieutenant, I didn't hear you." Ortega's voice turned cold.

"Yes, ma'am."

"And were you taught proper uniform appearance for both officers and enlisted personnel?"

"Y-yes, ma'am."

"Master Sergeant Adamson, please inform the good lieutenant of the number of uniform violations you spot on him with just a cursory inspection."

"Yes, ma'am." The blonde stepped forward and glanced almost casually at the young lieutenant who was starting to look more than a little green. "Without doing a proper inspection, Captain Ortega, I see at least eight violations of the uniform regulations."

"I see." She shook her head, her expression grim. "And the rest of the personnel in this room?"

"Ma'am, there are far too many to list without actually taking notes." Now Adamson's voice was as cold as Ortega's had been. "There is more than simple carelessness being shown in here, Captain."

"Master Guns, how many violations of protocol did you note as we entered the room?"

"Is the captain asking about what I saw as we immediately entered or since our arrival?" Talbot asked in return.

Ashlyn almost laughed as Young flinched and paled.

"Let's limit it to our immediate arrival."

"Then there were three actual violations of protocol and another two violations of common military courtesy," Talbot responded.

"And what would you do if someone assigned to the Devil Dogs failed to follow established protocol?"

"Well, Captain, I'd have them out on the O Course until they were ready to drop and then I'd have them standing watch, greeting every officer and NCO by rank and name for the next week."

Ashlyn considered telling her people that they had made their point. It wouldn't surprise her if, at any moment, the lieutenant either fainted or pissed his pants. No one enjoyed being dressed down the way he'd just been. If they were smart, they certainly didn't want it happening by two of the most well-respected NCOs in the Corps.

She held her tongue, however. Ortega was right to make an example out of him. He had violated protocol and his uniform, as well as most of the others in the room, did not come up to standard. If his CO wouldn't teach him the error of his ways, she'd let her XO and senior non-coms try.

"Master Sergeant, what would you do after seeing the sorry state of the uniforms in this room?"

"Well, ma'am, they'd be making sure every uniform in their company was properly cleaned and ready for wear. Then they would be polishing boots and brass until not only you but the major here were satisfied," Adamson answered, a slight smile touching her lips.

"Now, Lieutenant, I believe Major Shaw suggested you step aside so she can speak with your CO."

Ortega's voice was now deceptively calm, not that it would fool anyone with an ounce of sense in their head. Of course, Ashlyn wasn't sure Young possessed that much just then. She had a feeling he was too shell-shocked by the way he'd been handed his head to do anything but simply stand there, trying to look very small.

Young's green eyes flicked right and then left, as if he were looking for help or a quick exit, but neither came. Instead, silence filled the room as everyone waited for him to make his mind up about what he was going to do. As he did, Ashlyn fought the urge to smirk. The lieutenant had probably received the most thorough dressing down of his short Marine Corps career. What he eventually got out of it was up to him. Hopefully, it would make him a better officer. If not, he might just wind up getting people under his command killed should he ever see actual battle.

Before Young could decide what he was going to do, the door to the inner office slid open. A tall, grey haired man appeared. He took one look at the scene before him and shook his head, his mouth a firm line of disapproval. Then, with a curt nod to Ashlyn, he motioned for her to enter. When the others made to follow, he took a step to his right, barring their path.

"You really don't want to do that, *sir*." Ash rasped.

She might be skirting close to the edge of insubordination but she didn't care. Not after what happened during the sim. For whatever reason, this man had changed the parameters and, unless she missed her guess, had done so without proper authorization. She wanted to know why. Because of that, and because her temper was so close to boiling over, Ash was glad Ortega and the others had come with her. Their presence accomplished two things: it provided witnesses for whatever was said and it would keep her from doing something foolish.

Hopefully.

"Major Shaw." Lt. Colonel Kieran Brodsky's voice was cold, his expression hard. No doubt about it, he was almost as angry as was she.

At least he stepped out of the way and let the others enter his office. After closing the door behind them, he moved to sit behind his desk. Elbows on the desktop, fingers steepled before him, he pointedly did not invite Ashlyn to sit.

"You are skirting very close to finding yourself brought up on a charge of insubordination, Major," he said.

"Respectfully, sir, you are more than welcome to level that, or any other charge for that matter, against me. To be honest, I'd like to see you try to make it stick. Before you do, I suggest you remember that the ensuing investigation will force you to explain, on the record, why the parameters of the sim were changed without warning and why the new sim was nothing more than a replay of the mission that led to the false charges being brought against me and the surviving members of my team." The words were bitter in her mouth. "Then you'll be asked to explain why my son – my son, damn you! – was programmed into the sim."

"What?" Ortega's shock was mirrored by the stunned gasps from Talbot and Adamson.

"The boy at the end of the sim. I didn't realize it until it was almost over, but it was Jake." The fury and fear she'd felt in that moment returned and she fought the urge to take a swing at Brodsky.

"Colonel Brodsky?" Ortega turned a baleful glare on the man.

Not wanting her XO getting into trouble on her account, Ashlyn simply shook her head before indicating the woman should take a step back.

"Frankly, Major, I don't have to explain anything to you," Brodsky said. "You know as well as I do that we don't have to inform teams of a change in mission parameters. Part of the reason why we run these sims is to see how well our people can adapt and react, no matter what the situation they might be presented with. Sorry if you didn't like what we threw at you but you're a Marine. You know how to adapt." Venom dripped from his voice.

"What I know is that these training sims, when set up by the battalion CO – which I happen to be – are not to be changed without first informing said CO. The only exception is if someone higher up the chain of command orders it." Ashlyn ground out the words. "So, Lt. Colonel, who gave you the order to change the sim and to include my son in it?"

Brodsky didn't respond. Anger flaring, Ash took a step forward. Then she stopped. Something wasn't right. It didn't feel right. Not the way the sim had been changed on them and not the way Brodsky was dealing with her now. It felt like another test, one to see just how far they could push her before she broke. She might be wrong. There were several other possible explanations for what had been done. One thing was certain, however. She most definitely did not like the implications.

"Very well, Lt. Colonel." She drawled out his rank, her disgust and lack of respect obvious. "As battalion CO, I am entitled to a complete copy of the records of the sim for evaluation by my team. Master Sergeant Adamson will remain here until you have it ready."

As she spoke, Adamson nodded and moved to take up a position next to the door. Ashlyn felt sure none of them, Brodsky included, had any doubts about what she was doing. Adamson would remain there, and she'd make sure Brodsky did as well, until he turned the records over to her.

"Master Guns, go let the rest of the team know that we will be discussing the sim as soon as Captain Ortega and I return. Inform them that I expect full after action reports from each of them within the next two hours."

"Yes, ma'am."

"Colonel Brodsky, you are lucky that I happen to respect your rank since I don't particularly respect you right now," she continued. "Never play this sort of game with me or my people again."

With that, she turned and left the office, Talbot and Ortega on her heels. No one said anything until they were in the elevator, safely away from prying eyes and ears.

"What the hell was that all about?" Ortega demanded, her eyes flashing with anger.

"I wish to hell I knew." Ash drew a deep breath, held it for a count of five and then released it. "And I plan to find out. Loco, go make sure our team knows I want to see all of them as soon as I get back. We'll do our own debrief on the sim as well as discuss what happened and, hopefully, why."

"There'd better be a damned good reason for what went down, ma'am, or you're going to have a bunch of angry Devil Dogs on your hands and I don't mean just our team."

Ashlyn nodded. Talbot was right. Marines stood together. Devil Dogs did that and more. Unless she missed her guess, she had a feeling Talbot – and Ortega – would be leading the Devil Dogs if she didn't get answers for them all.

"And us?" Ortega asked.

"I'm going to see what our Division CO has to say about this. I want you to find out everything you can about Brodsky and any scuttlebutt there might be about how he is running the sims."

CHAPTER THREE

FURIOUS, ASHLYN STEPPED OUT OF THE LIFT AND STARTED DOWN the corridor in the direction of her office. Anger still burned deep inside her. Two hours later and she had yet to discover why the sim's parameters had been changed, much less who had ordered it. That didn't sit well with her, especially since she would have to tell her people she didn't have the answers to their questions.

It would be so easy to fall back into the doubts and paranoia she had lived with after the Arterus mission. Then her questions – and objections – had fallen on deaf ears. At least that wasn't the case this time, at least not yet. Not that it made her feel any better, especially when she thought about the rest of it.

When she had arrived at the office of FirstDiv's commanding officer, it hadn't taken her long to realize something was going on. For the first time since returning to active duty, she hadn't been passed straight through to see Brigadier General Elizabeth Shaw. Before she could even ask why, the general's aide told her he was under orders not to interrupt her conference. No, he didn't know how long the general would be.

The niggling concern Ash felt grew when she received the

same sort of greeting upon her arrival at General Helen Okafor's office. The Commandant of the Fuerconese Marine Corps was in a meeting and had left orders that she wasn't to be disturbed. No, there was no explanation and none had been asked for. The none-too-subtle verbal slap had done more than sting. It had warned Ashlyn that something had happened and she would bet her next month's pay it meant the Devil Dogs would soon be shipping out. That meant she needed to be prepared, as did the rest of the battalion. She would just have to worry about the sim later, after she found out what was going on.

Doing her best to push down her concerns, Ash entered her office. One look around the anteroom and she stopped short. A young corporal sat behind the desk across the room and gave her an apologetic look. Before she could ask what was wrong, the door to her private office slid open and Ortega appeared. One look at her XO's expression was all Ashlyn needed to know she wasn't going to get the few minutes to collect her thoughts that she'd hoped for.

"Nolan, send notice out to the battalion of PT at 0500 in the morning followed by a briefing of company commanders at 0630. Uniform of the day will be BDUs. Then confirm with Colonel Johnson that Captain Ortega and I are to meet with him at 1100 hours."

"Yes, ma'am." The young man quickly noted all she said and she nodded in approval.

"Captain Ortega will have changes to the training schedule for the next week to you shortly. Once she does, confirm everything with the O-Course and the like. Then send it out. Make sure you get confirmation not only from our company commanders but the individual platoon commanders as well."

"Understood, ma'am."

Trusting that he did, she turned her attention to her XO. Ortega held her gaze for a moment and then moved aside so she could step through the doorway. As she did, Ash didn't know whether to sigh or pound her head against the wall in frustration. What she did know was that she should have expected this.

This was finding not only her XO but also Adamson and Talbot waiting for her. At least the rest of those who had been part of the sim weren't there as well. Before she could say as much, Ortega handed her a mug of coffee and motioned for her to be seated.

"Consider yourself lucky it's just the three of us, Ash," Ortega said as she made sure the office door was securely shut. "MJ and Kevin managed to convince the others to let them handle this *debriefing*. But I warn you everyone is ready to go straight to General Okafor to demand an explanation for what happened. So, what did you find out?"

For a moment, Ash didn't reply. It didn't surprise her to learn the rest of the team wanted answers. If their positions were reversed, she'd feel the same way. That was one reason the team was as strong as it was. They looked out for one another, had each other's back. Hopefully, they would give her and their superiors time to find the answers they all wanted.

Setting her mug on the desktop, she leaned back, glad Ortega had made sure the door was securely shut behind them. The last thing she wanted was for someone to overhear what she had to say.

"Nothing." She shook her head when Ortega started to speak. "When I got to my mother's office, her aide wouldn't let me talk to her, wouldn't even tell her I was there. When I asked how long before she'd be available, he told me he didn't know." She paused, giving the others a moment to consider what she said.

"While I can't tell you why or what was so important that he wouldn't even let her know I was there, I can tell you he was tense and worried. More importantly, so was Lt. Garrity when

I tried to speak with General Okafor. So I left my report on the sim as well as a request to meet with both my mother and the Commandant before returning here."

She lifted her mug and sipped. As she did, she waited. From the troubled expressions worn by the others, she had no doubt they were as worried as was she. But would they come to the same conclusions?

"The Callusians?" Ortega asked simply.

"That would be my guess," Ash replied. "If we're right, I expect we will be shipping out very soon. So we need to make sure everything is ready. That means not only making sure the Devil Dogs are ready but that we have a line on what happened today and why."

"I may have a few answers where that's concerned." Ortega produced her datapad and briefly consulted it. "I did a little research into Brodsky and I don't like what I've found so far."

Concerned, Ash motioned for her to continue.

"I'll start by saying this isn't the first time he has changed the parameters of a sim without first informing the CO. I've uncovered at least three other times he's done so. Each time, when called on it by the brass, he has responded much as he did today. Two of the instances involved Marine exercises."

"Why hasn't he been disciplined then?"

Or had he?

"My sources tell me he explained it away each time by saying he was following orders."

"What? Whose orders?" Ash leaned forward, hands on her desk, eyes flashing.

"Dr. Jay Hines."

For a moment, no one said anything. Ashlyn leaned back, stunned. Then Adamson surged to her feet. Anger flashed across her expression. Without a word, she crossed the office to the far wall. For a moment, Ashlyn wondered if the master sergeant was going to put her fist through the wall. It certainly looked like the blonde was considering it, not that Ash blamed her. She'd actually punched the wall in her mother's office during the retelling of what happened and she had the sore knuckles to prove it.

"That bastard," Adamson rasped as she turned back to face the others.

"Why did he do it?" Talbot demanded.

"You want to know what he told the brass or what I think his motive was?" Ortega asked

"Both," Ash said.

"According to those I spoke with, Hines ordered the change in mission parameters because he had concerns about the various COs. In each case, they had been on restricted duty prior to the exercise. According to him, the only way to determine whether or not the officers, you included, should have been reinstated to active duty status was to put them into situations where all the stressors would be present."

"But she'd already been cleared to return to duty," Talbot said. "Not only by the medical review board but also by the top brass."

Ash nodded, her expression serious. She'd hated the sessions with the shrinks she'd been forced to attend. They'd poked and prodded and kept wanting her to talk about what had happened, not only before her court martial but after she'd been sent to the military prison on Tarsus. One of them had even required her to sit through the vid of her sentencing hearing, just to see how she'd react. But she'd done it and had managed to convince them that she was all right. The funny thing was, she really was all right as long as you didn't count the occasional nightmare and the need, a very primal need, to see those responsible for the deaths of her people brought to justice.

"True but, from what I can tell, in each case Hines told the review board that he was against any attempt to return the

COs, including Ash, to active duty. Each time, his recommendations were ignored by the others doctors. So he went to the review board with his objections and, when it ignored him, he went to Brodsky. Together they would alter the parameters of the upcoming sims, all in an attempt to prove Hines was right."

"What the hell!" Now it was Talbot who pushed out of his chair and paced the length of the office. When he turned back, Ash held up a hand, silencing him.

"Stand down, Kevin. I knew that bastard had tried to keep me from returning to duty. He actually took his objections to the commandant when the review board shot him down." She inhaled, striving to keep her temper in check as she remember being called to Okafor's office not that long ago. "Fortunately, at least in my eyes, she pulled the reports from my primary physician as well as the other doctors who had seen me and the medical review board. None of those records contained any concerns, outside of the normal ones they always have about Marines in general and Devil Dogs in particular, about letting me return to duty. Dr. Ahern was very careful to document not only my medical progress but the reports he'd gotten back from the shrinks. And, no, there was no report from Hines on the record, not that I expected one since I only saw him once."

And that had been one time too many. There had been something about the man that had rubbed Ash wrong from the moment she entered his office more than a month earlier. Of all the other doctors and counsellors she'd seen, Hines had been the only one who hadn't gotten to his feet to greet her and try to put her at her ease. Instead, he'd watched with what could only be described as a sneer of disdain as she moved across his office to one of the two chairs in front of his desk. She'd given him a moment to invite her to sit. When he didn't, she finally took it upon herself to do so, noting the aggravation that crossed his expression as she did.

The next hour had been an exercise in frustration. Hines had proven, in Ash's mind at least, that he had no desire to help her cope with any remaining problems she might have had. Instead, he spent the time poking and prodding, trying to get her to admit that she'd joined the military, the Marines in particular, because her parents had forced her to. Then he suggested in no uncertain terms that she'd been insubordinate on her last assignment, deserving the reprimands O'Brien and Sorkowski had put in her record. Worse, he'd tried to make her admit it had been her own negligence that had caused the disaster that had been the Arterus mission. In short, he had taken a page out of the prosecution's handbook and had run with it.

Her response, as soon as she'd left his office, had been to contact Dr. Ahern, as her primary physician, and tell him not only that she would not agree to see Hines again but also why. Ahern had been quick to assure her that she would not have to meet with Hines again. There had been something in the doctor's voice during that short conversation that had caught Ash's attention but she hadn't dwelt on it. Now, after the events of the morning, she knew what it was. Ahern hadn't been surprised by what she'd reported and that was something that, after the morning's events, bore looking into.

"I still don't get why Hines would tell Brodsky to alter the sims or why Brodsky would do it." Talbot shook his head, frowning. "It just doesn't make any sense."

"No, it doesn't. But I have a better question, Kevin. How did Hines even know about the sims, much less know about their parameters?"

The moment she said it, Ashlyn saw understanding dawn on her companions. Sim missions were not something talked about in public circles, at least not before they had been run. In the case of this particular sim, no one outside of the team, the sim crew, and a few others should have even known about the *mission*. That Hines had meant there was a security leak somewhere, one that needed to be found before any real harm was done – if it hadn't already.

"Damn it," the master gunnery sergeant said.

Ash nodded. "That's why we aren't about to let this drop. Luce, I want you to write up everything you've learned and suspect. I will attach it to my full report and send it, along with a full recording of the sim to both my mother and Okafor. MJ, Kevin, get reports from each member of today's team and I will include them as well. Hell, I think I'll copy everything to JAG as well. It's past time for them to open an investigation into what's been going on."

"Let's hope they move faster on that than they have everything else," Ortega murmured in ill-temper.

"Luce, I need you to do something else for me." Now she smiled, the predator scenting its prey. "I want you to put your skills in intelligence gathering to use and find out what you can about Brodsky and Hines. See where their paths cross, if they do. If they don't, then find out how Hines learned about the sim. Talk to Rico Santiago. He might have an idea about what's going on. Hell, knowing him, he's already got an investigation running into one or both of them."

"You're right there. Besides, he'll move faster than JAG once he realizes there is a real problem and, with this breach of security, there is," Ortega said.

Ashlyn nodded. Her own frustration with the JAG had been building over the last few weeks. Part of her understood the need to proceed carefully, making sure not only that they had an airtight case against Sorkowski and O'Brien for dereliction of duty, falsifying records and perjury, as well as all the other charges she'd been assured would be leveled against the two she held responsible for the deaths of those under her command. She recognized the need to keep the investigation under wraps as the JAG looked into who else might have been involved in making sure she and the other survivors of the Arterus mission were court martialed and sent to the Tarsus penal colony. But, with each week that passed, it had gotten harder and harder to believe they would give her justice any more than she'd seen when brought up on charges.

But, fortunately, that might be about to change.

"Speaking of the JAG, I guess I ought to let you know that Lt. Liu did ask if there might be any volunteers from the battalion, and preferably from Alpha Company, to help with some security details he will be putting together shortly."

A smile touched her lips as her companions sat up, suddenly even more alert than before.

"Ash—"

Ortega didn't finish what she had been about to say. Her expression betrayed her conflicting emotions. Hope and dread, determination and resignation: all emotions Ashlyn had experienced since her release from the military prison on Tarsus and, if she were being honest, emotions she'd felt during Okafor's conversation with the JAG officer in charge of her case. Now all she could do was nod, letting her XO and best friend know she understood.

"Don't jump to conclusions yet. Lt. Liu didn't go into specifics. My guess is that he's finally decided there's enough evidence to move against Sorkowski and O'Brien."

How much more should she say? These three had stood behind her and for her when she'd been court martialed. They'd fought, often at the risk of their own careers, to prove she and the others were innocent of the charges leveled against them. There were no others she'd trust at her back than them. More importantly, she would trust them to care for her son should anything happen to her and her parents. They deserved to know everything, even if it was only speculation.

"It wouldn't surprise me to find out that they'll be moving against others as well. Lt. Liu has made it clear whenever we've met to discuss the case that he believes others are involved in Sorkowski and O'Brien's operation. He's been able to tie them to the smugglers and pirates operating in the Arcterus Sector. Their bank accounts, the ones they don't know he's discovered, show deposits coming from some more than questionable sources. He has no doubts those two were doing more than turning a blind eye to the illegal activities in the sector. Believe me, he wants the ones they were working with almost as much as I do." She shook her head, a slight smile touching her lips. "I'll be honest, as much as I want to be there to see them slap the restraints on both Sorkowski and O'Brien, part of me wants to be off-planet when it happens. The media circus that will follow will be a nightmare I'd just as soon not be part of.

"And along that line, there's something I didn't tell Nolan earlier. We are final push mode. I want the battalion ready to move out at a moment's notice. That means we all have a great deal of work to do."

"It's about time we got our orders," Adamson said and the others nodded in agreement.

"Agreed. But it does mean we have a lot to accomplish and probably not much time in which to do it. I want full reviews of our personnel and your final recommendations on our officers and senior non-coms by morning. If we need to rearrange billets or transfer anyone, let's do it now, before the shit hits the fan.

"MJ, I want you to put together the PT for morning. Push everyone, especially the officers. If anyone gives you a hard time about it, send them to Lucinda. I'll step in if necessary. Just remember that I want every person in the battalion ready for battle. That means physically as well as mentally. Any questions?"

"Negative, ma'am," Ortega assured her.

"There's one more thing I want the three of you to do."

"Name it," Talbot said.

"While I need to know what the story is where Hines and Brodsky are concerned, we have more pressing matters. If I'm right, we're going to be shipping out sooner rather than later. I've been expecting our orders to come for the last two weeks. Whether we'll be sent to try to liberate the Cassius System or to the front lines, I don't know. But I do know we aren't ready. There are still slots in the battalion that need to be filled. Hell, there are still slots on my staff that need to be filled. I want the three of you to review the headquarters staff. We'll discuss your recommendations after the briefings."

"Understood." Ortega turned to the others. "I'll go have a chat with Santiago when we finish here. Kevin, you talk to the team and let them know the major has things well in hand and will brief them later. MJ—"

"I know some folks who have had the *pleasure* of dealing with Hines. I'll reach out to them," Adamson commented.

"Good." Another knot of tension eased and Ash smiled slightly. Her companions would get the job done, just as they always did. "Now get out of here and get busy. I have a feeling the brass is going to put us through the wringer just as we're going to be putting the battalion through it come morning."

She watched the others leave her office. As the door closed behind them, she leaned back and lifted her booted feet onto the edge of her desk. She was still angry about what happened that morning but the anger no longer consumed her. Now she could channel it and that was exactly what she planned to do. There was a great deal she needed to take care of before she could leave for the day.

*   *   *

The three men looked at one another, silence hanging comfortably between them as they waited for the page to leave. The young man, really nothing more than a boy, sketched a bow in their direction before backing out of the room. A moment later, the reinforced door slid shut behind him, locking out all prying eyes and ears.

Even so, personal and professional paranoia had kept the three alive and had become such a deeply seated part of their lives that it might have well have been part of their genetic makeup. There was a soft buzz and a quick flickering of the lights as shields went up inside the room. Designed not only to prevent surveillance by artificial means, it would also warn them if anyone tried to tap into the room or if they tried to make entry. It was just one of precautions they had agreed upon before deciding to meet face-to-face. There were simply too many people, both on Midlothian and elsewhere, who would view their current activities with scant favor.

"Have we received any information from Cassius Prime?" the man sitting at the head of the table.

"No, but then I didn't expect to hear anything yet." The man to his left, Mikhail Federov, reached out and entered a quick command on the virtual keyboard in front of him. He took a moment to scan the information he'd called up before continuing. "So far, everything has gone according to plan. Our *allies*—" He spat out the word. "—did exactly as told. They took out the orbital defense and communications platforms before starting the planetary attack. As you know, they followed their usual tactics there. They pounded what they could with bombs and then sent in the ground troops. It was a bloodbath and they are now stripping the capital of tech, anything they can sell or use themselves and rounding up prisoners. As I said, all according to plan."

"And the courier ship they reported entering the system as the attack began?" Alexander Watchman, Commissioner of Intelligence Services for the Republic of Midlothian, looked from Federov to the third member of their group, Admiral Horace Boniface.

"We can't be sure one way or the other, sir," Federov said. "The reports from Commander Hughes are inconclusive. All he

32

could confirm for us was that the courier came out of hyper right on the edge of the *Anubis'* detection range. They didn't pick up anything on sensors to indicate a message had been sent but we all know the Callusian communications hardware leaves a great deal to be desired."

"But?" Watchman prompted, his voice soft, his eyes glinting dangerously.

"Fuercon knows about the invasion. Whether the courier got word out or they found out through their own intelligence network, we don't know. But they are taking steps to not only keep their home system safe from another attack but to take the fight to the Callusians."

"We know that there is a taskforce comprised of ships from Fuercon's Second Fleet that has taken up a defensive picket near the Cassius System," Boniface said. "Third Fleet has moved closer to Callusian space and joined forces with the Badenberg Confederacy. Unless I miss my guess, they will soon be launching an all-out attack on the Callusian home system."

Waterman leaned back, his expression thoughtful. Federov and Boniface hadn't told him anything he didn't already know or suspect. Still, it would have been nice to have received some good news for a change. This entire operation had seemed cursed from the start. But they were too deep into it now to call it off. If they withdrew their support, both in military advisors and in money, the Callusians would be quick to betray them. Worse, if the Callusians decided to attack, Midlothian would fall. Its military was too small, despite a technological advantage. So they had to at least stay the course. Besides, they would make their own luck. It was how he'd risen to the position he now held and how he'd managed to stay alive as long as he had.

It was time to apply that to their mission.

"Federov, contact our operatives on Fuercon, specifically in the capital. They are to work their contacts and get us all the information they can about what FleetCom is planning. Moreau is to understand that she will be terminated if she fails us again. Make an example of someone she's been working with, someone she assumes we don't know about. She's a good operative but she's gotten sloppy this mission.

"Boniface, tell our *allies* that they are to keep the pressure on. Phase Two is to begin just as soon as possible."

"Understood," the admiral assured him.

"Then, gentlemen, to success." Watchman raised his glass in a toast.

"Success!"

Federov and Boniface repeated and downed their drinks. If they also said a quick prayer for protection, that was fine with Watchman. He didn't care if they were scared as long as they did their jobs. Besides, he knew something they didn't. Halstrom's Landing had already been attacked. The Callusians were doing exactly what he wanted. All he had to do was make sure Fuercon didn't realize what was happening until it was too late.

*　　*　　*

The sound of ice cubes clinking against the sides of the crystal high ball glass broke the silence of the apartment. Frowning, not remembering draining the whiskey, Evan Moreau walked across the thick carpet to the bar and reached for the matching crystal decanter. She shouldn't have a second drink. Or was it the third? Whatever, she didn't care. Just then, she needed the whiskey even more than she needed to be clear-headed. After all, she had more than an hour before her next *appointment*. That was more than enough time to have another drink and still pop the necessary pills to counteract the effects of the alcohol.

Unfortunately, an hour wasn't enough to figure out how to deal with what was bothering her. She wasn't sure there was enough time in the world to deal with her concerns. All her carefully laid plans seemed to be unravelling. Damn it, she'd known when she first accepted this mission that it was rife with risk. That had been part of its appeal. The other part had been the opportunity to strike back at not only Ashlyn Shaw and her family but at so many of those who had denied her her due. But now, one by one, those she'd had to use in order to carry out her mission were being swept up by either local security or FleetCom. Sooner or later one of them would talk in an attempt to save their own skin. Even though she'd taken precautions to make sure nothing could lead back to her, no plan was foolproof. That meant she had to take precautions, not only to protect herself but to make sure her mission was successfully concluded. If she failed to do the latter, nothing would keep her safe in the long run. Her employers were notorious for their swift and very permanent solutions for those who failed them.

Damn it! She was so close to completing the mission. It wasn't her fault that the idiot mercs she'd hired to run the attack on the capital had failed miserably. Not only had they failed to take out their targets, they'd managed to let FleetCom recover several of their fighters. The only good thing that happened was that none of the mercs themselves had survived. Most had been killed in the fighting. Others had died "as a result of their injuries." She had made sure her contact would never be able to broker another deal. So far, his body had yet to be found and, unless she'd lost her touch, it never would be.

Not that it had satisfied her employers. Fortunately, not only were they on another planet, there was also a vast expanse of space between them. She'd not hesitated one moment to point out in her report on the attack that she'd used people they had recommended. She knew that had been all that had kept her alive just as she knew her time was limited and another failure would mean death – or worse.

Now this. Another failure to jeopardize her mission.

Damn it, did she have to do everything herself?

CHAPTER FOUR

ASHLYN REACHED FOR HER MUG AS THE LIGHTS IN THE CONFERENCE room came up. From her place at the head of the table, she waited as her companions processed what they had just seen. She had certainly needed a few moments after viewing the vid-feed the first time. Even after reviewing it several times, the contents of the vid still affected her. How could it not, when it presented incontrovertible proof of the sadism of their enemy?

Not that that was anything new.

Looking at the ten men and women seated around the conference table, she saw the same horror and anger – no, the same fury. Anger was much too mild a word. – she had felt when she first watched the vid. It wasn't as if they'd never witnessed such cruelty from their enemy. Far from it, in fact. Most of them, herself included, had seen it firsthand too many times to count during the previous war.

Previous war.

Ashlyn almost snorted aloud. What a farce. Oh, there had been a truce, on paper at least. But every one of her companions knew different. The fact there had been no formal declaration of war and no major incursion into Fuerconese or allied space meant nothing. The only difference between what had been happening during the *truce* and a war was that the Callusians had run their operations under the guise of piracy and smuggling. Shipping lines had been disrupted, usually to such an extent that the ships and their crews were never heard from again. Even so, former President Markham had allowed the farce to continue. He'd refused to do anything to protect Fuerconese interests outside the home system, much less that of their allies. That decision had come back to bite all of them.

Not that it surprised Ash any. The previous war had been marked by politicians pushing their own personal agendas, no matter what the cost to those who trusted them to take any and all action necessary to protect Fuercon and her allies. Worse, there had been a few members of the military who had used the war to line their own pockets. That was something Ashlyn knew all too well. Good people, Marines and civilians alike, had died due to greed and incompetence. It very well could have continued had those same politicians and corrupt members of the military hadn't tried to make scapegoats out of Ash and the surviving members of her unit.

Fortunately, the public, tired of a war the politicians weren't trying to win, had finally had enough. When the elections came around, Markham and most of his cronies had been voted out of office. The new administration, led by President Derek Harper, had immediately put plans into action to not only free Ash and her people but to clear them of all charges leveled against them.

That had been just the first step in a long-range plan by the president to finally end hostilities with the Callusians once and for all.

After two years in the hellhole on Tarsus, Ash had suddenly found herself back on the planet where she'd been born and where she'd grown up. There had been no explanation and now warning. One day she'd been escorted from her cell and placed on a transport to Fuercon. But Fate was a fickle bitch and she wasn't about to let Ash's homecoming be an easy one. Without warning, the Callusians had launched a limited attack on the capital. At the time, FleetCom hadn't realized the significance of the attack. But now they knew. The vid had confirmed their suspicions. The attack on Fuercon had been a feint, designed to keep the Fuerconese military close to home while the enemy moved into position to attack Cassius Prime.

It was video of that initial attack on Cassius Prime that Ash and her senior advisors had been watching. If anything about the attack could be called good, it was the fact one of Fuercon's courier ships had entered the Cassius System just moments after the attack had begun. The ship's commanding officer, Lt. Commander Julia Sykes, had done what she was supposed to do. Instead of ordering her ship to retreat before it could be detected by the Callusian fleet, she'd ordered probes launched. Then she'd instructed her tactical officer to grab as much data on the invaders and their attack as possible. Ash had no doubts Sykes knew it was suicide for her ship to remain in-system. But Sykes and her crew had managed to not only get word back to Fuercon and its allies about the attack but had managed to get the video feed of the invasion, including video of the groundside fighting, and its immediate aftermath back as well.

Unfortunately, it had taken almost two months for the data to get back to Fuercon. Then FleetCom's intelligence experts had combed over it, trying to glean everything possible from the feed. While the video confirmed their preliminary reports about the invasion, it didn't tell them what the current situation in the system might be. Not that it would be good, at least not for those living there before the invasion.

"What about the *Tarrant*, Major?" Adamson asked from down the table. The blonde's eyes flashed as she studied the final image sent back by the probes Sykes and her crew had dropped.

"All contact with the *Tarrant* was lost shortly after Lt. Commander Sykes broadcast her warning. FleetCom dispatched ships to the area but search and rescue never happened. By the time we had ships in the area, the Cassius System had been interdicted by the Callusians. Task Force 227 did send a fighter squadron in-system but they were forced to pull out after picking up readings of Callusian LACs as well as a carrier on an intercept course. The task force commander determined, and rightly so, that they needed to exercise caution until reinforcements arrived."

As she spoke, Ash punched up a new image and waited as it appeared on the holo plot over the table. "Here is the latest intel we have from the system. It is, at best, three weeks old. But you can see that the Callusian fleet holding the system has taken up standard orbital placement. It's nothing we haven't seen before." Another quick command sequence and half a dozen lights appeared on the plot, all shining green.

"The best information we have is that the Callusian attack force was comprised of three destroyers, two heavy destroyers and a single cruiser, along with lighter elements. Orbital defenses were taken down and then they lay siege to the capital. FleetCom is assuming they managed to somehow get someone inside the defense ministry or were able to hack into the defense platforms because they were offline and the capital was being bombarded before an SOS could get out and before ships in a parking orbit could respond or groundside defenses could get online."

"That has pretty much been the enemy pattern from the beginning." Ortega commented thoughtfully.

"But?" Ash prompted. She recognized Ortega's tone of voice. It meant something was bothering her XO and past experience had taught her to pay attention.

"Have the Callusians made any sort of announcement that they've *liberated* the system?"

Good. Ortega had caught it as well. That had been something bothering Ashlyn since she first learned of the invasion. Fortunately, it had been bothering those higher up the chain of command as well, and not just the military chain of command. President Harper had studied the previous war, as well as the events leading up to it. He probably understood how the Callusians operated better than all of the former administration's military strategists put together. That was fine with Ashlyn. She knew Fuercon and its allies needed politicians who understood the enemy just as they needed military leaders who weren't afraid to do what was necessary to put an end to the war once and for all.

"They have not and that bothers not only me but FleetCom as well." She waited, letting that sink in. "Ladies and gentlemen, we have a situation where we have a number of unanswered questions. Of those, there are several we have to pay special attention to. First, why did the enemy suddenly attack the Cassius System? Until then, it had apparently been satisfied using the ruse of the cease fire agreement to raid commerce shipping and conduct their slave trade. So what changed?

"The second question is why hasn't the enemy announced that it has, as Captain Ortega put it, *liberated* Cassius Prime? The so-called liberation of territories from the hands of the oppressors has been their justification for invasion since before any of us were born. I'll be honest. The failure to make such a pronouncement now worries me more than the fact that they openly violated the terms of the cease fire agreement. There are too many possible explanations and none of them make me happy.

"Whether the attack on Cassius Prime represents a change in tactical thinking or just something they did for this particular mission I don't know and that bothers me. For longer than any of us have been alive, the Callusians have followed one basic plan of attack. That's why it has been relatively easy to defeat them whenever we've engaged and have had similar force sizes – and if we had good intelligence."

She didn't try to hide the bite in her voice. Every man and woman in the room knew what had happened back on Arterus. They knew the basic details of how she and the rest of her team were set up. They'd been given incomplete intelligence information and had walked into a trap as a result. Worse, once the few survivors made it back to the ship, those responsible had done their best to not only alter the orders Ash had received but had intercepted her communiqués back to her own commanders. O'Brien and Sorkowski had done their best to hide their own illegal activities while setting up Ash and the others.

And it had worked, for a while at least. Not that she could let herself dwell on it just then. There would be time for that later, when the two were finally brought up on charges and made to pay for the deaths of her people.

Ash glanced at her now empty mug and gathered her thoughts before continuing. "The fact that the attack on Cassius Prime followed a different order of battle from before is something we have to assume is a signal of a change in Callusian tactics. Other than the brief attack on the capital, this is the first time they have struck so close to our home system. It is also the first time they have attacked such a close ally, both in distance and in economic and political ties to Fuercon.

"And let's not forget that they also ran a limited attack on our own capital. We were lucky that it was only a feint, a diversion meant to keep our attention focused on the home system instead of what was happening in neighboring space. They might not have launched a full-scale attack but they managed to plant the seed of doubt into the minds of some of our people. The belief that we would never come under attack here, in our own space, has forever been shattered.

"In a way, that is a good thing because it means home system security will be increased. Our leaders aren't going to risk a full-scale attack taking place."

"Is all this leading up to something, Major?" one of the officers down the table drawled.

Ash frowned, her eyes quickly seeking out the speaker. There had been more to the question than simple interest or even the relief to know they might finally get their orders to ship out. While she wouldn't say anything to the speaker about his attitude just yet, she would make a mental note to discuss it with her staff later.

For a moment, Ashlyn didn't reply. Instead, she remembered the coded message she had received late last night. It had been short and sweet and it had confirmed at least part of what she had suspected after the events of the previous day.

"As I was about to say, FirstBatt has been put on alert. I expect to receive our orders within the next day or two. Until we do, I am not going to speculate on what those orders might be and I expect each of you to follow my example. What I will do is remind you that we are Devil Dogs. We are Fuercon's elite SpecOps battalion. That means we don't get the simple missions. So get your people ready for immediate departure. Expect all training to be stepped up. We will be prepared for any eventuality."

"Any idea what our destination will be, ma'am?" Talbot asked.

"That I can't say, not yet at any rate, Master Guns." She held up a hand to forestall the protests she saw forming. "It's not that I don't want to. It's because I can't. I haven't been told anything more than to get the battalion ready."

"Did the brass give you any indication as to whether the entire battalion will be heading out or only part of it, ma'am?" Lt. Aron Mitchell asked.

"Again, I don't know. I would assume the entire battalion and so should you. Remember, FleetCom, as well as President Harper, is determined to show the Callusians that they will no longer be allowed to run rough shod over this sector of space. So, while we wait for our orders, we prepare. We prepare mentally and we prepare physically. We make sure our equipment is ready and we do what Devil Dogs always do. We protect our homes and our people."

She waited, giving them time to process what she'd said. Seeing how several of them made quick notations into their datapads, she nodded slightly in approval. Unfortunately, that approval was tempered by the fact that three made no notes. Two were from the same company. The third was the one company CO she didn't personally know. Reaching for her own datapad, she made a quick note to talk to Ortega and Talbot about the three. But that would have to wait until later, after the briefing was over.

"While I don't know for sure how long we have until we ship out, my best guess is that we are looking at two weeks or less. That means you can't waste any time getting your companies ready. Along those lines, Captain Ortega will be setting up sims for each company. They will be based not only on scenarios from what we've known the enemy to do in the past to sims based on what little we know of the attack on Cassius Prime. Scenarios will be both dirtside and boarding parties. Have your people ready for everything from squad-based sims to company vs. company. Some will be scheduled and some will not be.

"Those who have been with the Devil Dogs and who have seen real combat know that Lt. Colonel Pawlak liked to prepare for any possible scenario. I happen to agree with him on that. So expect the unexpected." She paused and glanced around the table, her expression serious. "Ladies and gentlemen, we are at war. If you aren't prepared to take the fight directly to our enemy, put in for a transfer now because, sooner or later, each of us will be shipping out and I only want those in the battalion who are willing to make the ultimate sacrifice to protect our homeworld and allies.

"I doubt we will have long to wait before we learn what ships we are being assigned to. That said, I want everyone ready to bug out at a moment's notice. So, from now until further notice, all leaves are cancelled. No one is to be more than an hour's travel from the capital without my authorization. Understood?"

The same seven who had made notes earlier, responded with a quick "yes, ma'am!" while the others simply nodded. That did not sit well with Ashlyn. The lack of respect, if not for her then for her rank, bothered her.

"Before you continue, ma'am, I have a question."

Ashlyn's eyes narrowed and she didn't try to hide her frown. Instead of speaking, she inclined her head.

"When will the additional training begin?"

"Immediately after the briefing, lieutenant." She hadn't planned on it starting that soon but the lieutenant's question changed her mind.

"We just did a full workout, ma'am!" Captain Landry Hotchner protested.

Without a word, Ashlyn made another note. Then she stood, the palms of her hands resting on the tabletop, her expression hard. "If you think what we went through this morning was a full workout, you've forgotten the workouts Lt. Colonel Pawlak put the battalion through. You have also forgotten – or somehow managed to avoid – the workouts I've had the sergeant major put the battalion through since I assumed command. If you feel you or any member of your command cannot keep up, then transfer out. That goes for all of you. I hope I've made myself clear."

"Ma'am, yes, ma'am!"

"Review your rosters and let Captain Ortega know of any slots you need filled, particularly any specialty slots. Include anyone currently assigned to your companies that you feel will not be assets on the coming mission."

Just as she planned to do with regard to those company commanders and their senior noncoms.

"Captain?" She glanced at Ortega and nodded.

"Thank you, Major." The dark haired Ortega punched in a command and the holo changed to show the schedule for the next few days. "Let's start with today's exercise. . . ."

*　　*　　*

Evan Moreau paused and watched two couples enter the restaurant. Doing her best to be as unobtrusive as possible, she studied the restaurant entrance before glancing up and down the street. So far, she had seen nothing to indicate she was about to walk into a trap. Not that she was about to let her guard down. She hadn't managed to stay alive this long by getting careless.

Perhaps she was being paranoid – better that than dead. Especially since her employers were getting impatient for results and her pawns were running scared. It was only a matter of time before someone demanded something from her she wasn't ready to give and, if her luck had finally run out, that time had come.

Still, she had to wonder about Sorkowski choosing to meet in such a public location. He might not have been especially effective as an admiral but he knew how to save his own skin. His real problem was that his greed had led him to rely on others who weren't as competent at covering their tracks as was he. Not that it would help him if he tried to turn on her now.

Moreau blew out a breath. It was time.

A moment later she stepped inside the restaurant and glanced around. Before the maitre'd could do more than nod in greeting, she waved him off. She'd spotted Sorkowski almost immediately. Maybe she had reason to worry about why he'd chosen such a public place for their meeting. She'd assumed he'd think himself safe there should she decide he presented a danger. But there he was, sitting almost directly across from the door where anyone entering could see him. Then there were the security monitors and the fact the table could be seen from the street. It was either a stroke of genius or the move of a man who didn't have an ounce of situational awareness to him.

Unfortunately, she wasn't sure which and that only put her more on edge.

Schooling her features so none of her uncertainty or displeasure showed, Moreau crossed to the table. As she neared, he looked up and nodded. Her jaw tightened when he just sat there instead of standing to greet her. The few times before when they'd met, he had been the consummate gentleman. So much so, in fact, that it had grated on her some. So what had brought about this sudden change? More important than that, what did it mean?

She didn't like it but she took her cue from him, Evan Moreau reached out and waited until his hand closed around hers. Hopefully, anyone glancing their way would think this was nothing more than a simple business meeting. In some ways, they wouldn't be wrong. She was there to discuss business with the man. But simple it would never be. Too many lives and too much money depended on what happened in the next few minutes.

Almost as soon as she sat, a waiter was there to fill her water glass and ask if she wanted anything else to drink. Without a word, she waved him off. Because of the early hour, no one would think it strange she didn't allow herself even a glass of wine. The truth was, however, that she was already slightly off-balance by her companion's change in attitude. She wasn't about to dull her senses with alcohol until she knew what was going on.

"All right, *Admiral*," she drawled. "I'm here."

For a moment, Admiral Alec Sorkowski (ret.) said nothing. He didn't need to when his expression spoke volumes. He no more liked her lack of respect for his rank, or for himself, than she did his change in attitude. Well too bad. He was risking both their lives with this meeting.

"I need to know what's going on."

Interesting. His outward attitude might have changed but his demand showed he was still just as worried as ever. Good. She could work with that. His arrogance and failure to cover his tracks in the first place was what led her to him. She'd not hesitated a moment in using him as one of many cogs in her mission. But that same arrogance and carelessness now made him dangerous. So did his demands to be kept in the loop.

Unfortunately, she couldn't remove him – yet. But that day was coming and she looked forward to it.

"What do you want to know?"

He opened his mouth and then shut it with a snap. She watched as he ground his teeth in frustration. If both of his hands hadn't been visible, she'd have been reaching for her weapon where she'd carefully secreted it that morning. Instead, she waited, hoping he wasn't so foolish as to call more attention to them than he already had by demanding this public meeting. He might not have been brought up on charges yet but the whispers were there. People knew that he'd either been behind what happened to Ashlyn Shaw and her people or had been so derelict in his duties that he'd let it happen without stepping in to stop such a "grave miscarriage of justice" as the media was calling it.

"Damn it, you know what," he growled.

"Calm down." She leaned in and placed her hand over his. To anyone looking on, it would look like she was simply trying to reassure a friend or colleague. At least she hoped it did.

"And keep your voice down. Or do you want everyone here to know what you and O'Brien did?"

He hissed in a breath, his hand fisting under hers. "What have you heard?" he demanded, his voice soft enough that no one at the nearby tables could hear.

"First tell me what has you so worried." She leaned back and reached for her water.

For a moment, it looked as if he'd refuse. Then he nodded, as if to himself. "I had another *visit* from a JAG investigator yesterday."

Her heart beat a bit faster and she fought to keep her expression from changing. That fool! If she had known about his latest visit from the JAG, she would never have agreed to meet him in public. She had no doubt the JAG had eyes on him now and that meant they had eyes on her.

Damn him!

"What did they want?" She shifted slightly on her chair and casually looked around. Anyone curious enough to be watching would think they were discussing business – or setting up an assignation for that afternoon or evening. At least she hoped so.

"What do you think?" he demanded.

"Just tell me what they said."

"More questions about Shaw, of course. They didn't ask about the discrepancy in her copy of her last orders and what was entered at her trial. But they did ask about our patrol patterns and O'Brien's service record."

Interesting. That could mean the JAG was starting to focus on O'Brien as the one behind what happened to Shaw and her people. If that were the case, it would suit Moreau just fine. O'Brien always had been the weak link. Unlike Sorkowski, who would keep his mouth shut unless he saw no other way out, O'Brien would sell either or both of them out at the first sign of real trouble. If JAG had decided on him as the focus of their investigation, it would be easy enough to have an "accident" happen to him, closing the investigation as well as ending a danger to the rest of her mission.

But, before she thought too much about that, she needed to reassure Sorkowski.

"Sounds to me like they have decided your former Marine commander is the one responsible for what happened," she said. "So encourage that belief. Tell them that you had concerns about him but did not have anything concrete to put your finger on. As for your patrol patterns, they were influenced by what O'Brien told you based on his intelligence sources. The discrepancy in the orders, that's easily explained away as well."

"How?"

She heard the desperation in Sorkowski's voice and did her best to look and sound reassuring. "You were in command of the entire task force. The Marines onboard your ship were under O'Brien's command. You gave him the orders and it was up to him to relay them. Even though you had concerns about him, you never expected him to be foolish enough or cocky enough to actually change your orders. Pull out your personal copy of the orders you issued regarding Shaw's last mission."

"But I've already turned them over and they were the altered ones." Sweat now pricked out on his forehead.

"Again, easily explained. You gave the JAG officers your access codes and they pulled the orders off your command terminal. You didn't know they were altered until the trial. Since then, you've been trying to find out what happened and how. You just now were able to recover the original orders. I can make sure you have the right experts to back up your claim."

She waited, watching as he processed what she said. The fear that had been reflected in his eyes slowly disappeared as he visibly relaxed. The fact that he so quickly accepted her explanation and her offer for help proved he was getting desperate. That meant sooner, rather than later, she'd have to deal with him. But not yet. Not until she was sure she had to and especially not if she was about to offer up O'Brien as a sacrifice.

"But wait until they contact you again. Don't offer up anything because that will make it look like you are trying to cover something up. Understand?"

"Yes." He nodded and then tossed back the glass of wine he'd been toying with since her arrival.

"Good. Now let's order lunch and make sure anyone watching thinks we are simply having a nice business meeting. Then go home. Don't do anything to bring any more attention to you – or me – than you have already."

"And O'Brien?"

She almost missed his look of expectation. No, excitement. He wanted her to deal with the Marine. Could it be that O'Brien had been pushing Sorkowski the way the admiral had been her? That was something else she needed to find out.

"Let me see what I can find out about the JAG investigation. If he is their target, good. If not, we will re-evaluate what needs to be done. But, for the moment, let me worry about him."

Just as I'll worry about you.

* * *

Ashlyn watched as most of the others left the conference room. Once the doors slid shut behind the last of them, she shook her head, her expression troubled. But she stayed silent, making sure no one returned for something they might have left behind. The last thing she needed was the wrong person overhearing what she was about to say.

"You're not looking any happier than I feel right now, Ash," Ortega commented as she reached for the carafe across from her. She gave it a quick shake and then sighed. "We need to remember to have more coffee on hand for these meetings."

"I'm not happy and that's putting it mildly," Ashlyn said. "But, before I explain why, I want to know what's bothering you, all of you." She motioned to include Adamson and Talbot who had been preparing to leave.

"You mean other than wanting to take a two particular officers who have more attitude than common sense outside to teach them a lesson or two?" Adamson's disgust roughened her voice and Ash fought the urge to smile.

"Not to mention a certain sergeant who ought to know better," Talbot added.

"Luce?" Now she looked at her XO.

"I'll admit that Sergeant Tutola surprised me. He's been with the battalion for the last eighteen months. I've not served directly with him, but I haven't heard anything to raise any red flags where he's concerned. But I promise I will be taking a very close look at his record before the day is out." As she spoke, her fingers flew across the virtual keyboard, typing in a series of commands.

"He's a paper pusher and pretty damned good at it," Talbot said. "But that's about it. I'm not sure he knows the butt from the barrel of his weapon."

Ashlyn ducked her head to hide her smile. It was clear Talbot approved of the sergeant's organizational skills but it was just as clear he had little use for the sergeant as a Devil Dog. That, in and of itself, spoke volumes.

"Recommendation?"

"I wouldn't want him on the front line, ma'am, but he'd be good as part of the HQ Company."

The hint of humor in Talbot's eyes didn't fool Ashlyn one bit. She could read in his expression what he really meant. His unspoken recommendation was to transfer the sergeant out of the battalion, if not the division. But Talbot wasn't above teasing her a little by suggesting the man be assigned to her staff. Well, two could play that game.

"Very well, Loco." She let a slow smile touch her lips as his eyes narrowed at her use of his call sign. "I'll leave it to you to explain to both our division CO as well as General Okafor why I'm on the front lines and you are in command of HQ Company."

Both Ortega and Adamson burst out laughing as the master gunnery sergeant paled and held his hands up in surrender.

"Not a chance, ma'am."

"Then, Luce, it looks like you need to find a reason to transfer the good sergeant out of the battalion. Talk to my mother's aide to see if the transfer should be out of the division as well. I don't want to put a black mark on the man's record if we don't need to. But I will not have our people endangered by having him on the line. Of course, that means you'll need to find us a replacement and quickly."

"I should have it done by morning," she promised.

"Good. Now, what can you tell me about the two officers in question?"

"Both are new to the battalion. They were transferred in not long before you returned to us. I know Pawlak had at least vague concerns about them. But, as long as we weren't having to go in force into battle, he didn't have reason to transfer them out," Ortega replied.

Ashlyn frowned, wishing she'd had more time to discuss battalion personnel with Pawlak before he'd shipped out to his new assignment.

"All right. Here's what we're going to do. Put Gamma and Delta Companies through their paces this afternoon, Luce. I have no doubt that you'll get objections, especially after what we heard in the briefing. I don't care. I want you to push them, especially the COs and XOs. Put them through advanced boarding and ground assault sims. Add in that sim we worked on last week. Let's see how they respond when the ship's CO and senior officers are taken out of the mix and the ship is still in the middle of a battle. Then I want their companies, led by the officers and non-coms, to do the O-Course at the Academy. Let's see what their individual and group scores are. I want you supervising it all. Brief me on the results in the morning over breakfast."

"I understand, Ash, but that's not going to give me much time to deal with the other personnel matters."

Ashlyn nodded and thought for a moment before speaking. "MJ, you're with her on this assignment. In fact, I want you to be one of the onsite referees. I need to know if there is any breach in protocol or any attempt to bypass the rules. You know what I'm looking for."

"I do."

A devilish gleam lit Adamson's eyes and Ash smiled slightly. The master sergeant would miss nothing as the sims progressed and then she'd probably run the O-Course herself, beating all of them in the process.

"Kevin, you get to deal with getting the sergeant transferred out. Write up your recommendation and reasoning. I'll approve it. Then you can take it to Personnel Command. If needed, I'll tag my mother's aide to expedite it all. I'll let him know while I'm there for the briefing she's called."

"Briefing?" Curiosity tinged Ortega's voice. Ashlyn understood. Ortega knew her schedule better than she did and the briefing had not been on it earlier. "Do you think it's about our orders or what happened yesterday?"

"My guess is both."

She would certainly feel better if that were the case.

"When do you leave?" Talbot wanted to know.

She glanced at the time. "Right now unless I want to be late. Luce, I'll touch base with you later today. MJ, set up the use of the O Course for this afternoon. If any of you need me for anything, comm." She paused, making sure she hadn't forgotten anything. "Let's hope we are wrong to be concerned."

Not that she expected them to be. If she'd learned anything since taking over as CO of the Devil Dogs, it was that very little went as expected. Not that it surprised her. She'd learned a long time ago never to take anything for granted. If that meant trying to anticipate everything that could go wrong, so be it.

"Will do," Adamson promised.

"One thing before you go, Ash," Ortega said. "How hard do you want me to push on these exercises?"

"Luce, I'll leave that to you." And how Ortega handled it would tell Ashlyn a great deal about how her friend would do as the battalion's XO. "But, from what little I know of the three we have concerns about, they have been with the DDs long enough that they should be able to handle anything you throw at them. I need to know how they react in situations where they are out of their comfort zones. For at least part of one of the exercises, have the senior non-coms taken out of the mix. Let's see how the officers, and not just the captains, respond to having the backbone of their companies removed. Then, take out the COs. Let's see how the rest of their people react without them at the lead."

"Understood. I'll keep you posted."

Ashlyn thanked her and reached for her datapad. Unless she missed her guess, the next few days were going to be interesting and not necessarily in a good way.

CHAPTER FIVE

"HAVE A SEAT, MAJOR," BRIGADIER GENERAL ELIZABETH SHAW said as her daughter entered the office.

Ashlyn nodded and did as she was told. As she did, she smiled slightly. It was still difficult at times to remember that her mother was also her commanding officer. That meant she had to be careful to avoid the sort of response anyone else who might be present would see as insubordinate. At least when they were alone, her mother didn't usually require her to stand on formality. Not after the first few moments, anyway.

Like her daughter, Elizabeth was dressed in BDUs. That was just one of the many changes General Okafor had put into place when she took over as Commandant of the Marine Corps. Until she had, those assigned to the HQ staff and all members of the Corps stationed planetside wore their "service" uniforms, complete with coats and covers, most days. But at least once a week, mess dress was the uniform of the day. Most Marines, *real* Marines as far as Ashlyn was concerned, had hated it. Neither uniform was as comfortable as their BDUs. The other uniforms might look fancier but Marines weren't supposed to be fancy. They were supposed to get the job done. Nothing else mattered. Fortunately, General Helen Okafor happened to share that belief and she'd quickly made that clear once assuming her post as Commandant of the Corps.

Elizabeth made her way around the desk to her own chair. Then she waited until her aide served coffee and withdrew. "Ash, let me start by apologizing for not being able to meet with you yesterday. Right now my schedule is even more hectic than your own. And, from what I heard of your conversation with Lt. Hawther, it sounds as if you had an *interesting* start to the day."

Ash didn't know whether to smile or groan. The last thing she wanted was for her mother to think she'd come running to tell tales out of school. That was the only real problem about being in Elizabeth's direct chain of command. There were times when it was difficult to separate the daughter from the Marine. Then, seeing the way her mother nodded in understanding, she smiled slightly. A moment later, as she thought about why she had told the lieutenant to expect a comm from Talbot, her smile faded.

"That's one way to put it, ma'am."

"Relax, Ash. It's just the two of us. There's no need to rest on niceties and protocol." As if to prove her point, Elizabeth leaned back and lifted her feet onto the corner of her desk. "I will say that it is important for me to know what happened and I promise to explain shortly. So, tell me about the briefing and what you plan to do about it. Then we will discuss yesterday's sim."

For a moment, Ashlyn didn't respond. Then she leaned forward, elbows on her knees, her expression serious. Since her mother had said they weren't standing on protocol, she'd take advantage of the opportunity to speak freely.

"Let's just say the briefing has left me with some concerns." Without waiting for her mother to comment, she continued. "There are two COs, both new to the battalion and who I've never worked with, that worry me. I'd be lying if I didn't admit my concern increased after finding out Pawlak had concerns about them. From what Lucinda said, the only reason he hadn't transferred them out was because the Devil Dogs weren't going to be on the field any time soon – or so he thought." She leaned back and once more wished she'd had a chance to talk more in-depth with her former CO about the battalion's staffing.

"Specifics?"

"One of them was openly insolent in the briefing, almost to the point of being hostile. Add to that the fact that neither of them took notes or even seemed to pay much attention to what was being said and, well, let's just say I don't want them anywhere near my people in a firefight. If I can't trust them in a briefing, I sure as hell don't want them at my back.

"If that's not enough, one of them actually protested when I said there would be additional training today. It seems PT this morning was more than enough for him.

"Add to that a sergeant who is nothing more than a paper pusher. According to Talbot, the man's really very good at admin but he wouldn't want him at his back. That's enough for me to want him out of the unit. I need combat vets, not admins. That's true especially of the HQ staff."

Unlike many other battalions, all of the Devil Dogs went into battle, including the headquarters staff. Shortly after the battalion had been formed, it was decided that all officers would hit the battlefield. It was a decision Ash had always agreed with. Being in the thick of the battle meant the commanders understood exactly what was going on and were setting the example for all the Marines in the battalion.

"Also, the two officers in question have habitually been the last to file their reports and the training records for their companies are laughable and I don't think I have any choice but to get rid of them."

Elizabeth's expression clouded. Seeing it, Ashlyn swallowed hard. She'd seen that expression many times when she was younger. It was the expression her mother had worn whenever Ash told her about something going wrong at school. At least this time she hadn't done anything wrong. – she hoped. All she could do now was wait as Elizabeth considered everything she'd said and either agreed with what she wanted to do or told her no.

Instead of commenting, Elizabeth remained silent. Ash waited, her pulse beating a bit faster. Then, her mother nodded, indicating she wanted Ashlyn to continue.

"I'll admit I'm a bit sensitive to my position in the Corps – and the battalion – right now. So, to make sure I'm not overreacting, I've ordered Luce to set the two companies the officers and sergeant are assigned to through their paces in sims and on the O Course today. We'll be meeting over breakfast in the morning to discuss how they did."

"What parameters did you put on the sims?"

"I told her to push them. Ground and space sims. Variants are to include senior noncoms being taken out of the mix as well as the officers, at different times. I want to see how the companies respond when they have to act without their officers and vice versa. I also told her to set one sim for shipboard where the senior naval personnel are taken out. I want to see what the officers have their people do in that sort of an emergency."

"Excellent. There is a reason why most of our people are cross-trained with naval personnel." Elizabeth nodded in approval. "What else?"

"Well, MJ Adamson will be setting up the O Course for them and, if I know her, she will run it with them as well."

Now Elizabeth threw her head back and laughed. "That's just evil, Ash. MJ is one of the best we have at the O Course. She'll not only run them in the ground but she will probably scare them to death as she does."

"I have no problem with that, Mom." And she didn't, at

least not in a metaphorical sense. "We're Devil Dogs. That means we have to be the biggest and meanest sons of bitches to take to the battlefield, no matter whether it is in space or on the ground. You and Dad taught me that when I was just a kid. Pawlak drummed it into me as a new member of the battalion when I transferred in."

"But there's more, isn't there?"

Now it was Ashlyn's turn to remain silent. Except her mother was better at waiting her out and always had been. Finally, realizing Elizabeth wasn't going to speak until she did, Ash nodded.

"There is." She sipped her coffee, trying to find the right words to explain what she had in mind without making her mother worry more than she was already. "I'm going to run the course with them and, no, MJ and Lucinda don't know.'

For a moment, Elizabeth didn't say anything. Then she nodded, a look of understanding on her face. "Ash, I'd probably do the same thing, were our roles reversed. However, I have a feeling my reasons to do so would be less complicated than yours." She held up a hand before Ashlyn could interrupt. "Yes, you are doing this to show the members of the two companies that not all officers are like their COs. But you are also doing it to prove to yourself and anyone else who might have doubts that you are more than ready to take over the Devil Dogs."

"Mom—"

"Don't." There was a bite to Elizabeth's voice and Ash closed her mouth with an almost audible *snap*. "You wouldn't be having these second thoughts, at least not to this level, if that bastard Hines hadn't pulled that crock of shit with the sim the other day. Admit it, you've been stewing about what he said since then." Now she pinned Ash with a firm look, waiting until Ash nodded reluctantly. "Damn it, Ashlyn, I wish you'd get it through your thick head that no one but you doubts your ability to return to duty."

"Don't give me that, Mom." Now it was her turn to hold a hand up. "You know as well as I do that I have my doubters. That's only natural. But they've never really bothered me. I've had to deal with their kind my entire career. Unfortunately, you are right about how I've reacted to Hines and what he said and did. I'm not sure it would have hit me this hard if he hadn't had Brodsky put Jake into the sim. But it did show a weakness, one I can't afford to have on the battlefield. I froze when I saw Jake. That weakness could cost lives and I don't want to be responsible for anyone else dying needlessly."

Instead of saying anything, Elizabeth activated the virtual keyboard on her desktop. Ash watched as she typed in a command sequence. A moment later, the holo screen over her desk activated and the vid of the training sim appeared. Ash watched, her stomach tightening, as her mother fast-forwarded to the end of the sim. As much as she wanted to look away, Ashlyn forced herself to watch.

"Look." Elizabeth paused the vid and highlighted the time code at the bottom of the holo display. "This is where you have gotten the child to safety. You haven't figured out who he is and you are still doing what needs to be done. Right?"

Ash studied the display, remembering how it had felt to run toward the safety of the barricade with the child cradled against her battle armor. She slid when Talbot told her to get down. At the same time and other members of the unit had opened fire on the remaining enemy. There hadn't been many of them. Her people had done their jobs well and most had already been killed. But there were still stragglers, still danger to her people and the civilians they were trying to protect.

"Now, watch how much time passes from when you realized who you held and when you called an end to the sim."

Elizabeth started the vid and Ash fought the urge to look away. Instead, she focused on the display and watched as the seconds ticked away. There! She looked down as the child refused to go with another member of her unit. One second. He looked up at her. Seeing his face on the screen was like being hit in the solar plexus. Two seconds. Recognition dawned on her. She could see it on her face, the disbelief followed by the anger. Three seconds. She looked around, her eyes scanning the area. Four seconds. She called for the sim to end.

Four seconds from start to finish.

God, it had felt like an eternity when it happened. Now, watching it replay on the vid, it had been nothing more than a few seconds. Could that be right?

"Now, will you please quit beating yourself up for something that didn't happen?" Elizabeth asked. "Before you answer, think about this: you identified, reacted and weighed the situation in less than four seconds from the moment you first looked down at the boy's face. In that time, your senior NCO and your XO didn't respond to the situation. Neither did anyone else on your team. So, if you persist in condemning yourself, you'd better get used to condemning them as well."

For a moment, all Ashlyn could do was look at her mother in disbelief, anger and resentment flaring. How dare she speak that way about her team! Then Ash realized it hadn't been her mother talking to her. It had been Elizabeth in full senior officer mode. Swallowing hard, she did her best to think about what she'd just seen, not as the person involved but as a Marine. If it had been anyone else, she would have said pretty much what her mother had. Unfortunately, it was difficult to remove emotion from the equation, especially when that emotion was based not only on seeing her son inserted into the sim but also on the betrayal by Sorkowski and O'Brien that had cost so many their lives and had sent her and six others to the Tarsus penal colony.

Damn it, how long was that going to whisper doubts in her

ear?

"You made your point." She blew out a breath and leaned back, reaching for her mug. The coffee had grown cold but she didn't care. "Since you brought up the sim, have you had a chance to review my report and the other information I sent?"

"I have and I've forwarded my recommendations to General Okafor. Until she decides whether or not Brodsky will remain in charge of the sims, I've issued orders that no FirstDiv sims are to be run through him. I have also asked Rico Santiago to look into what happened. The information Captain Ortega gathered raises the question of security breaches and, if they do exist, I want them plugged.

"There is one other thing. I want you to quit worrying about Hines and what he's said in his reports. He is wrong and you need to accept it. The rest of us have already."

Ash sighed and closed her eyes. Intellectually, she knew her mother was right. But knowing the doctor had voiced the same concerns she privately held didn't help.

"You're right about one thing, Mom. What Hines said – and what he insinuated – has been eating at me."

"Now you've admitted it, it will get better." Elizabeth smiled slightly in reassurance. "Ash, what he did was nothing more than an attempt to undermine your confidence. If he managed to do that and could point to sim or test results showing it before you ship out, he could claim that you aren't ready to return to duty, much less to assume a command position. But you've realized what he was trying and you won't let him win. Right?" She cocked her head to one side and waited.

"Right."

I'll be damned if I let him or anyone else pull that sort of crap on me again.

"Good." Elizabeth gave a decisive nod and dismissed the holo display.

"I want you to consider this as well the next time you start doubting yourself. If I had any reason to worry about your fitness to return to duty and to command the Devil Dogs, I'd find a reason to keep you here in the capital. Remember, I've been there for your nightmares and for all those sleepless nights. I know the demons you are fighting. I also know that you have not given in to them and that you aren't going to. You have beaten them just as you've beaten those who tried to take you down.

"However, think about this. I have my own demons and know that they still come to haunt me even now, years after the fact. That's why I understand they are just part of the healing process and they don't make you unfit for duty."

Ashlyn stared at her mother, not understanding what she meant. What demons? She didn't think she asked it aloud but the look on Elizabeth's face was enough to know she had.

"I may not have been betrayed like you and your people were, child, but I'm like any number of Marines. I've been in situations I wish I could forget. I've seen too many of my friends and innocent civilians die because of a careless order or an officer out for glory. Those are bad enough but seeing what those we fight against are capable of is much worse." She paused and licked her lips, a haunted look clouding her expression. "Some of my demons stem from a time before I met your father. There's a very long two week period I spent as a prisoner of some pirates. I won't tell you all that happened, to me or to my fellow Marines. Hell, Ash, I've never told your father about it. Just know that it was bad enough to make me want to wipe every pirate and slaver out of existence in the most painful manner possible."

For one long moment, Elizabeth just sat there. Then she shook herself and it was if the memory of that time was gone.

"Mom." Ashlyn's voice broke and she swallowed hard. It was no wonder her mother had been so understanding after her return from Tarsus.

"As for the doctors, I'll be honest. They are concerned that you're holding too much inside." Now she shook her head, a slight smile touching her lips. "You know how they are, darling. If you've been through Hell – and you have been – they want you to pound your chest and scream in anger. They want the tears and self-recriminations and condemnation of everyone who didn't immediately come to your aid. But they don't understand Marines, much less Devil Dogs. You haven't played by their rules but they don't have a reasonable medical excuse to keep you from returning to full active duty status.

"So, they signed off on it and will testify if needed that Hines is full of shit when it comes to you. All I want is for you to promise me one thing."

"What?" Ash asked when her mother didn't elaborate.

"That you will continue to let the JAG and the rest of us deal with Sorkowsi and O'Brien and any others who were involved in what happened on that last mission."

Ashlyn blew out a breath and climbed to her feet. She should have expected her mother to ask just that. They'd danced around the subject often enough. The only problem was that she didn't know if she could make the promise. All that had gotten her through the two years of hell on Tarsus was her determination to make the ones responsible for the death of so many of her fellow Marines pay for their crimes. She wanted to mete out justice by her own hand. Even now that she and the six sent to the penal colony with her had been cleared and their records expunged, it was difficult to trust the system. After all, that system had been more than willing to convict them in the first place.

But she also knew her mother would – and could – keep her on the planet while the rest of the battalion left on their next mission if she didn't give her word. She didn't want to lie to the woman but she couldn't say she'd continue to wait until the JAG decided it was finally the right time to make the arrests. However, it did appear that she knew something about the current state of the investigation her mother didn't.

"Mom, I'm doing my best." She shook her head. She wouldn't lie but she had to find a way to reassure Elizabeth enough that her mother wouldn't beach her. "I know things have changed since those bastards brought me and my people up on charges. I know the JAG isn't under the same leadership it was when we were tried and convicted. But the distrust is still there. I'll give them some more time because I want them to do it right. I don't want Sorkowski or O'Brien or anyone else who worked with them to ever see another day of freedom. Hell, I want them dead, slowly and painfully. It won't bring my people back but they will rest easier then."

She clinched her teeth and moved across the office. She knew she might be saying too much but now that she was talking about it, she couldn't stop. "I also want to be sure they haven't betrayed the Corps, Fleet and Fuercon. If they have, they need to be treated like the traitors they are. But we need to know who they have been working with. But my patience isn't infinite. JAG will need to act before much more time passes or I won't be responsible for what I do."

"Or what the rest of the Devil Dogs, and much of the Corps, will do." Elizabeth moved to stand before her. "I understand that and I'm glad you've finally admitted it." She reached out and pulled Ashlyn into a quick hug before once more stepping back.

"But with regard to your question, I will hold on a little bit longer, mainly because Lt. Liu implied the last time we spoke that JAG is about to make a move. Seems they asked her if there might be some members of the battalion, and especially of Alpha Company, who would be interested in assisting them in an upcoming mission."

Elizabeth grinned, wry amusement lighting her expression.

"No wonder you're willing to be a good girl, at least for the moment. Not that you won't have to answer to both your father and me for not telling us this last night. But I'll let it go as long as you promise to let me know if you have any second thoughts about your current assignment."

"I will but, at least right now, there are none."

Elizabeth nodded and motioned for Ash to wait before saying anything else. Curious, Ashlyn watched as her mother reached up to activate her earbud. A moment later, Elizabeth smiled at her daughter.

"Sorry," she said even though there was nothing apologetic about her expression. "I know you're scheduled to meet with General Okafor in a few minutes but that just changed."

"Ma'am?" Ashlyn frowned, not sure what to think about her mother's sudden comment.

"That was her office. The general will be joining us shortly. Unless, of course, you don't want to hear what the Devil Dogs' next assignment is going to be."

A slow smile spread across Ashlyn's face and now her pulse quickened with anticipation. "I most definitely do want to hear what our assignment is to be."

"That's what I figured." Elizabeth grinned and Ashlyn felt her lips turning up in an answering smile.

It was about time the Devil Dogs got into the war.

*   *   *

Damn it, can this day get any worse? First that brat who only wanted to go shopping – and who wanted me to pay for everything she bought – and now this.

Major Thomas O'Brien stood rooted in place, hatred coursing through him, as the lift doors opened and the three women stepped out. A split second later, instinct kicked in and he took a step back, hoping to move out of their line of sight. Even as he did his best to become as small and invisible as possible, one part of him wanted to move closer. The three were so intent in their conversation, they wouldn't notice him until it was too late. They might not even notice him then. The shock and horror of what he wanted to do would slow their reactions and keep their attention focused away from him as he made his escape.

Hell, if he was lucky enough and quick enough, he could kill all three of them before anyone else figured out what was happening.

God, it was so tempting. He'd spent the last two years living in fear that Shaw would find someone to listen to her. In the months since she had, he'd been constantly looking over his shoulder, waiting for the moment when someone would finally act against him. She cost him so much, everything that had meant anything to him. Now, finally, she was close enough to strike. Those wonderful dreams of vengeance could finally come true. But only if he was brave enough to act.

His fingers itched as they slowly crept toward the folded blade in his thigh pocket. It would be easy to pull it but it wouldn't solve anything. Not really. Even if no one identified him as the attacker and even if the security cams didn't catch him and assuming he didn't leave any forensic evidence behind, the accusations against him would still be on the record. The damage had already been done. All he could really hope for now was to find a way to mitigate the damage before it was too late.

Fighting the urge to pull the blade, he watched as the three moved ever closer to where he stood in the shadows cast by two large planters. His jaw clinched so tightly he knew his teeth would shatter as Major Ashlyn Shaw threw her head back and laughed gaily at something her mother said. How dare she laugh about anything! She was the cause of all his troubles.

Damn it, why hadn't she died back on Arterus like she was supposed to?

Unfortunately, she hadn't and, somehow, she'd managed

to survive not only her court martial but two years at the Tarsus penal colony. Worse, her champions had gotten all charges against her tossed out and her name, as well as the names of those who'd survived the Arterus mission with her, had been cleared. They'd been proclaimed heroes while he'd been shunned by his fellow Marines and relegated to nothing more than a glorified babysitter for the brats of foreign dignitaries. He knew she wouldn't be satisfied until she completely ruined him.

The smooth stone wall was cool through the material of his BDUs and he shivered slightly. Until that moment, he hadn't realized he had all but knitted himself to the wall in an attempt to remain invisible to the women. As they drew closer, he held his breath. The last thing he wanted was for them to look his way. It was bad enough when he had to salute either General Okafor or Brigadier General Shaw. But if he had to be civil to *Major* Shaw, he wouldn't be responsible for what happened.

Instead of looking his way, the three women continued through the lobby in the direction of the doors leading outside. As they passed, O'Brien heaved a silent sigh of relief. Still watching as they moved away, he reached up and wiped his brow. That had been too close. He either had to find some way to deal with Shaw, and in such a way it would never splash back on him, or he needed to get off-planet and soon. He had no doubts his time as a free man was quickly coming to an end and he had no intention of taking Shaw's place at the penal colony.

The thought of the JAG inquiry into the events leading up to Shaw and the others being brought up on charges had his anger flaring once again. He had no doubts she'd known he was there. Hell, it seemed like everyone in the Corps knew his schedule and made an attempt to see him in his ignominy. What else explained why they kept showing up as he played escort to all the snot-nosed brats the brass assigned him to?

Damn them all.

And damn Ashlyn Shaw most of all.

She'd been nothing but trouble from the moment he first laid eyes on her. She'd been too much by the book and too diligent to look the other way and leave alone the special arrangements he and the admiral had made with certain *businessmen* in the sector. So she had become the mouse to his cat as he and Sorkowski carefully set their trap for her. But they'd failed and now they were the prey.

This was really all the old man's fault. If Sorkowski hadn't been such a coward and had let him space the bitch when they had the chance, they wouldn't be in the positions they were now. Well, the old bastard had better have a plan to keep them both safe from whatever Shaw and her supporters had up their sleeves. Otherwise, he would take things into his own hands and it was a sure bet he would save his own neck before anyone else's, Sorkowski's included.

* * *

"Well, that was interesting," General Helen Okafor commented with a grin as the aircar moved away from the curb.

Ashlyn leaned against the back of the seat facing the Marine Corps commandant, her head cocked to one side. "I wondered if you'd seen him skulking in the shadows."

"It was hard not to," Elizabeth chuckled from where she sat next to her daughter. "Despite the way he tried to make himself very small."

A smile played at the corners of Ash's mouth as she remembered the sight of O'Brien staring at them, his eyes darting from one side to the other before he did his best to become invisible.

"Though I will admit I did wonder for a moment if he wasn't going to try something," Elizabeth continued.

Ash nodded, her expression serious. From the first

moment she'd spotted O'Brien standing near the lift, she had done her best to keep an eye on him without tipping him off that she had seen him. She had realized the first time they'd crossed paths that he wouldn't hesitate to try to sacrifice her again as long as it meant saving his own skin. Not that it wasn't expected. Still, she'd have expected him to have better self-control than to let his emotions show so clearly on his expression whenever she was near.

But that inability to hide his emotions was a weapon she was more than willing to use. She had no doubt he'd try to slip a blade between her ribs or something equally as fatal given the chance. This time had been no different. She had seen the battle he'd fought with himself to remain where he was, safe in the shadows. She'd watched as his hand inched ever closer to his pocket and, she assumed, some sort of weapon. Thankfully, whatever he'd thought about doing, he had decided not to. The last thing she wanted was to have a firefight in the lobby of Corps HQ.

"He's close to breaking," she said softly. "That makes him more dangerous than ever."

"It also makes him careless and that will work for us. At least I hope it will," Okafor said. "Don't look so worried, Ash. I assure you, Rico Santiago has him under constant surveillance."

The worry that had been knotting Ashlyn's stomach eased a bit. If Lt. Colonel Rico Santiago, FleetCom's head of intelligence, had eyes on O'Brien, she doubted the man could sneeze without someone knowing. "That does make me feel a bit better, ma'am." Of course, knowing JAG was finally ready to arrest O'Brien and Sorkowski – as well as anyone else who had conspired with them – would make her feel even better. "Now, will one of you tell me what's going on? I expected you to brief me about the Devil Dogs' next mission when you arrived, General."

"And I will once we reach our destination," Okafor assured her. "But before we get there, answer me this. How long do you need to make sure FirstBatt, in particular Deimos and Nike Companies, is ready to ship out?"

Okafor's use of the companies' battle names had Ashlyn sitting up straighter. Long ago, according to division lore, it had become tradition to call the various companies by names of ancient deities aligned with war and peace. The only time those names were used were when the Devil Dogs were about to drop into situations any normal Marine would consider Hell. The fact that Okafor used the battle names confirmed Ash's suspicions not only that they would soon be moving out but that they were heading straight into action. But knowing her suspicions had been right didn't answer the general's question.

"To be honest, I'd like another month to get to know the strengths and weaknesses of all the members of the battalion. But I can probably get the most pressing matters dealt with in ten days to two weeks." She produced her comp and glanced at Okafor, waiting until the woman nodded in approval before switching it on. She quickly checked her notes on the companies to make sure she wasn't forgetting anything.

"However, I do have concerns about both Deimos and Nike Companies, ma'am, and I've already discussed them with my mother. I should know more later today whether my concerns are justified or not. If they are, and depending on what our assignment is, I will be recommending that they be replaced on the mission."

"And the other companies?"

"On the whole, they're good, ma'am. There are a few adjustments to assignments that need to be made. Nothing too serious."

I hope.

"Very well. Let me know come morning if you feel we need

to make changes to the assignments. But, for now, we'll assume the issue either isn't as bad as you think or is something you can deal with in the week or so you'll have before they have to ship out."

"All I can do is promise to do my best, ma'am."

"And that is all I'm asking of you, Ash."

Ash considered what little the general had said and everything she hadn't. As she did, she glanced out the window. She noted the passing buildings and the distinct lack of uniforms on the people moving along the sidewalks. They had left the area around FleetCom Headquarters. But where were they going?

"General Okafor, who are you planning on sending as CO?"

She hated the uncertainty she felt as she asked. There had been a time there'd be no question about who would be going. If the bulk of the battalion was sent somewhere, the battalion CO would go with them. But that had been before she'd been named CO and after everything that had happened, she couldn't help wondering if Okafor had the same confidence in her that she had had in the Devil Dogs' previous commanding officer.

Okafor didn't answer. Instead, she glanced at Elizabeth and nodded. Trying not to let her nerves show, Ashlyn turned slightly so she could look at her mother. Elizabeth's expression was serious. Swallowing hard, Ash waited. Then, as her mother smiled slightly, the knot in her stomach began to unwind.

"Unless you have a very good reason not to go, you will be going with them. That means you'll need to carefully choose what part of Ares Company and your staff goes with you and what part remains here to make sure the rest of the battalion is ready for the next phase of your mission," Elizabeth said. "I'll need to know your decision on staffing by end of day tomorrow."

Ash nodded and tried to ignore the way her stomach once more tried to tie itself in knots. She didn't like having to split her staff up, not this soon. It wasn't that she didn't trust them. She did. But she'd feel better if they were all together on their first mission under her command. Still, her mother was right. She needed to leave someone in command here who would keep the rest of the battalion working to prepare for the next phase of their mission, whatever that might be.

"All right. Let me talk to my people. However, it would help to know what the immediate and long term goals of our mission are." She glanced at Okafor, hoping the general understood and agreed.

"You'll be fully briefed shortly, Ash." Okafor held up a hand to keep her from interrupting. "Be patient a little bit longer. We'll be there soon."

What could she do except nod?

"One more question, General?" she asked a few moments later.

"Of course."

"I am getting the feeling that this is going to be anything but a standard mission you're sending us on. Because I have some concerns about certain officers and non-coms for the companies you've identified to take part in the mission, I would like to be present for at least part of their training today. Do you think we will be done in time for me to get back to the O-Course to see how they're doing?"

"You should be able to. I don't think the briefing will take more than a couple of hours. At least most of the afternoon will be yours. But be ready to meet with the mission's senior naval officers tomorrow morning."

"Understood, ma'am."

"Ash, there's one more thing," Okafor said. "You won't be the senior Marine on the mission. Colonel Isaiah Johnson will be. However, he understands that the Devil Dogs will have their own mission parameters and that you are in charge where they are concerned. It's just that in the chain of command until you reach your destination, he will be senior."

Ashlyn nodded. That didn't surprise her. Whatever their ultimate destination, the Devil Dogs were still SpecOps. They would serve to assist the Marine contingent assigned to the task force or fleet transporting them but, once there, they would take over. It was something she'd been part of time and again when serving with the Devil Dogs under Pawlak.

"Johnson's a good man, General, and an even better Marine." Sensing her mother relaxing at her words, she turned her head and smiled slightly. "Don't worry, Mom. I know O'Brien and Sorkowski are the exceptions. I won't hold what they did to me and my team against Johnson."

"We never thought you would, Ash." Elizabeth's hand closed over hers and gave it a quick squeeze. "But we also want you to understand that this decision is in no way an indication that we think you aren't capable of leading the full Marine contingent. It's just that you are going to have your hands full with the DDs' mission."

"Mom, I understand, truly." She looked back at Okafor. "Ma'am, I mean it."

"I know you do, Ash."

Okafor fell silent as the aircar pulled into a parking garage. Ashlyn looked around and felt the color drain from her face as she realized where they were. Of all the potential destinations that had come to mind, this was the very last one. Hell, it hadn't even been on the list of the most improbable destinations. What in the world was going on?

"Easy, Ash," Elizabeth said softly. "This is necessary. You'll understand soon."

Not trusting herself to speak, Ashlyn nodded and watched as their driver slowed and finally stopped at a security checkpoint. Two heavily armed Marines stepped forward and asked everyone to hand over their IDs. After closely checking them and confirming that they were expected, the Marines stepped back and waved the aircar through. Because she knew not many in her position ever made this journey, Ashlyn breathed deeply and tried to calm her nerves. As she did, she chuckled softly. Now she understood why her mother and Okafor had refused to tell her where they were going. If she'd known they were on their way to meet with the president, she'd have probably run for the hills. Now she had no choice but to see what her companions had up their sleeves next.

CHAPTER SIX

ASHLYN PAUSED OUTSIDE THE DOOR TO THE CONFERENCE ROOM and breathed deeply. How quickly things could – and did – change. That was a lesson she had learned early into her career as a Marine. That lesson had been drummed home when she joined the Devil Dogs. Now it was a lesson she planned to drill into her company commanders, whether they liked it or not.

Three hours ago, she'd been sitting in the back of the aircar with her mother and General Okafor. Her biggest concern had been getting through the upcoming briefing and then back to the Obstacle Course. She'd been so worried about the potential problems with Gamma and Delta Companies that she hadn't thought too much about why they were leaving Marine country for the briefing. Then they'd pulled into the parking garage under the Capital building and all concerns about the battalion had disappeared.

For more than two hours, she had stood behind her mother's chair as Secretary of State Linden Klingsbury briefed them. Then President Harper had taken over. Over the next few minutes, he'd made it very clear that he wanted to put an end to the war. FleetCom was to implement a plan to take the fight directly to the Callusians. While they were pushed on their own homefront, missions were to be run to help liberate both the Cassius System and the newly invaded Nystrom System. If FleetCom learned of strategic targets, they were to be hit and hit hard. The time for Fuercon and its allies to sit back and watch as system after system fell to the Callusians was over. The war was going to end now and on Fuercon's terms.

While Ash agreed wholeheartedly with the President, she had concerns. The morning briefing of company commanders had shown a weakness – well, two weaknesses – in the battalion. She was going to have to deal with that at once. Otherwise, the battalion would be at a disadvantage when it shipped out. The only problem was, she didn't know what to do. Not yet, at any rate. Hopefully, by the time this briefing was over, she'd have an idea.

Squaring her shoulders, Ashlyn reached out and opened the door. As she stepped inside, she glanced around. In the center of the room was a long conference table. Around it sat the company commanders and members of her staff. Standing nearby were the company XOs. Unlike the morning's briefing, the senior non-coms had not been sent for. She'd leave their briefing to Talbot and Adamson, but that would come later.

Ashlyn frowned at the sight of two empty chairs at the table. Damn it, she had really hoped the concerns she'd had since morning had been a temporary blip in the way the battalion ran. Now she knew better. Just as she knew she should have insisted the doctors release her to full active duty status sooner than they had. With only a month or so on the job, she simply hadn't had enough time to get to know her commanders, much less their officers and the enlisted personnel.

"'Ten-hut!"

Adamson's voice rang out as she called the room to attention. Instantly, all conversation halted and boots scraped against the floor as chairs were pushed back and those gathered got to their feet. At least those present showed no hesitation in following the master sergeant's order.

Ashlyn moved to stand at the head of the table and took the time to look each of her captains in the eye. "Where are Captains Hotchner and Rhydderch?" Her voice was cold and her eyes hard. Any doubts she'd had about the necessity of transferring the men out of the battalion disappeared as she waited for someone to answer her question.

"Unknown, Major. They have yet to report in. Nor did they send word that they would be delayed," Ortega reported from her place at Ash's right.

"Did you confirm receipt of the change in orders for Gamma and Delta Companies?"

Of course she had. Why else were the XOs from those companies present?

"I did, ma'am," Ortega confirmed.

"Call the roll, Master Sergeant." If Hotchner and Rhydderch wanted to play games, she'd teach them that she would win every time – and she'd do it by following the rules.

Ashlyn remained standing, her gaze moving from person to person as Adamson called the roll. Starting with Alpha Company, the name of each commanding officer was called. Then Adamson repeated the process with each of the executive officers. With only two exceptions, everyone answered. Ash nodded, grateful for small favors.

"I want to make one thing perfectly clear," she said as the room once more fell silent. "I expect each and every officer to act like a Devil Dog. That means obeying orders and never being insubordinate. I will not tolerate non-coms being thrown under the bus to save an officer's career nor will I stand by and let officers or non-coms abuse the enlisted members of this battalion.

"The Devil Dogs are the best of the Marines. So I expect the best from each of you. It was obvious this morning that two company commanders had a problem understanding that. They have now shown they do not deserve to call themselves Marines, much less Devil Dogs. I will not allow insubordination such as they have shown to go unpunished.

""Lt. Taffer, where is Captain Hotchner?"

From where he stood four places down the table, Taffer swallowed hard. But that was the only indication he gave that he might want to be anywhere but there.

"Begging the Major's pardon, but I don't know."

Ash forced herself not to clinch her fists at her side as her anger once again flared. "When did you last see or speak with him, lieutenant?"

"Shortly after we received the change in orders for this afternoon, ma'am."

"And?"

"That's it, Major. He instructed me to make sure the company knew of the change in orders and told me to be sure to be here. Then I was dismissed."

"Same question, Lt. Rossi."

Unlike Taffer, the petite Rossi stepped up to the table and looked Ash square in the eye. As she did, Ashlyn had a feeling the redhead had grown tired of covering for her captain.

"I received basically the same orders, Major."

For a moment, Ash didn't say anything. Then she nodded once, her mind made up. She was about to make an example of the missing captains, one they wouldn't soon forget.

"Master Guns." She looked to where Talbot stood near the door. "Step outside and contact the MPs. Captains Hotchner and Rhydderch are to be located and brought immediately to my office. If we are still in the briefing, they are to be held there until I'm done."

"Yes, ma'am." He executed a perfect about face and left the room.

"Lt. Taffer, Lt. Rossi, you are in temporary command of

Gamma and Delta Companies until new COs have been found. You will meet with Captain Ortega after the briefing and you will detail for her everything you can about the behavior of your former COs. You will answer each of her questions fully and without hesitation if you wish to remain with the battalion."

"Yes, ma'am!"

If they hadn't already been standing at attention, Ash had no doubts they would have braced to it.

"Now, understand one thing, ladies and gentlemen. I will not tolerate behavior such as Hotchner and Rhydderch have exhibited today. I will repeat what I told each of you when I assumed command from Lt. Col. Pawlak. If you do not feel you can follow my orders, if you are not willing to give your all – including your lives – to the battalion, to the Corps and to Fuercon, then leave. I will approve your transfer immediately."

She sat and waited, giving them time to think about what she had said. Then she looked at Adamson and motioned for her to once again call the roll. One by one, those gathered announced their intent to remain with the battalion.

Good.

"Be seated." She watched as they did as she said. "There have been some changes since our briefing this morning. Ladies and gentlemen, there is no longer any room for doubt that the Callusians are intent on waging an all-out war. They have now sent ships to the Nystrom System. Halstrom's Landing has been attacked but is, at least so far, holding out. Second Fleet is dispatching units to assist the Nystrom Navy in holding off the invaders until more help can arrive.

"There has also been movement in the Cassius System. The latest word from our picket is that it appears at least some of the Callusian ships have moved out. What that means, we don't know – yet."

Ash leaned back and frowned. By the time she'd left the

briefing with Okafor and the others, she had been worried about whether or not the Devil Dogs would be able to meet the challenge set for them. Now that worry had blossomed and she was going to have to admit to the brass that at least part of the DDs weren't up to the challenge – yet.

And that was on her because she hadn't anticipated the problem before now. That was one mistake she'd never again make.

"The battalion, or at least most of it, will be shipping out just as soon as FleetCom has determined ship assignments for the upcoming mission. It was to have been the full battalion but, after the events of this afternoon, I anticipate we will be at least one company short." She held up a hand to prevent anyone from interrupting. "If that is the case, a skeleton HQ staff will remain as well. I'll be meeting with Captain Ortega and the rest of my staff later to discuss how we'll handle it.

"Alpha and Beta Companies will go into immediate training for the mission. Focus is to be on boarding parties as well as ground combat. You will receive your training assignments within an hour of the end of this briefing. Be aware that orders are going out to all members of the battalion that we will be moving on base tomorrow. That gives you tonight to say your goodbyes. There will be limited comm privileges to all Devil Dogs but we are basically going into a blackout until launch. FleetCom does not want to tip their hand to the enemy.

"Delta and Gamma Companies will continue training as well. However, after today's events, those companies will have to prove to me that they are battle ready. Lt. Taffer, Lt. Rossi, you need to tell your people just that."

"Yes, Ma'am!"

"Do you know where we're going, ma'am?" Ortega asked.

"I do, but until we have relocated on base, I'm not at liberty to disclose it. Just know that it will be more than enough to get some of our own back from the enemy and to remind them of just how foolish it is to take us on.

"Now, here is what we know about the current situations in both the Cassius System and the Nystrom System. . . ."

* * *

"Major, they're here."

Ashlyn looked up at the sound of her XO's voice. Then she glanced at the time. Two hours had passed since she'd issued the orders to find and bring Hotchner and Rhydderch to her office. That was longer than she'd hoped but not as long as she'd expected. Whether it meant they hadn't expected her to take direct action or not, she didn't care. All she wanted was to deal with them and get them out of her battalion before they managed to do any further damage.

But, before she did, she wanted to make sure she had everything covered. There would be no mistakes where they were concerned.

"Let Lt. Liu know they are here and ask if he will listen in. Assure him I will let them know he is taking part." She chewed her lower lip, thinking. "I want MPs on the door, on the outside. Kevin and MJ are to be inside. You and I will deal with getting Hotchner and Rhydderch out of the battalion. Then I want you to be sure all recordings, documentation, interviews, etc., are transmitted to my mother and to General Okafor. Let's make sure these two never see higher rank."

"I'll let you know what Liu has to say."

Ashlyn nodded and turned her attention back to the list of potential replacements for Hotchner and Rhydderch. If she got lucky, she might find at least one officer she could transfer in as company CO. Preferably, it would be someone who had served with the Devil Dogs before. But as long as they had the needed combat and command experience, and the right attitude, she wouldn't require it. Unfortunately, it was proving more difficult than she'd expected.

SAM SCHALL

Ten minutes later, Ash sat behind her desk, her expression hard, as the MPs escorted the two captains into her office. She thanked them and then told them to wait outside. As the door closed behind them, Adamson and Talbot took up positions on either side of the doorway. Looking at their serious expressions, Ash found herself almost wishing the captains tried to make a break for it. She had no doubts her senior non-coms would make quick work of the two of them.

"What is the meaning—" Hotchner began, his face flushed with anger.

"Quiet!" Ortega snapped. "And stand at attention. You haven't been put at ease."

Rebellion crossed both men's expression before they obeyed. Without a word, Ashlyn stood. As she moved around her desk, she made no attempt to hide her contempt. Nor did she try to disguise the fact she was inspecting every aspect of the men's appearance. Standing close, she sniffed, her upper lip curling back as she caught the aroma of alcohol on them both.

"Captain Ortega, inform Medical that I require a technician here on the double to take blood samples from these two *officers*." She spat out the word. "I have reason to believe they have been drinking while on duty and want to be sure they haven't been abusing other substances as well."

Rhydderch stiffened and looked like he wanted to speak. But one look from Ash seemed to quell whatever he'd been about to say.

"For the record, this meeting is being recorded. Lt. Jianyu Liu from the Judge Advocate General Corps is taking part via link at my request. Upon the conclusion of this meeting, copies of the recording as well as all other documentation relating to it will be forwarded to the offices of the commanding officer, First Division, as well as the Office of the Commandant of the Marine Corps. Do you each understand?"

She waited until they both answered in the affirmative.

"To begin, I have one question for the two of you. Did you receive the change in orders issued by Captain Ortega at my behest stating that the afternoon training session had been postponed and that you, along with your XOs, were to report for a briefing at 1500 hours?"

As she waited for them to respond, she returned to her chair.

"Answer aloud," Ortega told them when Rhydderch nodded, his expression grim.

"Yes." Anger roughed Hotchner's voice.

"Yes what?" Ashlyn prompted. She would not allow their insubordination and lack of respect to continue.

"Yes, ma'am," he ground out.

"Did you understand those orders?"

"Yes, ma'am," they answered almost in unison.

"Was there anything in those orders that led you to believe you could skip the briefing?"

No answer. Not that she expected one.

""I think you can take that as a negative, Major," Ortega said.

"Captain Ortega, at any time, did either Captain Hotchner or Captain Rhydderch inform you that they would not be at the briefing?"

"Negative, Major."

"Do either of you have anything to say for yourselves that might excuse your actions? You have disobeyed orders and have been insubordinate and that's just taking into account your actions today. Do you have anything you to say?"

"We've done nothing to deserve this sort of treatment, *Major*." Disdain all but dripped from Hotchner's words. "So we missed a briefing. We'd already been to one today. We made sure our XOs were present. If you said anything of import, they'd let us know. Whether you want to believe it or not, we had better things to be doing than watching you massage your ego."

"Captain—" Ortega began. She stopped when Ashlyn shook her head.

"What was so important that you didn't feel you needed to make the briefing?" Ash wanted to know. When neither man answered, she turned her attention to Talbot. "Master Guns, ask the MPs to come in."

He nodded and stepped out of the office. A moment later, he returned with the MPs. They approached the desk and then braced to attention.

"Sergeant Morgan, where did you find Captains Hotchner and Rhydderch?"

"They were at the Officers' Club, ma'am," the older of the two MPs answered.

"Were they alone?" She wasn't sure she wanted to know the answer. If they had been there with other members of the battalion, she'd have to look into those Marines as well and, damn it, she didn't have time for it.

"Negative, ma'am. They were sharing a table with Major Thomas O'Brien."

O'Brien!

Ashlyn's head snapped up and her eyes flashed. Well that certainly threw a whole new wrench in the works.

"Major." Lt. Liu's voice interrupted her thoughts and she glanced at the display to her right. "Major Shaw, I am hereby authorizing the MPs to take Captain Hotchner and Captain Rhydderch into custody. They are to be escorted to my office where they can explain to me not only why they disobeyed orders but why they were consorting with someone currently under investigation."

"Thank you, Lt. Liu." She nodded to the MPs who moved to stand on either side of the two men. "Before you leave, there is one thing you need to understand. You are both relieved of your commands in FirstDiv and you will be transferred out just as soon as I can push the paperwork through. While you have your *discussion* with Lt. Liu, your offices will be cleaned out. Your personal belongings will be forwarded to you, just as soon as they have been checked." She paused and wished she dared to more. "Sergeant Morgan, get these two sorry excuses for Marines out of my office."

"With pleasure, Major."

"Liu," Ash began as Hotchner and Rhydderch were escorted out.

"Don't worry, Major. I have every intention of seeing what connection they have with O'Brien," the JAG officer assured her. "I will let you know what comes out of my interview with them. But rest assured, I will support your decision to remove them from the battalion." With that, he ended the transmission.

For a moment, Ash stared at the blank comm screen. Then she turned her attention to her executive officer.

"Luce, let's not take any more chances. Run a check on all officers and senior non-coms. If there is more than a passing connection with either Sorkowski or O'Brien, I want to know about it. This is one instance where I will let myself be paranoid. If we're about to drop into battle, I need to be able to trust the officers under my command."

"Understood."

"Now, it's going to make for a long night and a very early morning, but we need to find replacements for those two bastards and we need to finish filling out the HQ staff." She leaned back, her expression thoughtful. "Luce, you and MJ get together first and set up training sessions for Alpha and Beta Companies for tomorrow. We'll do a full battalion exercise day after tomorrow. Hopefully by then we will have new COs for Gamma and Delta Companies."

Hopefully. If not, she was going to have to tell General

Okafor that, for the first time, the Devil Dogs wouldn't be able to answer the call to serve and that was something she intended to avoid, if at all possible.

CHAPTER SEVEN

"MA'AM, WOULD YOU MIND TELLING ME WHY WE'VE COME TO THE *Aisling*?" Talbot asked.

Ashlyn looked up from the report she'd been studying and set her datapad to one side. Then she glanced around the shuttle's main cabin. She and Talbot had the first rows of seats to themselves. The next two rows had been left empty. But beyond that sat half a dozen men and women. They all wore naval uniforms. While their presence wasn't unusual, it did make it more difficult to discuss not only the reasons for the trip but her concerns about it.

"There are several members of the Marine contingent onboard who have requested transfer to the battalion, Master Guns. I figured it was easier for me to come to them to conduct the interviews and discuss their service records with their CO than to have them brought to us."

For a moment, she wondered if Talbot would ask something else. He didn't. Instead, he nodded, his eyes flicking to the rear of the shuttle. Good. He'd understood why she was being a bit circumspect. Not that she'd expect anything else from him.

She wished there had been time to fully brief him, as well as Lucinda Ortega who was holding things down for her dirtside, before they had to catch the shuttle. But there hadn't been. She had awakened to find orders from General Okafor. In no uncertain terms, she'd been instructed to make her way to the *Aisling* in its parking orbit. The public reason for her visit was to meet with those Marines who had requested transfer to the Devil Dogs. Since she had already planned to interview one of them as a replacement for Delta Company's CO, she'd not objected.

Then she'd learned the other reason for her visit. Not only was she to evaluate the Marine complement onboard but she was to determine if the ship would meet her needs as battalion CO for the Devil Dogs' upcoming mission. Okafor had made it very clear that only ships, and their personnel, that Ashlyn was comfortable with would be going on the mission.

That had surprised her. It hadn't taken long after her return from Tarsus to realize that FleetCom was being very careful where she was concerned. The medical personnel she'd seen had almost all been associated with the Devil Dogs. General Okafor had made sure those first few weeks that Ash only dealt with Devil Dogs and former Devil Dogs. Ashlyn had a feeling part of it was to make sure she understood that they meant everything they were saying about knowing she and the others had been set up. Another part had to have been an attempt to reassure her that the Corps was now and always had been behind her. But this latest was almost too much. Then she'd gotten a quick message from her mother. Elizabeth had said it best. Fleet was simply acting as transport for this mission. Ash, as well as the task force commander, had to be confident that every ship, and every man and woman onboard, would do whatever was necessary for the successful completion of the mission.

The shuttle seemed to give a shudder and a moment later a soft chime announced the completion of the docking sequence. The red light over the hatch turned green, confirming pressurization of the compartment beyond. As the hatch slid open almost silently, Ashlyn climbed to her feet, Talbot at her side. It was time, ready or not.

Squaring her shoulders, Ashlyn stepped into the aisle. She took a moment to make sure there wasn't a seam out of place or a medal hanging askew on her chest. Usually, she did all she could to do away with protocol that didn't serve any purpose but to add unnecessary time to an assignment. She hadn't had a choice this time. Okafor had *requested* she wear mess dress for her inspection. Hopefully, it would be enough to head off any trouble that might be waiting for her.

A few moments later, she stepped off the shuttle and into the docking bay of the *Aisling*. As she did, she glanced around. The sounds of a crew working on a nearby shuttle reached her. They appeared to be the only ones present, barring the BBOD and two Marine privates standing just behind the BBOD. Something about that seemed wrong but Ash didn't dwell on it. This wasn't her ship – yet – and she wasn't Navy. The two branches might be related and they certainly relied upon one another, but there was no disputing that they did things differently.

But she was a Marine and the sight of the two privates did bother her. It wasn't that they were privates, at least not completely. What bothered her was the fact they were the only Marines present. It was a breach of protocol to have privates there without an officer to meet someone of her rank. There could be a reasonable explanation. She simply couldn't think what it might be, not under present circumstances at least.

Then she noticed the state of their uniforms. Eyes narrowed, she took a moment to study them. Neither seemed to be paying that much attention to what was going on. That apparent lack of interest in doing their duties added to her unease. She knew first-hand that this kind of sentry duty was boring. After all, the chances of any real danger occurring while in a parking orbit over Fuercon was slim to none. But that didn't mean it was impossible. The attack on the capital just a few months before had proven that. However, these two weren't under her command, not yet at any rate. All she could do was take note of their demeanor and mention it to their CO later. It would be up to him to take action – or not.

Putting her concern on the mental back burner, Ash took three steps forward and then stopped, the toes of her boots almost touching the red line marking the official change from docking area to shipboard.

"Permission to come aboard?"

The very young looking second lieutenant stepped forward, his left hand resting on the butt of the gun at his hip and his right hand extended. "Orders and ID."

Without a word, Ashlyn handed over the datachip containing the information he requested. Then she watched as he slid it into his datapad. He studied the readout for a moment before motioning the Marine guards forward to take his place as he moved away.

Not liking what was happening, Ashlyn glanced over her shoulder to where Talbot stood one step behind and to her right. It reassured her to see how the man watched the two Marines. Anyone who didn't know him well wouldn't notice anything out of the ordinary. But she recognized his expression. He was on guard and ready to react to a threat from any quarter.

As they waited for the BBOD to return, Ash reached up and gently rubbed her right cheek with the first two fingers of that hand. Such an innocent seeming gesture and yet to a Devil Dog it was anything but that. It was their signal to be on the alert. Out of the corner of her eye, she saw Talbot nod slightly. Good. Whatever might happen, they'd be prepared.

"Welcome aboard, Major Shaw," the BBOD finally said a few moments later as he handed back the datachip she'd given him.

"Thank you, lieutenant."

She waited, wondering if he would explain the delay in approving her request to come aboard. When he didn't, she frowned. One part of her wanted to press the issue, especially when she looked around the docking bay again and that feeling something was wrong continued to grow.

God, she wished she could put her finger on what was bothering her. Even though the *Aisling* was not one of the newest cruisers in the Fleet, it was only a few years old and had not seen any major fighting. Yet there was an air of age about the docking bay that didn't fit what she knew of the ship. Add that to the fact not a single senior officer, Navy or Marine, was present to greet her as well as the delay in allowing her to come onboard and it all added up to the very real possibility that something was very wrong on the ship.

"If you'll wait for a moment, Major, I'll arrange for an escort—"

Before the lieutenant could finish his statement, Talbot stepped forward, his expression closed, his dark eyes flashing. He made it very obvious he was looking at the young man's name tape and that the BBOD's failure to identify himself was a breach of protocol. "Lieutenant Soroyan, Major Shaw here by the authority of FleetCom and General Okafor. Her orders give her free access to every portion of this ship and its personnel. I assure you, no escort is needed nor required." Now he held up a hand when the young man was foolish enough to try to interrupt him. "In fact, I am sure I speak for the Major when I note that there have already been several major breaches of protocol. First, there is no senior officer here to greet her. Second, you failed to identify yourself to a senior officer. Third, you have yet to explain why she was not immediately cleared to board. I can go on but I won't. What I will do is suggest you not compound the problem any further."

"Stand down, Master Guns." Ash fought back her smile. "I'm sure the lieutenant simply misspoke."

The younger man nodded, his Adam's apple bobbing as he swallowed hard, his face almost as red as his hair.

"M-may I be of any help to the Major?" Soroyan asked, his voice cracking.

"You can tell me where I might be able to find Captain Loren Nichols."

Soroyan quickly checked his datapad before answering. "He is off-duty now, Major. You'll probably be able to find him either in his quarters or in the Marine's gym or mess."

"Very good, lieutenant." She looked past him to where the two Marines stood in poses that would never come close to regulation stances. "Master Guns, before we move on, would you care to enlighten these two privates about what it means to be a member of the Fuerconese Marine Corps?"

"With pleasure, Major." Talbot stepped forward.

Five minutes later, the lift doors closed and Ashlyn grinned up at Talbot. She had forgotten just how effective his dressing downs could be. Watching him as he pointed out every thread showing, every hair out of place and every crease that shouldn't be there had been more than entertaining. More telling, however, had been the reaction of the two privates. It was clear they suddenly felt like they had been tossed back into boot camp and were facing the world's most intimidating DI. Which, if she were honest, was pretty close to the truth.

"Remind me to never be on the receiving end of one of your dressing downs, Master Guns," she said as she programmed the lift for Marine territory.

"Ma'am, I'd be a fool to try to dress you down. I don't want to lose my stripes."

Even though he grinned, he didn't fool Ash. She knew he'd waste no time in giving her a dressing down shed never forget if he thought it would save her life or prevent her from doing something she'd regret later. That was why he was a member of her staff and why she trusted him at her back no matter what the situation.

"I'll remind you of that, Loco, when the time comes." She reached out and paused the lift. "I think it's fair to say there is something wrong onboard. It may simply be a breakdown in discipline. It may be more. So keep your eyes open. If you see or hear anything you think I need to know about, tell me. Use my call sign if you feel there is any danger and I'll do the same."

"Understood, ma'am."

She reached out and started the lift once again. As she did, she wished she had brought at least one other member of her team with her. While she didn't really believe there was the possibility of anything serious happening while they were onboard, she didn't want to run any risks.

As they stepped out of the lift and started down the corridor a short time later, Ash frowned once again. From the moment she'd come aboard, her sense of wrongness had grown. Now, deep within the bowels of the ship, she knew she had ample reason to worry. The air smelled stale, as if the scrubbers weren't working properly and hadn't in some time. A thin coat of dust covered every surface. The ship had the look and feel of something in disrepair, a once proud lady now brought down by an uncaring and heavy hand. Like it or not, Ash was going to have to pass on her concerns.

What bothered her the most was the possibility that she'd discovered yet another ship's CO who wasn't doing his duty. At least this time she had no reason to assume he was actively working against Fuercon's interests. More importantly, at least as far as she was concerned, she wasn't in his chain of command. So there was little chance of anything untoward happening.

"Major, did you send instructions not to have anyone

present to greet us when we arrived?" Talbot asked as they moved through the nearly deserted corridors.

"Negative, Master Guns."

And that was something that bothered her almost as much as the condition of the ship. The captain should have been informed of her impending arrival the moment the shuttle pilot radioed for clearance to land. Under normal circumstances, the moment the pilot contacted the ship, the senior officer on duty should have contacted the captain so he could be there to greet her. It seemed obvious that notification hadn't been made and, as far as Ash knew, it could mean only one thing. The crew was setting their captain up and that worried her. It worried her a great deal. How had he managed to lose the loyalty and respect of those under his command?

There was another explanation, however. It was entirely possible that notification had been made and the captain chose to ignore it. If that happened to be the case, the captain had committed a serious breach of protocol. Again, Ash had no answer for the why he might have done so. What she did have was a feeling in the pit of her stomach that it was going to become her job to get to the bottom of the problem and deal with it.

Now, as she stepped into the Marines' gym, Ash looked around and nodded slightly. The corners of her mouth lifted as she spotted the tall, slim young man working out against a sparring droid. His blonde hair, so light it was almost white, was close cropped. Sweat glistened on his bare arms and legs, his black PT gear was soaked with it. Naked fury marred Nichols' features. Hands and feet flew as he pressed his attack against the droid.

Before the junior officer nearest her could announce her presence, Ash shook her head and touched a finger to her lips. Then she stripped off her jacket and reached up to unbuttoned her shirt before toeing off her boots. A moment later, dressed only in uniform pants and tank, she collected a mouth-guard from the equipment shelf before stepping onto the mat.

Without warning, Ash's hand flashed forward. Her fingers closed about Nichols' wrist before the young man could renew his attack on the droid. Nichols spun, leading with a savage right hook. Grinning, Ash expertly blocked it with her forearm. With that, the fight was on.

* * *

His fist connected with the 'droid's jaw with a satisfying crunch and his lip curled back. Mentally, he visualized smashing his fist against the captain's jaw instead of the 'droid's. Disbelief still warred with hot fury as memory of the morning's encounter returned. If he didn't find a way off this bucket of bolts soon he wouldn't be responsible for what happened.

Ducking a round house, Loren Nichols fought for calm. He knew all too well that if he didn't find his center soon, he would do something foolish. Not foolish enough to land him in the brig – or worse – but enough to give the captain yet another reason to come down on him. Not that the bastard needed a reason. He had proven much too willing to come down hard on Nichols, or any of the other Marines, without good reason on too many occasions already.

Damn him!

Anger once more spiking, Nichols ducked under another round house. He jammed his fist into what would be the 'droid's right kidney if it were human. Then he followed up with a sharp upper cut, leaving his guard open for just one brief moment. His breath exploded as an artificial fist slammed into his stomach. Sucking in air, he moved away from the 'droid's follow up before it could land another blow.

Then he turned, intending to land a spinning backfist to the 'droid's face. Before he could complete the move, fingers closed firmly about his wrist. Reacting on pure instinct,

Nichols pivoted, right fist cocked and ready.

Furious to have his workout interrupted, Nichols sent his fist flying forward, intent on giving whoever had been foolish enough to grab him a lesson he, or she, wouldn't soon forget. Instead, he found his blow blocked and a fist landing a perfectly controlled strike to his solar plexus.

Snarling, Nichols feinted and then executed a perfectly timed sidekick. Or so he thought. A forearm connected with his leg, blocking the kick and leaving him off-balance. Before he could react, his feet were swept out from under him and he found himself falling. He landed with a heavy thud, the ceiling of the gym filling his field of vision.

Ready to take the fight to his opponent, glad to have a living outlet for his anger, Nichols quickly rocked to his feet.

And came up so short it felt like he had hit a wall. Or had completely lost his mind because what he saw was impossible. Maybe he had hit his head harder than he thought and this was a dream. That was it. He was really lying on the decksole unconscious and this was all a dream.

Then the dream erupted into a myriad of stars and his breath exploded as he was once more slammed to the mat. Lying there, waiting for his lungs to remember how to work, he became aware of the sounds around him. His fellow Marines called out encouragements, urging him to get up and get back into the fight. Then another voice, a voice from the past, mockingly asked if that was all he had, if he'd finally gone soft.

Climbing to his feet, Nichols ran a hand over his face. His eyes locked on his opponent and he shook his head in disbelief. The tall, dark haired woman in uniform pants and tank top couldn't be there. Absolutely couldn't. But the pounding in his head and the ache in his back told him that he was wrong. Somehow he was wrong.

"Cap?" His voice betrayed his uncertainty.

There was no doubt about it. Ashlyn Shaw actually stood

before him, hands on hips, laughter in her eyes. How many times before had they been in this same position – the captain enjoying the fact she had sent him onto his backside yet again? If it wasn't for the band of white in the dark hair and a hardness around her eyes, Nichols could almost have believed he'd gone back in time and none of the long nightmare had occurred.

"Hey, kid." Then the woman smiled again, affection touching her voice as she reached down to help Nichols to his feet.

"Is it really you, Cap?"

* * *

Ash considered the young man with a surprise that mirrored Nichols'. It didn't make sense. He should know the story. Everyone seemed to know the story. After all, the newsies had made sure it had been spread far and wide. Beyond that, FleetCom had issued full statements to each ship and posting with orders to make sure all personnel knew what had happened. So there was no reason why Nichols should be asking how and why she had gotten there.

Surely the ship's captain wasn't as foolish and stubborn as Ash was beginning to think.

Or was he?

"Nichols, are you saying you haven't seen the dispatches from FleetCom or the news coverage of the last two months?" Ash did her best to keep her voice carefully neutral as the others in the gym began to gather around them. As they did, she heard the murmurs as some of them recognized her as well as the speculation about what her sudden appearance might mean.

"Ma'am, we haven't seen a newscast in months. The captain doesn't believe they add anything to our duties." Now there was a definite touch of disgust in the younger man's voice and Ash felt her mouth draw tight.

"And the dispatches from FleetCom?" she prompted.

"Ma'am, with apologies, but none of us know what you're talking about nor do we understand how you can be here," a tall, muscular man who reminded her of a Fuerconese Mountain Bear said as he moved to Nichols' side.

For a moment, Ash stood there, thinking hard. Before she did anything else, she needed to be sure she understood what the Marines did and did not know. So she might as well start with the obvious.

"Listen up." She raised her voice and waited until every Marine either joined them or stopped what they were doing and turned in her direction. "For those who do not know me, the name's Ashlyn Shaw. Yes, that Ashlyn Shaw." She gave them a moment to digest that bit. "In case you weren't given access to the dispatches from FleetCom and from General Okafor's office, the cases against myself and the six surviving members of my unit were reopened and we have been cleared, our records expunged and we have been returned to duty. I have been promoted to the rank of major and am now in command of the Devil Dogs. Lt. Colonel Pawlak has been transferred to Second Division to help bring their Marines up to the standard of FirstBatt."

She looked around, noting the looks of surprise and approval, on the faces of the Marines surrounding her.

"Now, were you apprised of the fact that the capital was attacked less than two months ago by the Callusians? It was an attack we now know was a feint meant to keep our focus on the home system while the enemy prepared to invade the Cassius System."

That was all it took. Several of the Marines cursed long and, in one case, quite inventively. Another turned and slammed his fist into the sparring droid Nichols had been working against, all but decapitating the droid in the process. Some of the younger Marines paled even as their spines straightened. No matter what had been happening on the ship, these Marines, at least, appeared to be ready for whatever was necessary.

Good.

"President Harper has withdrawn our support for the truce and we are now at war. You should have been informed of all this by order of FleetCom and under the seal of the President's Office."

For a moment, no one spoke. Then Nichols squared his shoulders and took a step forward. When he stopped, he braced to attention. "Major, with apologies, but we had no idea any of this had happened."

Ash closed her eyes and counted to ten. The bad feeling she'd had since boarding just kept getting worse. How in the name of all that was holy could the ship's CO not have told his command that they were now at war?

"Master Guns, I think you'd better access the ship's computers so we can see what's going on here. Verify receipt of FleetCom's dispatches and that the captain viewed them." She turned to Talbot, not bothering to hide her anger. He nodded once and, with a signal to one of the Marines standing nearby, hurried across the gym in the direction of the sole office located off to one side.

"Now," Ash continued as she studied those gathered around her. She nodded slightly as she recognized a number of the faces and saw the eagerness, even hope, reflected on their expressions. She wanted to know what was happening onboard the ship and now she had her chance to do just that. "Let me begin by saying that the *Aisling* is under consideration for a mission FirstBatt will soon be embarking on. That is part of the reason why I'm here. The other part is that I'm here to speak with certain members of the Marine detachment onboard as well as to review the detachment as a whole."

Before she could continue, Talbot emerged from the small

office. One look at his face told Ash all she needed to know. The dispatches had reached the ship and the captain had read them. But, for whatever reason, he had chosen to disobey orders and had not released the information to his officers and crew. For that reason alone, Ash knew she had to act. If he had ignored that order, what else had he done and could she put it all to right in time for their scheduled departure from the system?

"Master Guns?"

"Major Shaw, I regret to inform you that the captain of this ship failed to follow orders from FleetCom concerning informing the crew of the fact that all charges against you and the surviving members of your unit have been dropped and your records cleared. It is also clear that he failed to inform the ship's company that charges have been leveled against many of those who had been in charge of the prisoners at the Tarsus military prison. Further, it is clear that the captain also failed to disclose to the crew the fact that the capital was attacked or that Cassius Prime was invaded. Finally, he has failed to inform the crew that we are once more at war with the Callusians."

For a moment, Ash looked at Talbot, unable to believe what she heard. Her suspicions about him had been confirmed. He hadn't told his crew about the attack on the capital or on Cassius Prime. Was he insane? What if they had come across a hostile force? He could have gotten them all killed. And for what? That was what she had to find out and there wasn't a moment to lose.

"All right, Master Guns. It is obvious there's more going on here than we knew when we came onboard."

Damn it, why couldn't anything be simple anymore?

"I need to report in. While I do, no one is to leave the gym nor are they to contact anyone else." She let her gaze rest on each Marine present. "Just so they understand, Master Guns, remind them about what it means to be a Marine and what it takes to be in Spec Ops, much less the Devil Dogs."

"Yes, ma'am."

"Nichols, you're with me."

With that, Ash collected her jacket, shirt and boots and made her way to the office. Once there, she quickly dressed. After running her hands through her hair, she reached for her comm and waited to be connected with her mother. She knew she was breaking protocol by not going through the *Aisling's* comms officer but this was one conversation she didn't want the ship's CO getting wind of. At least not yet.

"Shaw here," her mother said a few minutes later.

"Ma'am, we have something of a situation onboard the *Aisling*," Ashlyn said simply before quickly reporting what she knew so far.

"Hold one moment, Major. I'm going to bring both General Okafor and Admiral Tremayne in on this."

"Thank you, ma'am." She glanced at Nichols who stood uncertainly in the doorway. "Quick question, Nichols, who is the Marine CO onboard?"

"That would be Major Jasper, ma'am."

Ash nodded and quickly called up Jasper's record. A quick glance produced nothing to explain why the Marines seemed a pale reflection of what they should have been. Nor did it explain why he hadn't been on hand to greet her when she and Talbot arrived onboard.

"Go get dressed and meet me back here in five," she continued as her comm unit beeped to let her know her mother was back. Before activating it, she waited until Nichols nodded and left the small office. "My apologies, ma'am. I needed to deal with something before continuing."

"Understood, Major," Elizabeth said. "I have General Okafor and Admiral Tremayne tied into the comm."

"My aide, Captain Jareau, is also tied in," Miranda

Tremayne added.

"You said we have a situation onboard the *Aisling*, Major. What's going on?" General Okafor prompted.

"I don't know the full details yet, ma'am, but it is clear that there are problems onboard. First, Master Gunnery Sergeant Talbot has discovered that the ship's CO failed to inform the ship's complement of not only the attacks on the capital and on Cassius Prime but also of the events surrounding my being here.

"But the trouble runs deeper than that. There is an air to the ship, like the crew has either been broken or it has decided just to get by until they can transfer off. The ship itself is rundown and appears much older than it really is. It is as if the standard maintenance isn't being conducted. I can't put my finger on what exactly is wrong. I'm a Marine, not Navy, so I don't know all the nuances of commanding or maintaining a ship like this."

"What does the captain have to say, Major?" Tremayne asked.

"I can't tell you, ma'am. I haven't seen him or any of the senior officers, Naval or Marine, since arriving onboard."

"Where are you now, Major?" General Okafor asked.

"In an office off the gym in Marine territory, ma'am." She paused, her eyes going wide in disbelief, as Nichols returned to the office. "My apologies, ma'am, but something's come up on this end. With your permission, I'll be back with you in just a moment." She muted the comm and stood, her expression hard. "Mr. Nichols, would you care to explain to me why in the name of all that is holy you are wearing the insignia of a second lieutenant?"

And why hadn't the BBOD said anything when she asked for *Captain* Loren Nichols?

"Ma'am, it is my current rank." There could be no mistaking the anger and bitterness in the man's voice.

"You'd best explain, and quickly, since the last entry in your personnel jacket was a rank of captain with a notation that you were being recommended for promotion at the first possible opportunity." Ash inhaled, held it for a moment and then exhaled. Getting upset with Nichols wasn't going to help, at least not until she knew what was happening.

"Major, it was by order of Commander Kryzcek. I can't explain why it hasn't yet been noted in my file."

"And why is a Naval officer, ship's CO or not, busting down a Marine officer and why didn't your Marine CO object?"

"Major Jasper has been confined to sick bay for the last four weeks, ma'am. At that time, Commander Kryzcek took command of the Marine contingent."

Ashlyn's mouth grew tight and she fought the urge to curse long and hard. Instead, she keyed off the mute on her comm. This was definitely something she needed to pass along to the powers that be.

"My apologies, General Okafor, Admiral Tremayne, but things are most definitely not what any of us had been led to believe about the ship. I've just been informed that the Marine CO has been confined to sick bay for the last month. Since then, Commander Kryzcek, the ship's CO, has taken over command of the Marine contingent. He has busted Jasper's XO from captain down to second lieutenant. I know the Marines assigned to the *Aisling* are part of SecDiv, but I recommend they be temporarily reassigned to FirstDiv until this can be sorted out."

"Major, you are to take immediate command of the Marine contingent onboard. We'll sort out what's going on after you've had a chance to review the current situation and, hopefully, speak with the Marine CO," Okafor said. "Orders will be transmitted to you and to the ship within the next five minutes."

"Understood, ma'am."

"Major, you are also to assume command of the ship until Captain Jareau arrives. He will relieve you and begin an investigation into what has been going on onboard the *Aisling*," Tremayne put in.

"Admiral!" Ash stopped and forced herself to stay calm. "Ma'am, I'm a Marine. I doubt there is any way the CO will accept my assuming command."

"Then you will confine him to quarters and he will find himself brought up on charges of insubordination and disobeying orders." There was no give in the Admiral's voice. "Orders relieving him of command and putting you in charge of the ship pending Captain Jareau's arrival will come under both my signature and General Okafor's." She paused briefly. "Just don't go deciding you can take the ship out for a joyride."

"Not this time, ma'am," she chuckled.

"Ash, I'll be including orders as well. I want to know what happened to Major Jasper and why he hasn't been transferred to a groundside medical facility," her mother added.

"Understood."

"Major, remain in the gym until you receive your orders. Then get to the bridge and take command. Pick those of the Marines you feel most comfortable with to assist you," Okafor said firmly. "Any questions?"

"Not at the moment, Ma'am."

"Record on at all times. Tell Talbot the same."

"Yes, Ma'am."

"If you haven't received your orders in the next few minutes, let us know, Major," Tremayne told her. "Captain Jareau will get you his ETA as soon as possible."

"Thank you, Admiral."

"Get to work, Ash. Sounds like you have your job cut out for you," Okafor said and ended the transmission.

For a moment, Ash just sat there, staring into space. Then she gave herself a mental shake. Like it or not, she'd been given her orders. But, before she did anything else, she needed to know exactly what Nichols could tell her.

"All right, Loren, tell me what happened."

"Ma'am, right now I feel like I hit my head too hard in a fall and this is all a dream. I'm not sure I'd make any sense, at least not until you tell me how you happen to be here. So I guess maybe you ought to just look at this." As he spoke, he handed over his personal datapad.

For a moment, Ash simply looked at the younger man. Then she took the datapad and leaned back, not sure what she would find. The cynic in her was prepared to see personal justifications for what happened. Instead, she saw the official documentation behind Nichols' drop in rank. Part of her was relieved to know Nichols' sense of honor hadn't changed in the last several years.

Without looking up, Ash flipped through the official documentation to Nichols' personal log entries for the dates in question. A bitter smile touched her lips as she did. Nichols' log was detailed, including the names of witnesses to the events alleged in the allegations against him and, in some cases, recordings of what happened.

Good. If Nichols' log passed muster after being examined by the JAG, it would be enough to make sure the ship's commander never held another command again.

"I have two questions." Ash handed the datapad back and waited until Nichols nodded. "First, what would you say to returning to the Devil Dogs?"

Now it was Nichols' turn to say nothing. For several long moments, he simply stared at some point over Ash's head. Finally, he looked back at Ashlyn, a million questions reflected in his expression.

"Ma'am – Major, I meant what I said earlier about feeling like I hit my head too hard and this is all some sort of hallucination or something." He ran a hand over his hair and shook his head. "I don't understand how you can be here. But, to answer your question, I would like nothing more than to return to the Devil Dogs. I never wanted the transfer out."

"I know and that's one of the reasons why I'm here." She climbed to her feet and moved around the battered desk so she stood before the man. "Consider yourself back to the battalion, Mr. Nichols."

She produced her datapad. A few moments later, Nichols' datapad beeped. Ashlyn watched as Nichols checked the new message. Seeing the smile that slowly spread across her companion's face, Ash nodded slightly. Good. One hurdle cleared. But that was just the warm up.

"Now for my second question. I have received orders to take temporary command of not only the Marines onboard but of the ship itself, at least until Admiral Tremayne's aide arrives to relieve me. Starting with the Marines in the gym, who can I trust?"

Ash had to give it to Nichols. He didn't answer instantly. Instead, he glanced out into the main area of the gym, his expression thoughtful. Ashlyn waited, not wanting to rush her.

"Each of those present are solid, Ma'am. I would trust them at my back in a firefight anytime."

"Very good."

She smiled slightly. This next part would be tricky, but at least Tremayne and Okafor had been quick about making sure she had copies of her new orders. But before she announced them to the rest of the ship, she needed to see how the handful of Marines in the next room reacted. Orders or not, if she got the feeling things could go south, she would hole up here in the gym with Marines Nichols said she could trust until time for Captain Jareau to arrive onboard.

"Ten-hut!" Talbot snapped as she returned to the gym a moment later.

Instantly the Marines obeyed. Ashlyn left them braced to

attention. Before she could say anything, Nichols quickly took his place at the end of the line. Good. There was still pride in these few men and women and that was something she could work with. At least she hoped so.

With Talbot on her heels, Ashlyn moved down the line of Marines, her eyes missing nothing. Even in PT gear, there was an air of confidence and strength about them. Despite the concern and curiosity they had to be feeling just then, they didn't move, they didn't so much as let their eyes follow her as she moved past them. It was as if they were recruits at Basic and she was the meanest, baddest drill sergeant, the one they hated in the moment but who they thanked for giving them the skills that would one day save their lives.

"Stand easy," she said as she finished her inspection. "As I said earlier, for those who don't know me, my name is Ashlyn Shaw. I am the commanding officer of FirstBatt, the Devil Dogs. Since it is becoming all too clear that there is a problem onboard this ship, let me start by telling you what you should have learned two months ago. At the behest of President Harper, a full investigation into the events surrounding the court martial and conviction of myself and the six surviving members of my unit more than two years ago, all charges have been dropped, our records have been cleared and we have been reinstated to active duty. That is the short version. The long version is that the JAG is investigating the circumstances that led up to our convictions, looking not at us but at other members of the Navy and Marines. That is all I am at liberty to tell you at the moment. However, if you check your datapads, you will find copies of not only our pardons and orders reinstating us to duty but also statements from the President and from General Okafor.

"As for the Devil Dogs' former commander, Major Pawlak is now Lt. Colonel Pawlak. He has been transferred to Second Division. He left a pair of very large boots for me to fill but I will do my best to do so, starting with carrying out my orders from FleetCom to hold this ship until Captain Jareau arrives.

"Until FirstDiv's CO and the Commandant's Office can review the disciplinary actions that have been taken by the ship's CO, I am brevetting Mr. Nichols to his previous rank of captain. So, Captain Nichols, put three teams put together. One is to go to Engineering. Another is to go to Life Support. The third is to come with me to the Bridge.

"Understood, ma'am." He stepped forward and then turned to face the other Marines. "With the Major's permission, you have three minutes to get dressed and fall back in. Move!"

"Yes, sir!" they answered as one and raced to the locker room to do as he said.

Ashlyn nodded in approval. No matter what the ship's CO thought, it was obvious the Marines respected Nichols and that, as far as Ash was concerned, was all that really mattered.

Less than five minutes later, the Marines had once more formed up. Each looked as if they could have stepped right out of a recruiting poster, unlike the two in the bay. That reassured Ash. So did the way they snapped to attention as she and Talbot approached. As they neared, Nichols moved forward two steps and then braced to attention. His right hand snapped up in a salute.

"Orders, ma'am?" he asked once she returned his salute.

"Get me those three squads, Captain."

Nichols nodded and then turned to face the waiting Marines. Quickly, he split them into the three squads. As he did, Ash nodded slightly in approval. Nichols put the senior non-com, a staff sergeant, in charge of the squad heading to Engineering. A young second lieutenant would lead the squad going to Life Support. Nichols left himself to lead the squad escorting Ash to the bridge.

Nor did she blame him. By acting as her escort, he would

be able to show the ship's CO that not all officers had such little regard for his abilities as a Marine. She understood Nichols' need to get a little of his own back. She'd been hoping for the exact same thing since learning she had been pardoned and then cleared of all charges that had been leveled against her after the Arterus mission.

"Squad One, you are to take up positions inside Sick Bay and guard all entrances to it and to Life Support. As soon as you hear the ship-wide announcement of my orders from FleetCom, you are to secure the databanks there. You are to hold position until relieved," Ash said as the squads formed up. "Any questions?"

"Negative, ma'am," Nichols answered for his people.

"Then let's get moving."

With that, Ash moved toward the gym exit. As she did, Talbot quickly signaled to Nichols and his hastily formed squads. Instantly, Nichols barked out a series of orders and the squad designated as Ashlyn's escort fanned out around her. Ashlyn didn't know whether to feel flattered or worried when the largest of the Marines other Marines ranged down the corridor in front of her while the others brought up the rear. Nichols was all but stuck to Ash's side, sandwiching her between himself and Talbot. Obviously, they were preparing for the unexpected.

As they moved through the corridors, those they met quickly came to a halt and looked on in disbelief. Orders were quickly snapped out that they were to report to their duty stations and await further instructions. Before the onlookers could react, one or more of the Marines would growl out a warning of dire consequences if they should attempt to warn the bridge or the captain of Ashlyn's presence onboard.

As the lift doors slid open, Ash instantly pushed passed her Marine escort and stepped onto the bridge. The moment she did, Talbot barked out "Officer on deck!" Heads turned in surprise, eyes wide and mouths open. Two of the Marine escort peeled off and relieved the current watch. As they did, Ash moved purposefully toward the command chair in the center of the bridge.

"Major Shaw, this is Lieutenant Commander Archer Denman, the ship's second officer," Nichols announced as the small, whip thin man all but jumped to his feet.

"He is the officer to log in your arrival, Major," Talbot added softly.

"Very good." She paused long enough to look around the bridge. Then she shook her head, her expression serious. Even here, there were too many signs of neglect, both of the equipment and of the personnel.

Without another word, Ashlyn reached out and activated the comm-link on the command chair. Instantly, the chime sounded throughout the ship, demanding that all hands pause in what they were doing to pay attention. Datapad in hand, Ashlyn glanced at the orders she had received from General Okafor and FleetCom and then she drew a deep breath.

"To: Major Ashlyn Shaw, commanding officer, First Battalion, First Division, Fuerconese Marine Corps.

"From: General Helen Okafor, Commandant and Admiral Miranda Tremayne, commanding officer, Second Fleet.

"Major Shaw, you are hereby ordered to take temporary command of the *Aisling* and you are ordered to hold said command until relieved by Captain Justin Jareau. Until that time, the *Aisling* is to remain in its parking orbit. You are further ordered to have the commanding officer of the *Aisling* as well as all senior officers made ready for questioning by Captain Jareau upon his arrival. Failure by any member of the *Aisling*'s crew to obey your orders will result in appropriate disciplinary charges being filed.

"Signed, Admiral Miranda Tremayne, commanding officer, Second Fleet and General Helen Okafor, Commandant."

She paused briefly before continuing. "All hands, you will find further information pertinent to this action in the ship's databanks. It has now been cleared for all onboard to access it. You are under orders to review it immediately as we are now at war. I repeat, Fuercon and its allies are once again at war with the Callusians.

"At this time, all senior officers are to report to the ready room. Shaw out."

"Major, if –"

"Mr. Denman, I may not know what's going on here, at least not yet, but I do know you are a part of it." Her voice might not have betrayed what she felt but the way her eyes flashed angrily surely did. Denman might not be the cause of the problems onboard the *Aisling*, but she had a feeling he'd done nothing to prevent them. His actions by not making sure the CO knew of her presence confirmed that. "You are dismissed to the ready room. Master Guns, make sure he has an escort please."

"Yes, ma'am." Talbot signaled to one of the Marines who quickly peeled off and waited patiently for the Denman to salute and leave the bridge.

"Mr. Nichols, you know the rest of the bridge crew. Who would you put in command while we meet with the senior staff?"

"Major, because we are in docking orbit, any of them can do the job. However, if you're asking who is in the Commander's pocket and who isn't, all of the current crew look to the lieutenant commander."

That wasn't any better, as far as she was concerned.

"Very well. Captain Nichols, you have the conn. As you said, we are in docking orbit. You are also a certified LAC pilot. I think you'll be able to handle the job." The look she gave the others on the bridge as well as the inflection in her voice spoke volumes. She had faith in the young man and woe unto anyone who tried to buck that faith.

"Yes, ma'am."

Ashlyn had to give it to Nichols. He gave her one very quick look of surprise before squaring his shoulders. A moment later he took his place in the command chair.

"Master Guns, I believe it's time for us to report to the ready room as well."

With that, Ash turned and almost sedately left the bridge. Only those who knew her well realized just how much she looked forward to the upcoming encounter.

* * *

"Relax, Ash," Okafor said with a smile as she motioned the major to a chair.

"Ma'am, I hate to say it, but whenever you tell me to relax, things tend to get *interesting* pretty soon afterward." She smiled slightly, hoping the general understood she didn't mean to be insubordinate.

"I understand completely, believe me." Okafor's smile matched hers. "I've been in contact with Admiral Tremayne and it seems you walked into a situation she's found on several of the smaller ships assigned to Second Fleet. Apparently some of those officers who should have been cashiered out years ago but who managed to hold onto their ranks through political or other ties had been assigned to her Fleet. From what Tremayne said, these officers aren't nearly the cancer Sorkowski or O'Brien turned out to be but they are a danger nonetheless because they aren't keeping their ships and their crews in fighting trim."

Ashlyn nodded, her expression troubled. Why would any officer, especially a ship's commander, allow his crew to become lax?

"So she is reviewing the staffing of all ships in Second Fleet to make sure she's caught all the bad seeds." Okafor leaned back, her head cocked to one side as she studied Ash for a moment. "FleetCom has been apprised and has issued orders for all units of Second Fleet to return to the home system. That's going to impact your mission to some degree."

"Ma'am?" Ash leaned forward, suddenly alert.

"The initial plan was to use ships from Second Fleet to comprise the task force that will be part of your mission. However, with what you found onboard the *Aisling*, FleetCom has decided to send ships from First Fleet on the mission."

Ashlyn opened her mouth to interrupt only to snap it shut. There would be time later – she hoped – to voice her concerns. The thought of removing even a few of the ships currently assigned to protect Fuercon and the rest of the home system worried her, especially after the attack on the capital not that long ago. It didn't matter that the attack had been a diversion by the enemy, designed to keep FleetCom's focus on the home system, making it easier for the Callusians to attack the Cassius System. What the attack had proven was that Fuercon's defense systems weren't as good as everyone had assumed. Worse, now the enemy knew it. Did they dare risk another attack with a weakened First Fleet?

"You look like I felt when I was first read into the new mission parameters, Ash." There was little humor in Okafor's voice. "But, as much as I hate, it, I agree with their thinking. We can't risk the mission on a taskforce that might have one too many weak links. That's not a knock against Admiral Tremayne. Far from it. But think about your problems trying to bring the Devil Dogs up to your standards. Now multiply it to include all the personnel and ships the admiral has to deal with."

Ashlyn nodded, suddenly glad she only had a few officers and non-coms to worry about.

"So Admiral Collins is meeting with FleetCom and his senior officers to establish Task Force 119, codenamed Freedom Strike. You, as well as Colonel Johnson, will meet with Admiral Collins and his people tomorrow morning at 0800. What I can tell you now is that FirstBatt needs to be ready to move out, all of FirstBatt, in two weeks. You should be receiving a full timeline from your mother by morning."

"Yes, ma'am."

"That means you have to seal up any problems you see with the battalion without delay."

Ashlyn nodded. "I understand, ma'am. I removed two of my company commanders and they are being transferred out. I should have heard from Captain Ortega and Master Sergeant Adamson as to whether they feel we need to transfer anyone else out of the unit by the time I return to my office

"General, you've obviously had time to read my preliminary report." She paused, waiting until Okafor nodded. "I'd appreciate it if you'd help push through Loren Nichols' reinstatement to the rank of captain as well as his transfer to FirstBatt. Specifically, I'd like to put him in command of Delta Company. He's served with many of the company and I have full faith that he'll be an asset not only to the company but to the battalion as a whole."

"I happen to agree, Ash, and it is being taken care of as we speak."

"Thank you." That was one concern off her shoulders. If only all the others were as easy to deal with. "As for Gamma Company, I received a transfer request from Captain Teryl Monroe. She was CO for the company during the last war and was one of many of the Devil Dogs transferred out – against their wishes – during the build down. I'd like her back."

"Consider it done."

"Thank you." She felt better knowing the company command slots would soon be filled. But there were still the senior officers and senior non-coms she had to worry about and two weeks wasn't nearly as much time as she'd like to do those reviews and bring the battalion up to speed. But it was all she had, so she had to find a way to make it work.

"This is yours, Ash," Okafor said as she slid a datachip across the desktop in Ashlyn's direction. "Your orders are on that, along with all the intelligence we have to date. I will warn you now, the orders probably aren't exactly what you and your people expect. But they are necessary. Review them tonight. Discuss them with your mother, but no one else – yet. You'll be released to do so tomorrow after your briefing with Admiral Collins and FleetCom. If there are any questions you have of me, just comm."

Ash's fingers closed over the 'chip. As they did, her stomach did a slow roll. Even knowing the Devil Dogs would be shipping out in two weeks hadn't made it as real as knowing she now held their orders in her hand. Ready or not, when the two weeks were up, they would be off-planet and thrust back into the thick of things.

"There is one more thing, Ash," Okafor continued before she could ask permission to leave so she could study the data on the 'chip.

"Ma'am?"

"JAG will be moving over the next two days to make arrests pursuant to their investigation into the facts around the false charges that were leveled against you and your people."

The breath seemed to explode out of her as the general's words sank in. Finally! She'd tried telling herself that there was no reason to doubt the JAG. But she'd put her faith in the system once before and the results had been almost fatal, not only to herself but to the six who had survived the Arterus mission with her. But now, if it really happened, she would no longer have to live with the ever-persistent fear that the current administration was as apt to betray her and her people as the previous had been.

God, she prayed the general was telling the truth.

"Ash, breathe." Now Okafor did smile, a reassuring and

understanding smile. "They will move first on Sorkowski and O'Brien. They don't want to risk them learning of the warrants for their arrest and finding a way off-planet before they are in custody. Once they have been secured, Lt. Liu assures me there are others, around a dozen or so, who will then be picked up."

Damn, she didn't want to ask but she had to. "Any members of FirstBatt, ma'am?" Her voice was soft with concern.

"No. However, I have a feeling among those being rounded up will be your friends Brodsky and Hines."

Good!

Ashlyn grinned, satisfaction filling her. "That is most welcome news, ma'am."

"I thought you might think so. I certainly did." With a smile that matched Ashlyn's, Okafor stood. "That, too, is to be kept to yourself until JAG or my office says otherwise. Let's not risk tipping our hand just yet."

"Yes, ma'am."

"Good." She waited as Ash stood. "I'm sure you have something you'd rather be doing right now, Major. Dismissed."

Ashlyn braced to attention and left the office. Okafor had been right. There were several things she wanted to be doing just then. She wanted to see the Devil Dogs' new orders and the intelligence material included with them. She also wanted to spend time with her son. There wouldn't be much spare time over the next two weeks and she needed to spend it with him. She had to let him know that she was going to do her best to come home to him.

God, let me keep that promise this time.

MOVE OUT!

Chapter Eight

Ashlyn leaned back and rubbed her face as if that simple action could scrub away the almost overpowering exhaustion that gripped her. As she did, she sighed heavily. Somehow, without her knowing it, night had slipped away and dawn now crept into the room.

And she had yet to find her bed.

Breathing deeply, she pushed away from the desk and slowly stood. Her muscles screamed in protest, reminding her it had been hours since she had last moved. Hours? It seemed like days. Without meaning to, she had stayed up all night, reviewing her orders and the reports that had accompanied them, trying to digest all she read.

Stretching her arms over her head and arching her back, Ash worked to ease the kinks out of her shoulders. Then she walked to the window. She rolled her head from side to side, wincing slightly as her neck cracked. She simply couldn't believe it was morning. The last time she'd checked, it had been two. She'd poured herself another mug of coffee before promising herself she would go to bed soon. All she wanted to do was read one more report. . . .

Now the sun crept over the horizon, painting the sky with beautiful yellows and pinks. In the distance, the greens and golds of the trees seemed to come alive. Bird song filled the air, calling to her with the hope a new day brought. How magical dawn was and how beautiful.

She reached out, touching the window with the palm of her hand. Sunrise had always been her favorite time of day. How badly she had missed the simple pleasure of watching the dawning of a new day those nightmarish years on Sirocco. Now she could enjoy that magical time once again. But it wouldn't last. All too soon, she would be shipping out and there were no guarantees she would return. They were at war and, in war, people died. All she could hope for was that when her time came, her death helped secure a safe and peaceful future for her son and others like him.

Stop it!

Frowning, she forced down the doubt and the fear trying to worm its way into her belly. Any Marine with an ounce of common sense knew she might die in battle. That was part of being a Marine. But that wasn't what ate at her. There was still that nagging doubt born from betrayal that plagued her. She had to get a handle on it now, before it managed to take root.

Add in exhaustion and worry about whether or not the Devil Dogs would be ready for the mission and it was no wonder she was having doubts. But this was a new day, one in which those who had betrayed her no longer held positions of power. More importantly, those who had taken their places were dedicated to protecting Fuercon and its interests. She knew them and knew she could trust them.

A new day had dawned for her, figuratively and literally. It was up to her to remember that. She had to remember that each dawn promised a new day with new opportunities. Ash had grown up believing every individual had the almost sacred duty to make the most of the new day. For as long as she could remember, she had tried to do just that. Now, after the seemingly endless night of her time on Tarsus, it was especially important to make the most of each new day. One way to do that was to be the best commander the Devil Dogs had ever had and to come home safe to her son.

A soft knock at the study door interrupted her musings. She shook off the negative thoughts and turned. As she did, the door slid open and her mother stepped inside. Like her, Elizabeth wore a pair of BDUs. Unlike hers, however, her mother's were crisp and fresh. Her dark hair was pulled back into a braid and she carried two mugs of coffee in her hands.

Without a word, Elizabeth crossed to where Ashlyn stood. She handed one of the mugs to her daughter and then glanced at the desktop strewn with data chips. For a moment, she stood there, studying Ash, a slight frown playing at the corners of her mouth.

"I should probably be worried that you haven't been to bed," she said as she motioned to the sofa against the far wall. "But considering that I only managed to get a couple of hours of sleep myself." Now she shrugged. "I assume you were reviewing your orders and the information that went with them."

Ash nodded and then sipped her coffee, almost sighing in pleasure. Then she settled at one end of the sofa and watched as her mother sat at the opposite end and angled so they faced one another.

"I was." Another sip of coffee. "And I was trying to figure out the best way to get the battalion ready. Whether we want to admit it or not, there are bound to be some members of the Devil Dogs who still have doubts about me as their CO. Add in two new company commanders and several senior officers and senior NCOs who need to be replaced or reassigned and we aren't anywhere near the state of combat readiness I'd like."

Elizabeth opened her mouth to respond and then closed it. Ash smiled when she did. She had no doubt her mother had been about to tell her she had nothing to worry about. That would be Elizabeth's first reaction as mother. But, as Ashlyn's commanding officer, she would know better. There never had been and never would be a unit where someone didn't doubt its CO at some point.

"True, but there are several things you need to remember. First off, you're lucky Pawlak was their CO before you. You know he kept them as close to combat ready as he could. Yes, there are members of the battalion he had concerns about. I don't know of any unit larger than a squad where there isn't at least one member who doesn't quite fit in, at least at first blush.

"Second, because of who the Devil Dogs are and the missions they are sent on, most of the battalion are combat veterans. A great many of them served with you before, so they know they can trust you to lead them into battle. The others, they'll learn. Remember how you felt before going into your first battle under Pawlak's command. You didn't know him well and you weren't sure how he would do under fire. Those concerns disappeared pretty damned quickly once the DDs had their boots on the ground." She waited until Ashlyn nodded.

"Finally, and in a lot of ways most important, every member of the Devil Dogs know you are one of them. They know you've earned your rank and that you've earned the command. And, by the end of tomorrow, those who might still harbor some doubts will see that the Corps and FleetCom have no doubts about you."

Ash frowned, unsure what her mother meant and not sure she wanted to know. But then, not knowing could be even worse. She had never been a big fan of surprises and there had been too many of them of late.

"What?" she asked simply. When Elizabeth didn't answer, she cocked her head to one side and looked at her mother in suspicion. "What are you up to?"

"Let's just say that General Okafor and the powers that be at FleetCom have decided to make it very clear that they know they have the right person in command of the Devil Dogs and that those responsible for sending you and your people to

Tarsus are going to pay dearly for their actions."

For a moment, Ashlyn didn't say anything. The best news she'd had recently was learning it was only a matter of hours, maybe a day, before Sorkowski and O'Brien would be arrested. She would be lying if she said she wasn't relieved. A lot of the doubt that still lingered would be eased if she saw the two in custody before the battalion shipped out. It would also mean one less distraction on the mission, which was a very good thing.

Then she almost groaned at the thought of having to face the media once JAG announced the arrests. Maybe she could move onboard a ship, any ship, before that happened. . . .

* * *

Another day, another reminder of everything he'd lost.

Admiral Alec Sorkowski (Ret.), sat on the edge of his bed. Resentment filled him as it did most mornings. He missed starting the day onboard his flagship. He had grown used to having a steward there, robe in hand, before he even sat up. A mug of coffee would be waiting on the bedside table and the steward would inform him of anything he felt the admiral might need or want to know.

Then there were the other perks. The additional monies he'd made from his dealings with certain *businessmen* in the sector had been set aside, for the most part, for his retirement. Now those funds were beyond his reach. Some the JAG investigators had found and others he didn't dare try to access for fear they'd be discovered. He wasn't about to let them know just how much he had managed to put away over the years. Not when JAG and most everyone else at FleetCom suddenly seemed to think that bitch Shaw was exactly what they needed instead of dedicated officers like himself.

Shaw!

Just the thought of the woman left a bitter taste in his mouth and it was his own damned fault. He'd chosen not to take direct action when she started being *inconvenient*. Instead, he'd told that sniveling coward O'Brien to deal with her. All the fool needed to do was file the necessary reports with FleetCom, telling them that the taskforce's own Marine contingent was more than capable of handling any operations in the sector and recommending Shaw's SpecOps unit be transferred back to the front lines where it could do the most good. But no. O'Brien had wanted to break the woman. The Arterus mission hadn't done that and, worse, Shaw and the survivors of her unit managed to survive their two years in the penal colony and were now the darlings of the military.

Well, he wasn't going to let that bitch be his downfall. She had already cost him his command and his commission. Fortunately for him, JAG had been moving with its usual lack of alacrity. That had given him time to put his own plans in place. By this time tomorrow, he would be long gone from the capital. In another two days, he would be off-world and on his way out of the system. He had a very nice little hideaway purchased with some of the funds he'd made from his extra-curricular activities on that last tour Purchased through an intermediary and with nothing to lead back to him, he would be comfortable there as he assumed a new identity and began a new life well away from these fools who didn't appreciate all he had done for them.

Standing, he reached for his robe and slid into it. If he wanted to avoid any interruption in his plans, he needed to get moving. He might want to keep one step ahead of the JAG – not very difficult to do, as far as he was concerned – but it was Moreau who worried him. He knew she was much more of a threat than the JAG would ever be. He had known the first time they met that she would just as soon see him dead as to let him live. When he was still in command of the taskforce, he was of use to her. Now he was a loose end that he knew she planned to tie up. He had managed to keep her focused on

O'Brien, at least for the moment, but that wouldn't last.

He planned to be far away before she decided it was time to take him out of the equation.

As he entered the small kitchen, resenting once again the lack of a steward to have coffee waiting for him the moment he woke, the apartment comm beeped softly. A frown darkened his expression. He wasn't expecting anyone. For a moment, he considered ignoring the signal. But curiosity won out and he activated the comm, blocking video on his end.

"Yes?"

His heart beat a bit faster to see the image that appeared on the comm-screen. A serious faced captain, dressed in the daily uniform of a JAG officer looked out at him.

"Captain Lucas Waymouth to see Admiral Sorkowski," the younger man said. Nothing about his expression gave any indication about the purpose for his request.

Sorkowski didn't respond. For one brief moment, he considered telling Waymouth that the *Admiral* wasn't there. It was tempting but it wouldn't work. Building security would verify that he entered the apartment on his own late the night before and that he hadn't left since then. Besides, he had no doubts JAG had him under surveillance. It was what he would do were their positions reversed. So he might as well admit the man and find out what he wanted this time.

"One moment."

Sorkowski drew a deep breath and counted slowly to ten. He could do this. He had faced down numerous enemy in the past and had never backed down from a fight. No mere captain was going to intimidate him now and especially not in his own home.

Squaring his shoulders a short time later, he disengaged the locks and opened the door. He felt his mouth draw tight and the color drain from his face at the sight that greeted him. He had expected to find Captain Waymouth. What he hadn't expected was to see that little weasel, Lt. Liu, and three Marine MPs.

"Admiral Alec Sorkowski?" Waymouth asked formally.

"Yes."

Instead of bracing to attention and saluting, Waymouth produced a folded sheet of paper and extended it to the admiral. At the same time, he gave a jerk of his head and two of the MPs took up positions on either side of Sorkowski.

"Admiral, you are to consider yourself under arrest. Among the charges, all of which are outlined on the warrant I just presented you, are perjury, tampering with evidence, falsifying reports, collusion with the enemy, complicity in the deaths of ten members of the Fueronese Marine Corps, misappropriation of funds, abuse of authority, and treason."

Treason!

His mouth went dry and his knees turned weak. He had expected most of the other charges and knew he could either explain them away or bargain them down to nothing but minor violations of the Code of Military Conduct. But treason! He had never considered the possibility of that charge.

Damn Shaw!

Damn them all.

"Lt. Liu will advise you of your rights under the Code of Military Conduct. Then the MPs will escort you to your room to dress. You will not be allowed contact with anyone until you have been transported and processed into the brig."

"No!" He jerked his arm free of the grasp of the Marine on his right. "I will not be treated this way. You will contact my attorney and I will surrender myself only after conferring with him."

He pulled himself up to his full height and put on his best command face. He was damned if he would be marched out of there like a common criminal. He had rank, damn it, and they would damn well respect it.

"Secure him!" Waymouth snapped.

Before Sorkowski could react, the Marines twisted his arms behind him. Security cuffs were quickly fastened around his wrists.

"I'll have your bars, Captain!"

"You can try, sir." He turned his attention to the Marines. "Get him out of here."

Panic filled Sorkowski and he renewed his struggles. "At least let me get dressed. Please."

"You had your chance, sir. I am not going to risk you trying something foolish that could result in one of my companions being injured." Waymouth reached out and pulled Sorkowski's robe together. "I'll give you that much dignity," was all he said and signaled for the Marines to lead the admiral away.

Fury gave way to frustration which now gave way to fear. He'd overplayed his hand – again and this time the consequences would be much more than forced retirement. He would be lucky to get away with his life.

Damn it, why hadn't he left the planet weeks ago?

* * *

Major Thomas O'Brien stepped off the elevator and looked around. Something was wrong. He could feel it. From the moment he rolled out of bed that morning, things had felt off. But what? Nothing about his small apartment had been out of place. No one had attempted to tamper with his security. A scan of the headlines hadn't revealed anything either. It had to be his imagination working overtime.

So why wouldn't the feeling go away?

He crossed the lobby, scanning the area for any sign of trouble. Nothing. The same men and women he saw every morning were coming and going. No one appeared to by paying any more attention to him than normal. One or two, nodded in greeting if he caught their eye but, on the whole, they simply went about their business as if no one else was there with them.

Outside, he turned to his right and started the on the short walk to the transpo station. His eyes darted right and then left, scanning, searching for anything that might seem out of place.

His breath caught and his step faltered as two Marines fell into step on either side of him. Before he could react, a hand closed firmly on his shoulder from behind. A voice, soft but deadly serious spoke in his ear. "Major Thomas O'Brien, you are under arrest. If you try to resist, these Marines will stop you. At the corner, you will turn to your right and we will take you into custody there. Nod your head if you understand."

He swallowed hard. His hands fisted at his sides. There had to be an alternative to going along like a lamb to the slaughter. All he had to do was choose the right moment to make his move. The Marines would act to keep the civilians around them safe, even if it meant letting him get away. He didn't relish the thought of being on the run the rest of his life but it was better than the alternative.

"Please try something," the man to his right growled.

O'Brien canted his gaze upward. As he did, he knew he was lost, at least for the moment. From the cold expression the Marine wore to the way his free hand stayed close to the gun at his hip, O'Brien had no doubt the man wouldn't hesitate to shoot if he tried to escape. Worse, he had a feeling that the man would shoot to cause the most pain.

Damn it! This was all Shaw's fault.

Shaw's and that bastard Sorkowski.

Well, he'd show them both, starting with Sorkowski. But that meant he had to work fast. There was little doubt the JAG would be moving in on the admiral soon, if they hadn't already. So he needed to be the first one to try to make a deal. He'd gladly throw Sorkowski to the wolves then, once the heat died down some, he'd deal with Shaw the way he'd wanted to all along.

"Wait!" He stopped, pulling, at least temporarily free, of his escorts. "I have information you want."

"Major, you can plead your case with my superiors once we've processed you into the brig," the JAG officer said. "Take him."

*   *   *

Evan Moreau exited the Trade Building and paused. After a night of rain, the morning was crisp and the air clean. Under most circumstances, she might actually enjoy it. But any morning that started with a meeting before dawn was never something she enjoyed. Still, getting the contract had made it all worthwhile. Her bank account would appreciate the latest influx of cash. Besides, if she had turned down the meeting, questions would have been asked and that was the last thing she needed just then.

The juggling act was getting old. She had been on Fuercon for almost six years. The last five of them had been here in New Kilrain. For all intents and purposes, she represented one of many tech developers on-planet. She had carefully cultivated her contacts in the industry and in government. All the while, she had also been putting together dossiers on anyone who might be of use to her at some point in the future. It really was amazing how much people let slip after drinking too much or at the gaming tables or while sharing a bed.

She had even been luckier than she'd expected. With only a few exceptions, none of her *partners* had tried to refuse her *requests* for information or services. Those who had been so foolish had quickly met with *accidents*, but only after she'd made sure no incriminating evidence could be found among their effects that could link them back to her.

But now, well, it was different. She could feel it. There were too many loose ends and too many people she – or her employers – had pulled into the plot. All it would take was one talking and the trail would eventually lead back to her. She needed to make sure that didn't happen, at least not until she was well off-planet and secure in a new identification.

No, she had to make sure it didn't happen until her mission was complete and the Fuerconese government finally realized that it had been fighting the wrong enemy all along and that it was no too late to do anything about it. Her handlers kept telling her it was only a matter of time. Unfortunately, their sense of time didn't seem to correspond to her own.

Early as it was, there were still a number of people out. That was something she'd learned quickly about both the business district and the adjoining government complex district. Both always seemed busy. She guessed that most of those moving along the sidewalks with her were men and women hoping to get an early start on the workday, each of them worried about their latest deal and not once suspecting that their lives would soon be turned upside down.

God, she could hardly wait.

Turning the corner, Moreau came to a sudden stop. A man bumped into her and murmured an apology even as he stepped around her. She mumbled something in response – she thought she mumbled something – but her attention was focused on what was ahead of her. Three armored military aircars were parked in front of the exclusive apartment complex she knew almost as well as she knew her own. A Navy captain appeared from inside. Following close behind him were several Marine MPs. Sandwiched between two of them was a fairly nondescript man. He wore a robe and nothing else as far as she could tell. His fair hair, going grey and thinning, stood out in all directions around his head. Even from a distance, Moreau could see how he struggled against the hands holding him firmly.

Instinct for self-preservation had her stepping closer to the building on her right. She stood there, watching, straining to hear anything that might be said. But there was nothing other than the pounding of her pulse and a string of curses she hoped were only in her subconscious. Then, as the man was forced into the back of the middle aircar, fear kicked in. This was one of the worst possible things that could happen.

Damn it! She'd known it was only a matter of time before FleetCom moved on Sorkowski, but she'd hoped it wouldn't be quite so soon. Well, at least she wasn't completely unprepared. She had plans in place to make sure he knew better than to try to betray her. But to put them into motion, she needed to get off the street.

Fighting down the desire to curse long and hard – and at the top of her lungs – she pulled her comm and left a message for her admin to cancel her morning appointments. She wasn't feeling well but she planned to be in that afternoon. That done, she pocketed the comm and moved off in the direction from which she'd come. She didn't have any time to waste. She had to act before her handlers decided she was as much of a loose end as Sorkowski, O'Brien and the others.

*   *   *

Ashlyn entered the conference room and quickly shook her head as Talbot prepared to call everyone to attention. She couldn't stop smiling. She didn't care if no one knew why. Hell, she didn't care if they all thought she had lost her mind. She knew better. She hadn't lost her mind. Far from it. Instead, she had found her center again. No, it had been given back to her and, along with it, so had much of her confidence in the system and the institutions she had trusted and that had failed her. Oh, she knew there would still be times of doubt, just as there would still be the occasional nightmare. But she could deal with those. Hell, every Marine, every member of the military had those, at least the smart ones did.

What a difference a few hours could make. Then she'd been sitting at the table, eating breakfast and studying her orders one last time. Her only thought then had been figuring out the best way to make sure the Devil Dogs were ready to ship out. After that, she'd hurried to her briefing with Admiral Collins and reps from FleetCom. Her mind had been reeling as she thought of all she needed to do to get the Devil Dogs ready to ship out when her comm sounded. A moment later, the world looked a lot better than it had in a very long time.

Now she stood at the head of the conference table and looked at her company commanders, their XOs and her own senior staff. Their expressions ranged from mildly curious to concerned. Not that she blamed them. They knew enough to realize she had their orders, even if the grin on her face was at odds with going to war.

"Ladies and gentlemen, before we get started, there is one bit of news I want to share with you," she began as she was seated. "This morning, at approximately 0700, JAG officers, accompanied by Marine MPs, executed arrest warrants for Alec Sorkowski, Thomas O'Brien and approximately a dozen others. Charges range from treason to interference with an official investigation to bribery and accepting bribes to official oppression and more."

She leaned back and watched as the news sunk in. Ortega nodded, a satisfied smile on her face as she pounded the tabletop with her fist. There were a few none too quiet comments about how it was about time. Adamson punched Talbot in the arm and grinned almost as broadly as Ash. Best of all, no one, not a single officer present appeared to be anything but pleased with the news.

"JAG has assured me they will be sending over more information shortly. Once I've reviewed it, I'll release it so you can let your people know. I want every member of the battalion to understand that FleetCom and the Commandant's Office are fully behind the Devil Dogs and our upcoming mission," she continued. "Captain Ortega, let's start with staffing needs.

Before Ortega could stand, the door to the room slid open. Surprised and a little alarmed that the newcomer had managed to get past the two Marines standing post outside the door, Ash swung to face them. Instinct had her ready for anything.

Or almost anything.

"Ten-hutt!"

Her voice rang out as she shoved to her feet at the sight of both her mother and Okafor standing in the doorway. As she braced to attention, she knew the others did so as well. What she didn't understand was why the women were there. Her mother hadn't said anything earlier about sitting in on the briefing she the last she'd heard from Okafor, they weren't to meet until the next day.

Was it possible there had already been a change to their orders?

That possibility worried Ashlyn. If the Callusians were already escalating the fight, they had managed to build up their military more than suspected during the years of the so-called truce. Either that or they had help from someone. That possibility worried Ashlyn more than a possible buildup because it meant there was a player Fuercon was unaware of. It could be someone thought of as an ally or it could be one of the systems that had stayed neutral during the previous war. Hell, for all she knew, if there was a third player involved, it could be a group based out of Fuercon. That might, just might, help explain away officers like Sorkowski and support personnel like Hines.

"As you were," Okafor said as she approached the conference table, Elizabeth just behind her. "Major, have you had a chance to brief your people yet?"

"Negative, ma'am. I was just telling them about the latest from JAG."

Okafor nodded, a slight smile touching her lips. "Then I guess I ought to let you know that both Sorkowski and O'Brien are now in custody and are being processed into the brig. There will be other arrests made as well over the next few days."

"Thank you, ma'am." Ash's voice was soft and full of emotion.

"Well, you might not thank me when you learn that the President will be making a statement tonight, after the arrests have been made."

Now Ash groaned, the thought of what the media hounds would be like spoiling the pleasure of a moment before.

"Major, before we let you get back to your briefing, there is one matter that needs to be taken care of." She motioned for Ash to step forward. Then she glanced over her shoulder at Elizabeth.

"Major, stand tall," was all Elizabeth said but her eyes twinkled and Ash swallowed hard. They were definitely up to something. But what?

"Major Shaw, I hope you know just how much the Corps, FleetCom and the current administration value all you have done and sacrificed for Fuercon," Now she accepted a flat, black leather case from Elizabeth. "Events have not really given us a chance to do this formally. Besides, I know you prefer as little fanfare as possible where you are concerned. However, we aren't going to let another day pass without you receiving your due.

"Major Ashlyn Shaw, it gives me great pleasure as Commandant of the Fuerconese Marine Corps and acting at the behest of President Derek Harper to present you with Distinguished Service Medal for the actions you took not only during the Arterus Campaign but also during the time of your false imprisonment at the Tarsus Military Prison. You acted above and beyond the call of duty to protect those under your command, often placing yourself in danger to do so. You are a credit to the Corps, Major. Thank you." Ash managed a slight nod as Okafor opened the leather box, revealing the medal nestled against black velvet, before handing it to Ortega who now stood to the right and slightly behind Ash.

"President Harper sends his regrets for not being here to do this himself, Major," Okafor continued as she took a second box from Elizabeth. "But he said that he figured you would probably try to jump out a window if he suddenly showed up. There was something about you being a suspicious sort who doesn't like being the center of attention."

Snickers came from several of those gathered and Ash closed her eyes, counting to ten. Jumping out a window sounded pretty good just there. There were only two problems. One, there was no window in the room. Two, she doubted any of her people would let her make a break for the nearest window. So all she could do was stand there and take whatever Okafor had up her sleeve.

"It is my great honor to award you the Fuerconese Medal of Honor, Major, not only for your actions during the last war but for those upon your return to the capital. You did not have to act but you did and you did so without thinking. Because of your actions, numerous lives were saved."

"Ma'am." She couldn't help it. This was too much. She didn't deserve either honor but especially not the Medal of Honor. She hadn't done anything any other Marine wouldn't have done. If anyone deserved to be honored, it was all those people who had died as a result of the phony intel they'd had on Arterus.

"I know, Major. You think there are others who deserve this more than you."

Ash could only nod.

"I assure you, they are being recognized as well." She waited until Ash reluctantly nodded. Then she handed over the leather case she'd been holding.

"Thank you, ma'am."

What else could she say? Then, seeing how her mother looked at her with pride, she had a feeling the two of them would be having a very long talk about this before the day was over. Obviously Elizabeth had known about this when they left the house but had chosen not to say anything. Well, she would learn that it wasn't wise to pull this sort of a surprise on her eldest daughter.

"There's one more bit of business to take care of before we let you get back to your briefing," Okafor said and Ash groaned. From the amused look on the general's face, she'd been heard. "A battalion commander is almost always a colonel's billet. There have been a few exceptions where the Corps has put a lieutenant colonel in command. With the Devil Dogs about to ship out, it is time to correct that oversight."

Once again, she reached back to Elizabeth. This time, Ash watched as her mother placed a small box into the general's palm. As Okafor took one step forward, Ash unconsciously squared her shoulders. Her heart fluttered and she felt her face flush. Now she understood what her mother had meant earlier that morning when she'd said that soon everyone would know that the administration as well as the Corps and FleetCom had full faith in her.

"As of this morning, your proper rank is that of lieutenant colonel. Congratulations." Okafor smiled again. As she did, Elizabeth stepped forward. Ash stood at attention, wondering if this was all a dream, as they removed and replaced her rank insignia. "Now, before you say anything, Lt. Colonel, the only reason you aren't being promoted to full bird colonel is I figured you would either implode or kill your mother and me or both." A bigger smile this time before the women stepped back and braced to attention. Ash returned their salutes and then shook their hands, not quite trusting herself to speak yet.

"Captain Ortega, I think you were about to begin your part of the briefing when we interrupted," Okafor continued, a devilish glint in her eye. "Perhaps you'd be so good as to continue now. I have a feeling your CO needs a moment to catch her breath."

"Ma'am, if I might be so bold, I'd suggest you and Brigadier General Shaw get on your way before she recovers. She doesn't particularly like surprises and this has been a humdinger of one."

"Respectfully, ma'am, you and my mother pulled a fast one on me and I do promise to return the favor one day," Ash managed to say.

"I'm sure you will. But until then, you have an op to plan, Lt. Colonel. We'll let you get on with it."

And, with that, they were gone, leaving Ash to stare after them, wondering why she couldn't wake up from what was definitely one of the oddest dreams she'd ever had.

CHAPTER NINE

ASHLYN STOOD ON THE OBSERVATION DECK ABOVE THE MAIN landing bay for the *Cassin Young*. Below and to her right, heavy armor was being unloaded and checked. Directly below her, attack shuttles had been brought onboard and carefully locked into place. Their flight crews were now scouring them for any damage that might have occurred during the landing process. To her left, LACs, the newest in the Corps, were being checked. Everything looked to be in good order but she wouldn't relax until she'd seen the final reports for herself.

Not that a problem with any of the equipment would delay their departure. FleetCom had made it very clear that they had to depart on time. If the latest intelligence was right, they had a very tight window in which to arrive at their destination and execute their mission before enemy reinforcements arrived. That added pressure to everyone involved but it was nothing new to the Devil Dogs. Most of their missions seemed to have similar restrictions.

Ash winced slightly as a high pitched screech filled the bay. For a moment, all activity halted as everyone looked around to see what had happened. Then, before she could say anything, she saw Ortega stalking through the crates of weapons that had just been offloaded from one of the shuttles, her expression thunderous. Even though she couldn't hear what her Exec had to say to the hapless private she had honed in on, it was clear she was giving the young man the dressing down of his life. Then she turned and called one of the NCOs over. There was a calmer discussion and, as the Exec walked off, the sergeant laid a hand on the private's shoulder, his expression speaking volumes. Yes, the private had screwed up but now he knew better and would never do it again. Apparently he'd said just that to the younger man. The private nodded and looked at the sergeant with an expression that mirrored both relief and a determination not to repeat the same mistake. Good. Ortega had done her job and the sergeant had reassured him. Hopefully it would be enough to keep the young man from second guessing himself on the battlefield.

"Ma'am, Captain Nichols reports that Delta Company is now squared away," Corporal Nolan reported from her side.

"Send my compliments to the captain. Tell him to get his people settled into their quarters now that their gear and equipment has been stowed."

"Yes, ma'am."

"And let Captain Jareau know we should be finished here in the next hour."

A loud crash sounded below her almost before she'd finished speaking and she bit back a curse. Talk about "famous last words." She didn't need anyone to tell her what happened. She'd recognized the sound and had a pretty good idea who was responsible. Frowning, she scanned the area, looking for the source of the sound.

"Ripper, what the devil do you think you're doing?" she yelled. As she did, Ortega, as well as Adamson and Talbot, stalked across the deck in the direction of the power armor that lay on its side on the decksole.

"Sorry, Ma'am. The controls on this piece of shit are dodgy as hell," the burly Marine replied.

"Don't give me that, Rip. This is the second powered suit you've managed to drop today. Next one you drop, I'll assign to you. And make sure someone gives this suit a thorough going over ASAP."

"Yes, Ma'am!"

"I'll make sure of it, LC," Adamson called up, her expression as serious as Ashlyn's.

Ash nodded and turned away. Much as she wanted to stay and supervise, that was no longer her job. As battalion CO, she had to trust her command staff. If she didn't, the rest of the battalion wouldn't. Even if she did, if she gave the impression she didn't by always looking over their shoulder, the battalion would suffer. Besides, she knew Ortega was more of a stickler for details than was she.

If that wasn't reason enough for her to move on, she had a briefing with Admiral Collins soon.

"Are the latest status reports uploaded?" she asked Nolan.

"Yes, Ma'am."

"Then, Corporal, let's go see what the Admiral and his staff have to tell us."

She managed to take a couple of steps toward the lift when the sounds of another crash filled the bay. Cursing softly, Ash turned and hurried back to the edge of the platform. Anger and frustration spiked to see another powered armor suit laying on the deck.

"Ripper!"

"It wasn't him this time, LC," Adamson responded before anyone else could. "See?" She nodded to a second loader, this one operated by a Navy rating.

"Just be careful, everyone, and check that suit as well," she growled before turning back to Nolan. "Let's go before something else happens."

* * *

"Admiral on deck!"

145

Ashlyn quickly climbed to her feet and braced to attention. Around her, more than a dozen other Naval and Marine officers did the same. Out of the corner of her eye, she watched as one of the two civilians who were also present for the briefing followed suit. He might have been dressed in dark trousers and shirt but there was a distinct military bearing to him. She had noted it when he first entered the room and now she had no doubt he had spent a number of years in the military. What she couldn't figure out – yet – was why he and the other civilian were present.

Admiral Richard Collins moved to stand at the head of the conference table, his aide, Captain Julianna Jareau a step behind him. For several moments he held everyone at attention, his eyes moving from one to the other. Ashlyn knew he didn't miss a single detail about their appearance, their expressions and, more than likely, what they were thinking.

"Have a seat," he said.

Following protocol, everyone waited until he had taken his own seat before doing as he said. Then they waited, anticipation filling the air.

"I know each of you would rather be supervising the final preparations for our departure, so I promise not to take too much of your time," Collins continued as half a dozen young ensigns appeared and poured coffee for those who wanted it. A few moments later, they disappeared as quickly and silently as they had appeared.

"The first order of business is confirmation that we will be breaking orbit in twelve hours."

Groans sounded from around the table. That didn't surprise Ash. She couldn't remember a single briefing where a ship's commander hadn't wanted another day – or week – to make sure all the bugs were shaken out before breaking orbit. The fact that this particular taskforce had been put together such a short time ago probably didn't help either.

Collins had apparently anticipated the response as well and he held up a hand to prevent any interruptions.

"FleetCom has received new information that makes it imperative that we ship out immediately. So if you have repairs going on, make sure the yard dogs know they have ten hours to finish or they will be making the trip with us. If they give you any trouble, let Captain Jareau know."

"You might remind them that the last time a yard dog tried dragging his feet, he got a free ride to the front lines and saw more action in the few months we were gone than he had in a twenty year military career up to that point." Jareau's green eyes sparkled and almost everyone chuckled. "In the meantime, be sure to send me updated reports on any repairs or maintenance that is still being done on your ships."

"From this point forward, all personnel are confined shipboard unless their duties require them to go dirtside. If there is any breach in our security, if I find out that anyone has said when we are scheduled to ship out, not only is the operation in jeopardy but so will the careers of whoever is involved. That includes their COs all the way up to ship commanders."

"What the Admiral hasn't said is that FleetCom is confident that the enemy is monitoring local media broadcasts," Jareau took up. "A review of the events leading up to the attack on the capital shows that there had been increased media coverage of the fact that much of First Fleet would be out of their normal patrol patterns as it took part in training exercises. That coverage made it easier for them to sneak the ground troops in. It also gave them a timeframe in which to strike. So we don't want to give them warning that we are about to make a strike against them and especially not at a target they have started to assume we have no interest in."

"I'm afraid you've lost me, Captain Jareau."

Ash glanced down the table in the direction of the speaker.

Captain Gideon Afolayan, commander of the *Thanatos*, leaned back in his chair. His hands rested on the tabletop, his fingers laced. To the casual observer, he might look relaxed, almost bored. But Ashlyn knew better. She saw the way his brown eyes watched Jareau and Collins, waiting for one of them to answer.

"Our mission has, from the start, been to repatriate territory taken by the Callusians since hostilities resumed. However, after the invasion of the Nystrom System, part of FleetCom, not to mention the Administration, thought our best chances for victory would be to go to the Nystrom System. The thinking was that the enemy wouldn't have had as much time to dig in and set up their own defenses, not to mention that there might still be an active resistance we could hook up with."

That made sense. The Callusians had been in control of the Cassius System for two months now. That had given them time to do more than just interdict the system. They could have brought in more ships to hold the system as well as set up defense platforms, laid mine fields and more.

"But then we received information that makes it imperative that we move on Cassius Prime as quickly as possible. Jules."

Jareau nodded and typed in a quick command sequence using the virtual keyboard on the table before her. A moment later, the holo screen at the end of the room activated. Ash leaned forward, shocked, at what she saw. The 'feed might not be the best quality but it was good enough. She counted at least a dozen people wearing Fuerconese uniforms. Her jaw clinched and her stomach knotted. She had a pretty good idea what they were looking at. Hell, she'd spent two years in something very similar.

Anger flared only to die a quick death as disbelief replaced it. She shouldn't be seeing those uniforms. All the information she had seen up until now about the invasion of the Cassius

System had pointed to the *Tarrant* being destroyed with all hands onboard shortly after her commander managed to get off a warning about what was happening. Other than the Marine guards stationed at the Fuerconese embassy, there should have been no member of the military on planet at the time of the invasion. That meant only one thing – the crew of the *Tarrant*, or at least part of it, had managed to abandon ship before it had been destroyed.

Eyes flashing, she turned to look at Collins. For a moment, their eyes locked and he nodded, his expression betraying his own anger. Then he rapped his knuckles on the table, calling everyone's attention back to him.

"It is clear the crew of the *Tarrant* wasn't lost, at least not all of them," he continued, his voice hard. "Add to that the fact that it appears at least part of the Callusian picket is pulling out. So that is our target. We are going to retake the system, free the prisoners and bring our people home."

"Admiral, where did this 'feed come from?" Mikhail Volkov, captain of the *Kresnik*, asked.

"Fortunately for us, there is a resistance movement on Cassius Prime. It is being led by members of the government that were able to get into hiding before the Callusian ground troops took control over the capital and they have reached out for our help." He glanced down the table to the civilian Ash had earlier guessed was former military.

"Ambassador Joachim Gunderson, the Cassius System's representative here on Fuercon, has joined us as has our ambassador to the system, Collier Thomas-Hutchison. Both will be accompanying us on our mission. For the moment, we are to consider Ambassador Gunderson as the government's voice for his home system." Now Collins pinned each of them with a firm look. "Ambassador Gunderson."

"Thank you, Admiral," Gunderson said as he got to his feet. "I know there is a great deal we don't know about the current situation in the Cassius System. However, I am here to answer what questions I can and I will start by letting you know that I have the schematics for our defense platforms as well as the government and security buildings in the capital. Even if the Callusians have changed the security protocols, this information should be of help."

"Ambassador, what sort of support can we expect when we get there?" Colonel Isaiah Johnson, the Marine CO for the mission, asked.

"Not as much as any of us would like, Colonel, but certainly more than I'd dared hope for even a few days ago." He smiled grimly but it didn't reach his eyes. "Most of our military and government officials have either been killed or captured. There are a few who appear to be working with the enemy. My guess is that most of them are being coerced to do so, probably by threats to their families. But there are some collaborators and that means the resistance is having to be careful about who they approach. However, they are armed and they are working to find a way to take down at least some of the defense platforms when we arrive. They will also hook up with the Devil Dogs when they drop groundside."

That would help, as long as they could trust those they were hooking up with. But that wasn't a concern Ashlyn was ready to voice – yet. She wanted to hear more of what the ambassador had to say.

"We will, of course, refine the plan of attack as we approach the Cassius System and we get up-to-date readings on the system defenses. For now, plan for both boarding as well as groundside operations. If we can retake the orbital platforms without having to destroy them, we will. Colonel Shaw, we'll be relying on your people for that as well as for the groundside operation."

"Understood, Sir, and we'll be ready," she assured him. "Ambassador Gunderson, is there anything you can tell us that would make it any easier for the boarding parties?"

"With Admiral Collins' permission, I'll be glad to meet with you at your convenience, Colonel. I have information about each of our platforms as well as the orbital stations that goes beyond the schematics already mentioned."

"Of course," Collins said and Ash nodded in appreciation. Any additional information they had ahead of time could help them successfully conclude their mission. Taylor-Hutchison shifted in his chair, his frustration clear. For a moment, he reminded Ashlyn of her five year old son when he didn't get his way about something. Frowning, she waited to see if he did or said something to explain his attitude. As far as she could tell, no one had done or said anything to upset him. So what was his problem?

"While I understand why you have to be prepared to use force to retake the system, there are a few considerations you need to keep in mind," he began without waiting for Collins to give him the floor.

The moment the words were out of Taylor-Hutchison's mouth, it was as though time stopped in the room. Ashlyn watched as all eyes focused on him before shifting to Collins. No one interrupted a briefing without damned good reason.

"Ambassador." Collins' voice might have been soft but his eyes flashed. Seeing it, Ash was glad she wasn't in Taylor-Hutchison's shoes just then.

"It is just as important that we do nothing to interrupt trade in the region as it is that we retake the system."

Amazingly, he seemed completely unaware of the look Gunderson gave him. Not that Ashlyn blamed the ambassador. It was his homeworld they were discussing and she knew she wouldn't be worrying about trade routes if Fuercon had been invaded. Freeing her home would take precedence. Trade routes could be re-established afterwards.

"We also have to think about the economics of it all. If

retaking the system costs too much in terms of manpower and ships, well, I hate to say it but we are at war."

Ash ground her teeth, fighting the urge to speak. But it wasn't her place, even if it was her people who would be doing much of the fighting, especially once the fight went groundside.

For his part, Collins stared at Taylor-Hutchison as if he'd sprouted a second – and maybe a third – head. Then he slowly stood. He placed his palms against the tabletop and leaned forward, his attention focused solely on the man sitting midway down the table. The man who did not appear to understand what sort of trouble he'd just brought on himself. Leaning back in her chair, Ash relaxed slightly. It was obvious to her and, judging by the way most everyone else at the table reacted, to most of the others as well that Collins was about to *educate* Taylor-Hutchison on the error of his ways.

"Ambassador, I will say this only once. I am well aware of the fact that we are at war. I assure you that every man and woman in this room is well aware of it. But what you seem to have overlooked is the fact that Cassius Prime is our ally. We don't abandon our allies to the enemy any more than Colonel Shaw and the rest of the Devil Dogs leave any of their own behind." He gave Ash a quick nod before continuing.

"Unlike you, FleetCom and the Administration also realize the danger of leaving the enemy in control of the Cassius System because of its location in relation to us. If we don't retake the system and make sure it is held against further attempts by the Callusians to invade, it becomes a launching point for attacks against our own holdings. It would mean they could bring the war directly to us and to our home system." Collins paused, as if waiting to see if Taylor-Hutchison understood what he meant. When the man remained silent, he continued. "Ambassador Gunderson, I assure you that FleetCom has instructed me to do everything possible to free the Cassius System and return it to your people. We will make sure it is defended until your own navy is able to take over."

"I know, Admiral. Unlike my counterpart, I did make the briefings with President Harper and his staff, not to mention the representatives from FleetCom." Disdain filled Gunderson's voice as he glanced across the table to where Taylor-Huchison sat. "I am here to be of whatever assistance to you and your staff and crew that I can be."

"I beg your pardon!" Taylor-Hutchison puffed out his chest, outrage suffusing his expression.

"To get back to the matter at hand," Collins said, pointedly ignoring the smaller man. "Do any of you know of anything that might cause a delay in our departure?"

For a moment, no one said a word. Then someone cleared his throat before speaking.

"Sir, I mean no disrespect, but I have heard some things that make me wonder if the Devil Dogs are the best choice for this mission."

Ashlyn's fists clinched in her lap and her eyes flashed. How dare he question the Devil Dogs! Anger flared at the insult. As she opened her mouth to respond, she realized Ortega had pushed back her chair and now stood. Much as Collins had before, her palms were flat against the tabletop and she leaned forward, every fiber of her alive with anger and outrage.

"Stand down, Captain," she said before Collins could intercede. Then, knowing better than to say what was on her mind, she looked to the Admiral. How he responded to this slight would set the tone for the rest of the mission.

"Commander Powell, I assure you the Devil Dogs are more than the best choice for this mission. They are the only choice." Collins' displeasure was obvious.

"But, sir, it is common knowledge that two of the companies have brand new COs and that there hasn't been time for them to integrate with their companies, much less the rest of the battalion."

Ash felt sure her fingernails were digging holes into the palms of her hands as she fought to stay silent. This wasn't her show – yet.

"Colonel Shaw, would you care to respond?" Collins asked.

Ash pushed back her chair and stood. As she did, she almost choked to see the Admiral give her a slow wink. Unless she missed her guess, he was giving her permission to verbally – and possibly physically, if necessary – take Powell apart for his absurd allegations.

"Commander Powell, I assure you FirstBatt is more than ready and capable of handling this mission," she began. She kept her voice even, calm. She wouldn't play into his hands by showing how angry his comments had made her. "Yes, I did replace two company commanders as well as several NCOs. By doing so, I made the companies stronger and that, in turn, makes the battalion better able to carry out the parameters of our mission." She paused when she felt Ortega touch her arm. Her XO gave her a slight smile as she handed over her datapad. Ash glanced at the information on it and fought back a grin. She should have expected Ortega to find something to use to rebut the man.

"Both of the captains have served with the Devil Dogs before. They were transferred to new assignments at the end of the last war. Both had requested to return to the battalion and I was more than glad to have them back. They are credits not only to the battalion but to the Corps as well."

"But—"

"No, Commander, there are no buts. Both captains are welcome additions to the Devil Dogs and they will do a much better job than their predecessors on this mission." For the first time, she allowed some steel to show in her voice. "FleetCom has no concerns about giving this assignment to FirstBatt, nor does General Okafor. Admiral Collins has assured me that he welcomes the Devil Dogs on the mission. Why you have concerns when none of my people will be onboard your ship is, frankly, beyond me. Perhaps it is all in an attempt to hide shortfalls in your own staffing?"

He opened his mouth and formed the words but nothing came out. Then, as though realizing how ridiculous he looked, he snapped his mouth shut and stared at her. Before he could recover, Collins motioned for Ash to return to her seat.

"Colonel, would you care to elucidate?"

"Sir, Captain Ortega has pulled up the ship's roster and it would appear the commander is short several department heads. It isn't readily apparent at first glance but there are overlaps in assignments of half a dozen second lieutenants, as well as several NCOs, covering areas where there should more senior officers or NCOs in charge."

Collins held out his hand and she extended the datapad to him. Everyone waited, silence filling the air, as he studied the readout. When he looked up, his expression was even colder than before. Ashlyn leaned back, glad she wasn't the one who would be on the receiving end of the dressing down she felt sure was about to come.

The Admiral stood and handed back the datapad. Then he glanced at his aide. Captain Jareau stood and took up her position at his shoulder. Both worse matching expressions, serious and not about to accept any excuses from anyone.

"On your feet, Commander Powell."

Powell instantly complied. However, instead of bracing to attention, he assumed an at rest stance that had Ash and the other Marines in the room frowning.

"Commander Powell, you have all but accused Colonel Shaw of not having her battalion ready for the mission. By doing so, you have cast doubt on her ability as a commanding officer. That is bad enough. But when I see that the Colonel's observations about your own command appear to be correct, it smacks of much more. Fortunately, your ship is mainly a support vessel. Captain Jareau shall be accompanying you back there as soon as this briefing is concluded and she will determine what action, if any, needs to be taken to make sure you are ready to move out with the rest of us. I assure you, if your inaction – or worse – cause our departure to be delayed, you will not like the result."

Now he turned to face Ash. She quickly stood and braced to attention.

"The changes in company commanders Colonel Shaw made with regard to the Devil Dogs was done with the full support and approval of General Okafor as well as Brigadier General Shaw. But I have a feeling the *concerns* Commander Powell voiced are not what worries him. So let me make this very clear. I have no concerns about Colonel Shaw, the Devil Dogs or their ability to do the mission set for them. Colonel Shaw has proven in ways most of you will never know that she is more than worthy of the trust being put in her by FleetCom."

Ash's cheeks heated as a blush crept up from her throat.

"Now, let's finish this briefing so we can get back to work. . . ."

CHAPTER TEN

ASHLYN LEANED BACK AND SIGHED HEAVILY. THE LAST FEW months had been a roller coaster of emotion. First had been finding herself back on Fuercon without explanation. Then, just as hope had started to form that the charges against her and her people might be expunged from their records and they'd be freed, the capital had been attacked. She had managed to survive that and had even managed to push back her suspicion long enough to return to Tarsus to free her people. That had been just the beginning of the ride and she knew there was a long way before it was over.

Three weeks had passed since the taskforce had left Fuercon. Part of her had to give it to FleetCom and Admiral Collins. In an attempt to keep the Callusians from figuring out what their mission was, the taskforce had set off on a very round-about course to the Cassius System. Now they were only a few days out. Even though there had been no indication the Callusians had scouts in the area, the ships of the taskforce were on alert. No one wanted to take any chances now. Not when their goal was so close.

She also had to admit that she'd been pleased with the way the Devil Dogs had integrated into the crew of the *Cassin Young*. They stood watch and helped out wherever possible.

Ortega worked closely with Captain Jareau as they coordinated where the Devil Dogs would be at any given time.

Ash studied the latest intelligence report from the Cassius System and blew out a breath. It appeared that the survivors from the *Tarrant's* crew were still on-planet. Nothing indicated they had been separated from the other prisoners taken by the Callusians during the invasion. That was something she had to take into consideration when planning the assault on the capital. If they didn't get to the prisoners quickly enough, the Callusians would use them as human shields and that was only if they didn't kill them outright. But if she could get to them before that happened, they would be additional warm bodies who knew who to handle themselves in a firefight.

At least she hoped they would be.

But before that happened, they had to deal with the defense platforms protecting the system. That would be up to Collins and the taskforce. The LACs would be launched against the platforms and to help protect the ships making up the taskforce from groundside defenses. Attack shuttles would transport the Devil Dogs to the platforms. Then it would be up to the Marines to secure the platforms and hold them until Collins could get specialists over to relieve them.

A soft chime signaling someone's arrival interrupted her train of thought. Ash rubbed and hand over her face and then rolled her shoulders to ease the tension she hadn't noticed before. Then she reached out. A quick touch of a finger to the control console unlocked the hatch. A moment later it slid almost silently open and Corporal Nolan stepped inside.

"Ma'am, Corporal Donnelly is here as requested," the young man announced.

"Very good. Send him in," Ash said. "Once you have, ask Captain Ortega to send word to the company commanders reminding them of the briefing in one hour."

"Yes, ma'am."

The corporal gave a quick salute before turning sharply to leave the office. As the door slid shut, Ashlyn allowed herself a smile. Nolan had proven to be much more of an asset on the mission than she'd expected. Given time and experience, he would make an excellent NCO – assuming he lived long enough, something no one in the Marines, and especially a Devil Dog, could count on.

"Corporal Donnelly, Ma'am," Nolan announced from the doorway a moment later.

At Ash's nod, the young man saluted and backed out of the office, closing the hatch behind him.

Leaning back, folding her hands on the desktop, Ashlyn watched closely as Corporal Ryan Donnelly marched smartly across the office. He stopped precisely four feet from the desk and braced to attention. The corporal's expression remained correctly impassive. Even so, Ash saw the quick flash of nerves that clouded the corporal's green eyes before it was gone.

Suppressing an understanding smile, Ash nodded almost imperceptibly, pleased with what she saw. Tall, slender, giving the impression of both physical and emotional strength, the corporal could have been a picture on a recruiting poster for the Marines. The insignias at throat and sleeve marked his rank as well as his qualifications as expert marksman, sniper, and shuttle pilot. Like so many who found their way to the Devil Dogs, Corporal Ryan Donnelly had accomplished a great deal in a relatively short period of time.

Now she hoped he managed to maintain that same level of competence and professionalism. If he couldn't, she would not hesitate to keep him onboard while the rest of the battalion went dirtside.

"Have a seat, Corporal." Ashlyn motioned to one of the chairs situated before her desk.

"Thank you, Ma'am." He settled on the edge of the chair,

back straight, body tense.

"I hope I didn't take you away from anything, Corporal."

"Not at all, Ma'am."

"Good." She knew the corporal wouldn't have admitted it if she had but at least she'd asked. Now she leaned back and smiled slightly, hoping to put him at his ease. "Donnelly, take a deep breath and relax. We're off the record now."

Her smile turned into a grin as the young man visibly tried to relax. He sat back, crossing his long legs at the ankles. His expression went from one tinged with more than just a hint of concern. Ashlyn knew the young man's curiosity had to be running rampant. He had been with the Devil Dogs since before she assumed command and this was the first time she had sent for him.

"Ma'am, I'll admit I'm more than a little confused about why you've sent for me. Have I done something wrong?" His brow furrowed in concern but he said nothing else. Good. That showed a level of control he would need if he was going to make the drop with the rest of the battalion.

"No, Donnelly, you've done nothing wrong."

I just have to make sure you don't in the near future.

"Corporal, there has been some intelligence come to us from the Cassius System that will impact the upcoming mission."

"Ma'am?"

"Corporal, when word first reached FleetCom about the invasion of the Cassius System, it was assumed that the *Tarrant* and all hands onboard were lost. We now have reason to believe that might not be the entire truth. Our sources on Cassius Prime have provided information that seems to indicate that at least some of the crew might have survived and are currently being held by the Callusians on-planet."

She waited, watching as the news sank in. The color drained from Donnelly's face and then he leaned forward, an expression of hope on his face. Even so, Ash could see how he fought against getting his hopes up. She didn't blame him.

"My brother?"

"We don't know." She wouldn't lie to him. "All we know for sure is that some of the vid feeds we've received from the Resistance appear to show some men and women in Fuerconese uniforms. They are being held with prisoners the Callusians captured when then invaded the system. We don't know who they are or how many of them there might be. FleetCom's best guess is that they are members of the *Tarrant*'s crew because there appear to be more of them than would have been stationed at our embassy there."

"Why are you telling me, Ma'am?" His voice was soft, his uncertainty obvious.

"Because I need to know that your head is in the game when we go dirtside, Donnelly. I need to know if this will be a distraction for you."

"Ma'am, I can't say that it won't be a distraction," he admitted after a moment's though. "What I can say is that it won't keep me from doing my duty."

"And if we reach the compound and find that your brother isn't one of the prisoners – or worse?"

He didn't flinch even though she saw the quick stab of pain in his eyes. Good. He could control himself. Maybe she didn't have anything to worry about.

She hoped.

"I will follow orders and do my duty, Ma'am." His response was automatic and Ash frowned slightly. Not that it was unexpected. Instead of commenting, she gave him a moment. What he said or did next would tell her all she needed to know. "Ma'am, I'm a Devil Dog. I will follow orders. But if I find myself in a situation where I know for a certainty that the enemy harmed my brother or any of his crewmates and they give me the chance to exact a little revenge, I will do so. I promise you, though, that any action I take will be justified."

"Very well, Corporal." It would have to do, for the moment at least. "That will be all. Keep the information about potential prisoners to yourself. The battalion will be briefed on everything come morning."

"Yes, Ma'am." He stood and braced to attention.

"Dismissed, Corporal."

He executed an about face and left her office. As the hatch slid shut behind him, the hatch leading to Ashlyn's bedroom slid open. Lucinda Ortega stepped into the office. When she nodded at the far hatch, Ash shrugged. Before she gave her impressions of the meeting with Donnelly, she wanted to know what her XO thought.

"Well?" she asked as Ortega took the chair Donnelly had vacated.

"He'll do. But I'll put a word in Nichols' ear to keep an eye on him."

"Good." Ash lifted one foot onto the edge of the desk and blew out a breath. "If his brother is still alive, I want Nichols groundside. Not only will his presence reassure his brother but any other survivors as well." And that would go a long way in helping any survivors accept that they were really free. It was a lesson Ashlyn knew all too well.

* * *

Evan Moreau didn't even try to hide her frustration. Abel Kannady sat across the desk from her. He had arrived at her office without warning and demanded to see her. Under most circumstances, she would have told her assistant to give him an appointment and show him out. But nothing about Kannady fell into the "most circumstances" category. Instead, she had said to give her a few minutes to finish what she was working on before showing him in.

Those few minutes had been spent trying to figure out why the fool risked both their lives by coming to see her. They had been so careful that last month to do nothing that might cause attention to be brought to their relationship. It was bad enough that her real employers were starting to have concerns about the job she was doing. The last thing she needed was for Kannady to do something foolish. There were too many eyes and ears out there just looking into the attack on the capital – not to mention the false charges that had been brought against that bitch Shaw and her people.

"This had better be good. You risked both of us by coming here unannounced."

He bristled at her tone but she didn't care. He needed to understand just how serious the consequences of his actions could be.

"You forget your place, Moreau!" he snapped.

She bit back her retort. Much as she wanted to tell him he was nothing but a pawn in a game much bigger than he could ever imagine, she couldn't. She didn't dare. That would mean her life because he would be foolish enough to try to use it for leverage, if not against her than with her employers. Their response would be quick and fatal, for both she and Kannady. So, somehow, she had to diffuse the situation and then find a way to deal with this fool once and for all.

Damn it but there were going to be a lot of bodies before this mission was over and that meant more complications than she wanted to consider.

"No, but obviously you have forgotten how dangerous it is for us to be seen together," she countered. "So what is so serious you had to risk us both?"

Even as she spoke, she cursed herself. She knew better. She needed to keep him calm. His pride and overriding ego could very well cause him to strike out at her. If he felt threatened, he wouldn't hesitate to offer her up to the authorities. He wouldn't even consider the fact that she had more than enough evidence against him to have him facing the executioner. All he would think about was the need to prove to her that he was in control.

But she was damned if she was going to let him leave without making sure he understood just how foolish his actions had been. She just had to figure out how to do it without pushing him over the edge.

Pushing him.

The image of pushing him out the window and watching him fall the fifty stories to the ground below was an enticing one. Unfortunately, it would raise too many questions and have too many eyes focused on her. She wasn't ready to do a bolt – yet.

"You assured me you had everything under control and yet they are still making arrests. Arrests that have nothing to do with the charges that were leveled against Shaw and the others. Arrests that come much too close to my interests." He all but ground out the words. "What are you planning to do about it?"

She opened her mouth to reply and then shut it. He eyes narrowed and she tilted her head to one side as she looked at him. She had been so focused on making sure neither Sorkowski nor O'Brien said anything to the authorities that might wash back on her or her employers that she hadn't paid much attention to any other arrests that might have been made.

Galled that Kannady might actually know more about what was going on than she did, she did a quick search. Her frustration grew as she scanned the data scrolling across her screen. Kannady had a right to be concerned, not that she would ever tell him that. More importantly, her other employers would be more than a little worried when news of the arrests reached them. If she didn't do something quickly to alleviate the potential damage, she could kiss all she cared about, including her life, goodbye.

"I assure you, steps are being taken to protect your

interests. By the end of tomorrow, each and every one who has any tie, no matter how tenuous, to you will know how foolish it is to even consider betraying you."

All she had to do was grease the right palm and arrange for an *accident* or two. So simple, assuming she could find the right palm to grease.

"Don't try to talk your way out of this, Moreau. I've paid you good money to make sure my interests are protected. If just one investigator comes snooping around my interests, I'll hold you responsible."

Hold her responsible!

She didn't know whether to laugh or reach across her desk and throttle him where he sat. He actually believed he held the upper hand. The fool. Well, she would play him a bit longer and then she would take great pleasure in teaching him just how foolish he had been in threatening her. Perhaps she would even arrange things so that all paths led back to him where the investigation into the charges against Shaw and the others, as well as the attack on the capital, were concerned. It would be worth all the headaches and expense to see his expression when he learned he was being charged with treason.

But she couldn't let him know what she planned, not until it was too late – for him.

"I assure you that you are overreacting." She stood, a slight smile on her face. Let him think her the fool. It wouldn't last long but it would give her the time she needed to put the next phase of her plan in place. "By end of day tomorrow, you will see that there is nothing to worry about."

"You had better be right." He, too, stood. His expression was hard and she almost laughed as he did his best to look imposing.

"You need to get ahold of yourself, sir." Now she leaned in, her voice soft, her expression intense. "Fear is the enemy. It makes us careless and that is the one thing we cannot be, not when victory is so close to hand."

His nostrils flared and his color rose. But he said nothing. Good. That meant he was thinking about what she had said. Unless she missed her guess, it was probably one of the only times someone had dared tell him to think before acting. It really was too bad no one had beaten that lesson into his head when he was younger.

"Go back to work or go home. Get drunk. Whatever you do, do not draw attention to yourself. I haven't let you down yet and I won't now." She waited, wondering if he would say anything. When he didn't, she continued, modulating her voice into reassuring tones. "You hired me because I get the job done. I wouldn't last long if I didn't. So trust me to do what I'm good at."

"I want an update by tomorrow evening."

She assured him he would have it and then watched as he left her office. The moment the door slid shut behind him, she allowed herself the release of kicking her desk. The pain it caused helped focus her anger. She had gotten sloppy and that wasn't like her. She was being pulled in too many different directions with this job. If she hoped to survive it, she needed to focus. She would deal with the immediate danger, those who had been arrested, and then she would deal with Kannady. Hopefully, by then, the plans her true employers had in place to take down the Fuerconese government would be past the point where anyone would care about her. That would give her time to get off-planet and out of the system. A new life sounded better with every passing day.

* * *

"All right, Devil Dogs, this is it," Ashlyn said over the battle net as she stripped out of her BDUs. Her light armor rested nearby. Her weapons were laid out next to it. "The taskforce will be entering the Cassius System shortly. We are now at full alert. Gear up and head to your battle assignments. Beta and

Delta Companies, report to the attack shuttles. LAC pilots and support personnel, report to your posts. At the Admiral's orders, we will begin the assault on the planetary defense platforms. Company commanders, make it happen."

As she ended the message, the signal for General Quarters sounded. It was followed by Captain Jareau relaying basically the same information to the ship's crew that she just had to her Marines. Ready or not – and she prayed they were – the fight was about to begin.

Five minutes later, clad in her light armor, Ashlyn moved to her desk. Waiting to be added to the dispatches to be sent back to Fuercon was a letter to her parents as well as one to her son. She wanted them to know that she had been thinking about them should anything happen. Even though she had a good feeling about this mission, she had learned the hard way on more than one occasion that you never knew what a battle might bring.

Wishing she could talk with Jake before the proverbial shit hit the fan, she authorized the transmittal of both letters. She could trust her parents to make sure Jake saw her post as soon as it arrive. If something did happen to her, they would, when he was ready, show him the second message she had recorded for him, the one she included with their letter. Her son needed to know he was always close to her heart and she never forgot about him. But now she needed to tuck that part of her away so she could concentrate on the mission at hand.

"Ten-hut!" Adamson called out as Ashlyn entered the main bay a few minutes later.

"As you were." Ash moved through the knots of Devil Dogs as they checked their equipment and went over their assignments. As she did, she glanced around, making sure she missed no detail, no matter how small. "Master Guns?"

"All present and accounted for, Ma'am," Talbot said as he approached. "The shuttles check out and are a green for go."

"Very good." She nodded in satisfaction and then drew a breath. "Beta and Delta Companies, mount up! I want you in the shuttles and ready to launch the moment you get clearance.

"The rest of you, get to your assigned stations. Be prepared to assist Beta and Delta Companies if necessary. COs, if there are any questions or if you need anything clarified, now's the time to ask." She waited, looking to see if anyone spoke up.

"Ma'am, any restrictions on ordinance other than what was included in the preliminary briefings?" Nichols asked.

"That's a negative, at least so far. This will hopefully be a standard board and secure operation. So no heavy loads. We don't want you blowing out any bulkheads and killing yourselves in the process. However, if heavy arms are necessary to secure the station or to save lives, then don't hesitate to use them. Just take whatever precautions you can to protect yourselves and any friendlies who might still be onboard.

"The ROE is simple. Board, secure and hold until relieved. FleetCom would prefer that we not completely disable the platforms because we will need them to help hold the system. However, lives outweigh material. Remember that.

"Now get going. Time's running out."

"You heard the Colonel. Get your asses in gear, boys and girls, and let's take the party to those motherless sons of bitches!" Talbot said.

"Ooh-rah!"

The bay echoed with the call. Then the sounds of Marines grabbing their gear and moving quickly into position followed. Ashlyn watched for a few moments more. To the untrained eye, the sight of so many armored men and women might seem like chaos but, to her, it was a well-choreographed dance. In ancient times, they would have been warriors, dancing around the fire and chanting to the gods. Now they checked their battle armor and weapons, made sure they carried extra ammo and power packs. Comms checks were made as were checks of the battle net. Lives depended on what happened in the next few minutes and every member of the battalion knew it.

"Devil Dogs!" She waited until everyone silenced and all eyes were once more on her. "We will take the system back from the Callusians. We will teach them the lesson they should have learned in the last war. Most of all, we will serve Fuercon and the Corps with honor. From now until further notice, all comms within the unit are to refer to our individual call signs. Understood?"

"Ma'am, yes, Ma'am!"

"Then elbows and asses, Marines! Elbows and asses!"

"What are you doing just standing around, Marines? You heard the Old Lady. Get a move on!" Adamson shot Ashlyn a grin before moving off to help one of Beta Company with his gear.

"This is it, Luce," Ash said softly as they moved out of the bay. She wanted to check on the LAC pilots and then she had to report to the flag bridge. "Are we ready?" She could let her concern show with her XO and not worry that Ortega would think any less of her. They had known one another too long and had been through too much not to be honest now that they were once more heading into battle.

"We're ready, Ash. You've made sure of it." Ortega pulled her into one of the side corridors, away from the Marines and Naval personnel rushing to their stations. "Ash, I mean it. You've made sure the battalion is better prepared than it has been since before the end of the war. You've not only shaken off the rust but you've given FirstBatt a shine it hasn't had in a long time. So quit worrying. The Devil Dogs are ready, thanks to you."

"No, thanks to all of us." She smiled and laid a hand on her friend's shoulder. "I need you to go with the first wave, Luce. You are my best intelligence specialist and your experience and instincts may be needed over there."

"All right." Ortega didn't like it but she wouldn't argue.

At least not until after the mission. Then she'll give me an earful.

"Take MJ with you. You guys coordinate but leave it to the COs unless you have to step in."

"Understood."

"Luce, you're my eyes and ears over there. Keep the battle net open. I want to know what's happening at all times."

"Understood."

"Then go. I'll check with the LAC crews and then report to the Admiral." She paused, this time reaching for her friend's hand. "Good hunting, Sorceress."

"You too, Angel."

*   *   *

"Hang on! We're going in hot."

The pilot's voice remained calm even as the attack shuttle banked sharply. Lucinda Ortega felt the slight shudder she long ago learned to associate with a shuttle returning fire. Frowning, she quickly checked to make sure they had sustained no damage before leaning forward, straining to see into the cockpit.

"Report!"

"Platform weapons online, ma'am, and trying to zero in on us."

Ortega quickly keyed her comm. "We're taking fire, Viper, move your LACs in."

"Roger that, Sorceress," Lt. Burton "Viper" Iverson replied. "We'll clear you a path."

"We do this by the numbers, folks. The LACs will get us in close enough to make a hole. Once the shuttle gets into the bay, everyone out. Secure the bay and hold it as the second shuttle comes in. Then we will hand off the guard duty to them and begin clearing the station." Nichols spoke calmly, confidently and Ortega nodded slightly. Ashlyn had been right to put him in command of the company.

"Captain Ortega?" Now he looked at her, waiting to see if she had any other orders.

"This is your show, Captain Nichols. I'm just along for the ride." She fought a smile as Adamson snorted softly at her side. They both knew Ortega would not hesitate to step in if she felt it necessary.

Ortega focused on the reports coming in over the battle net as the LACs made their runs against the defense platform. Viper kept up a running commentary. His tone ranged from amused to insulted. According to him, whoever was manning the platform defenses had never taken a single tracking course, much less tactics or programming. Not that Ortega minded. She much preferred the inept weapons tech who couldn't hit the broad side of the proverbial barn than one who actually knew what he was doing.

"Platform defenses neutralized, Sorceress. Ramjet, get in the bay before they get back online," Viper said.

"Roger that, Viper. Stay sharp." Ortega let herself feel a brief moment of relief before nodding to Nichols.

"Take us in, Ramjet," he ordered the shuttle pilot.

"Roger that, Cap. Hang on."

The shuttle banked sharply as it began its approach. As it did, Ortega prayed the bays were still accessible. The Devil Dogs were prepared to make entry via the emergency hatches but the bay would be much quicker and less dangerous. No one liked making a space entry. Too many things could go wrong and there were already enough unknowns about the mission to worry about.

"Ma'am, you will stay put until the bay is reasonably secured," Adamson said softly over a closed channel.

Ortega opened her mouth to respond and then snapped it shut. Whether she liked it or not, Adamson was right. Besides, unless she was badly mistaken, Ash had told the blonde to make sure nothing happened to her. It was exactly the kind of order she had been giving both Adamson and Talbot since Ashlyn's return from Tarsus.

More than that, by hanging back, no one would think that she had any concerns about Nichols' ability to do his job. That was important. The last thing they needed at the beginning of a mission was for the rank and file to think the brass lacked confidence in their CO. Besides, any qualms she might have had about him had disappeared weeks ago.

"You can assure Angel that I'll be good," she answered.

For a moment, Adamson looked as if she didn't believe her. Then she nodded. As she did, the pilot warned them to be prepared to land.

It went as practiced in all the sims Ashlyn had ordered the battalion to run. As soon as the shuttle was down, the hatch cracked and the first members of the assault team poured out, weapons at the ready. For one moment, the only sounds to read those still inside the shuttle were those of the assault team moving across the decksole of the bay. Then the unmistakable sounds of a railgun being fired filled the air. It was followed by a curse and, almost instantly, the order went out to return fire.

The fight was brief and ended exactly as Ortega expected. The shooter was dead, his light armor shredded by the rounds fired from the Marines' battle rifles. By the time Adamson allowed her out of the shuttle, the Marines had secured the bay, guarding the various entrances, ready for any attempt to retake the bay.

"Let's get the other shuttles onboard," Ortega ordered as she glanced around. "Do we have a terminal I can tie into yet?"

"Over here, Captain," Nichols said.

By the time the other shuttles had landed and the Marines had off-loaded, Ortega had managed to hack into the station's computer system. The ease with which she had done it had her shaking her head. It was one indication that the Callusians hadn't completely changed their tactics from the previous war. This time, just as then, they came in, took over and assumed no one would push them out of the system. Because of that, with only a few exceptions, none of the security codes had been changed from what they'd been before the invasion. It would take her a bit longer to break the other codes, but the information she had already accessed would go a long way to helping them retake the System.

But first they needed to retake the station.

"It looks like there is a minimal presence onboard," she said as Nichols and several others gathered around. She punched in a command sequence and a map of the station appeared before them. "Here are our goals." Another command punched in and the command center, three defense platform control centers as well as environmental control where highlighted. "Comms has a backup control console here." A fourth area was highlighted.

"Defenses?" Sergeant Fabiano, Nichols' senior NCO, asked.

"Not quite as heavy as we expected in some ways and more so in others." She punched in another code and a series of red and green dots were added to the display. "Green represents flesh and blood defenses. Best guess based on the data is that we have two squads patrolling and then fire teams stationary at our targets. Red represents automated defenses. They are live but we should be able to bypass them. The question is can we do it quickly enough to keep them from destroying the station?"

"Sorceress, don't wait. Let the heavy armor go first into the areas where automated defenses have been noted." Ashlyn's voice came over the battle 'net.

Agreed. She tapped her response into the virtual keyboard that was part of her left gauntlet.

"Listen up, everyone. We aren't going to wait. The Old

Lady says to send heavy armor into the areas where we know the automated defenses are active. Captains, I leave it to you to make any adjustments to your assignments. We move out in two minutes."

*　*　*

Ashlyn stood to one side of the flag bridge, her eyes never leaving the plot. She had been waiting to see a response to their LACs launching. It had taken longer than expected but it finally happened. Part of her wished she could have been there to see the look on the face of the Callusian commander when he realized he couldn't call on the defense platforms. The reliance on the platforms was the only reason she could think for why the Callusian ships still in system had not instantly gone weapons hot and moved into position to intercept the taskforce.

Now those ships were moving in – finally. Collins had brought the taskforce to ready stations and it was now just a waiting game. As soon as the Callusian ships were in range, the fight would be on. It was a fight Ash felt out of place in. Marines should either be in their fighters or have their boots on the ground, doing what they did best – fighting the good fight. This waiting as others did the fighting cut against the grain.

At least Beta and Delta Companies had managed to secure the station along with the controls for the defense platforms. Even better, there had been no major losses doing so. Now they held the station and Ortega and the other Devil Dogs used the defense platforms to help protect the incoming taskforce.

"Sir, enemy ships are almost in range."

"Open a channel."

Collins leaned back and crossed his legs. As he did, Ash had to marvel at his presence. She knew he couldn't be as calm as he appeared. Yet, to the casual eye, he looked relaxed. She recognized what he was doing. He wanted the crew to believe he had no doubts about the eventual outcome of the mission. If they thought he was convinced of a successful outcome, they would be as well.

"Channel open, Sir," the comms officer said a moment later.

"This is Admiral Richard Collins, Fuerconese Space Navy, to the commanding officer of the Callusian ships illegally attempting to hold this system. You are ordered to stand down. Drop your shields and take your weapons off-line immediately. Your unconditional surrender will be accepted only if you do as I order and if you do nothing to wipe your databanks. Any act of aggression, no matter how minor, will result in the destruction of your ships. You have two minutes to give me your answer. Collins clear."

He sliced his finger across his throat, signaling for the comm to be cut off.

"Colonel Shaw, have your people ready to board. I doubt the enemy will be so cooperative as to do as I ordered but, just in case they surprise me, let's not give them time to change their minds.

"We're ready, Sir," she assured him. "Teams are waiting with the assault shuttles and LACs are ready to move into position."

"We have incoming, Sir!"

Ash swung to face the plot even as Collins did. Dozens of red dots lit the plot, moving in the direction of the taskforce. Each dot represented a missile, perhaps even a missile cluster depending on what sort of armaments the ships were carrying. Collins didn't hesitate. He ordered counter-measures launched to intercept the incoming missiles. Then he ordered the leading ships of the taskforce to open fire. It was time to end this and Ash couldn't agree more.

BOOTS ON THE GROUND

Chapter Eleven

ANTON KASUN, OCCUPATIONAL GOVERNOR OF THE CASSIUS SYSTEM, raced across the green outside the main administration building. Around him, others raced here and there. Some would be going to their posts. But some, too many he knew, would be going to ground, hoping to keep their heads low and pass unnoticed as the damned Fuerconese retook the planet. Much as he wanted to do the same thing, he couldn't. He had one job he had to do. He had to make sure nothing existed to tie what happened here to anyone besides the Callusians. The agreement his government had made with their so-called benefactors would bring ruin on them all if it were to come to light.

Damn it, he'd really thought this was going to be a good day.

The doors slid open and he burst inside. Instantly, his ears were assaulted with the blaring of the alert signal followed by someone, probably some low level rating, ordering all persons to their posts. The fact that the order sounded like it was meant for soldiers and not a bunch of bureaucrats and paper-pushers would have been funny under other circumstances. But not now. Not when he knew he was probably one of the very few with more than the minimum required military training left in the build.

But there should be others and, by the gods, he would make sure those left did their duties. They would hold this building and take as many of the enemy with them before they died.

"Peltier!" The head of security ought to be in his office by then. "Captain Peltier, get your worthless ass in here now!"

He turned and moved to the far wall. His hands shook as he punched a code into the almost hidden keypad at shoulder level. There was a soft snick and part of the wall slid away, revealing a safe. It took two tries to get through not only the biometric security level but the old-fashioned combination. His frustrated mumbling as he spun the dial right and then left before slamming his palm against the safe door filled the room.

He paused and closed his eyes, breathing deeply. He had to slow down, calm down. He didn't have time to panic. The Fuerconese were the enemy, yes, but they also played by the rules. His employers, on both sides, did not. So if he wanted to get out of this alive and with some chance of living after the war, he needed to calm down so he could do what needed to be done.

Finally, the door to the safe swung open. Without hesitation, he reached inside. His fingers closed around a stack of data chips and a single sheet of old-fashioned paper. Leaving the door to the safe open, he carried the items to his desk. As he did, he listened to the latest report coming in. Damn it, time was running short.

He hadn't believed it at first when his chief of staff woke him with news that the defense platforms were off-line. He'd actually been foolish enough to assume it was nothing more than a technical glitch, probably caused by the few members of the Resistance they had yet to round up. Then reports of the Fuerconese ships being spotted – well inside the System – came in and he knew time was up.

That had been half an hour earlier. Since then, he hadn't stopped. He couldn't stop. He'd thrown on some clothes and made his way to the office. Now he had to destroy the databanks and make sure there was nothing to lead the Fuerconese to the puppet masters pulling the strings in this new war.

"Where is Peltier?" he demanded as one of the lower level office drones appeared in the doorway.

"He is in the building, Governor."

"Find him and bring him here."

Damn it, he didn't have time to play games with Peltier.

Peltier had been nothing but a thorn in Kasun's side from the start. The security chief had made it very clear that he felt his *talents* were being wasted as part of the occupation force. He wanted to be on the front lines, fighting and causing as much pain and terror to others that he could. In the early days after the invasion, that sadistic streak had been of use. But now it only confirmed what Kasun had long suspected. Peltier was the worst sort of bully. He was a coward would didn't have the balls or the guts to stand up against those as strong, or stronger, than was he.

As he waited for Peltier to finally make an appearance, Kasun sat behind the desk and activated his data center. His fingers flew across the virtual keyboard as he brought up status reports and scanned the projections for how long they had until the Fuerconese landed troops in the capital. Gods above and below, how had all this happened?

He had options. He had to remember that. He always had options. To buy time to scrub the databanks, he could use the prisoners. He could use them as human shields and he could use them as bargaining chips. The Fuerconese proved during the last war that they would do almost anything to protect those they viewed as innocent victims – and he just happened to have a whole camp of innocent victims, including more than a few of their own.

He would and could use them. Hell, he might even get lucky and manage to disappear in the confusion that would follow the landing of Fuerconese troops.

Gods, let him be so lucky.

But where the hell is Peltier?

"You wanted me?"

A tall, swarthy man with a permanent sneer lounged almost negligently against the door frame. His uniform looked as if he had slept in it. His thick, dark hair stood out in spikes, as if it had rarely, if ever, seen a comb. But it was his insolent expression that spoke volumes. Kasun knew Peltier, like most of the security force, hated him. That was fine as long as they feared him.

Kasun knew exactly why they hated him. He had forbidden the troops from killing their prisoners simply for the fun of it. If a prisoner was to be *executed*, Kasun had to approve it. Even worse, he had put an end, at least temporarily, to the sexual *favors* the troopers had demanded from the prisoners, male and female alike. Now only those who proved themselves loyal to the governor could demand those *favors*.

Kasun glanced at his head of security and hid his own sneer of contempt. If Peltier and those like him had done their jobs properly, none of them would have anything to worry about. The Fuerconese ships would never have been able to slip in-system undetected and the defense platforms would never have fallen to them without at least squawking off a warning.

Not that all the blame fell to Peltier and his people. High Command had pulled most of their ships out of the system in order to join the fighting. Now he had too few people to hold the planet, much less the entire system, against the Fuerconese.

"Captain, we need to make sure the enemy is slowed

down," Kasun said coldly as Peltier dropped onto one of the two chairs situated in front of the desk.

"And?"

Again, insolence won out over discipline. It really wasn't surprising the man had been left behind when the cream of the occupation force had been pulled out. If they didn't have to worry about the Fuerconese landing troops at any moment, Kasun might actually allow himself to deal with Peltier once and for all instead of just daydreaming about it.

"We use the prisoners. The Fuerconese commander won't let them be harmed. You know how soft they are." Kasun noted the flash of anticipation that lit his companion's expression and knew he had to be careful about what he said next.

"How?" Peltier sat up straighter, his eyes alert as he waited for Kasun to explain.

"Have the dependents of the political prisoners rounded up. Bring in the old men and women too. We'll use them to convince the Fuerconese not to force entry into this building. I want the Fuerconese prisoners and the senior political prisoners held in the center of the camp. Let them be seen and let the invaders see that there is no way for them to get to the prisoners before they are killed by our people. I want them bound and secured so they can't flee. Then have your people dig in. I doubt we can hold the enemy off indefinitely but it will give us time to make sure they find nothing here they should not."

Peltier nodded, clearly enjoying the mental picture of it all.

"Have that son of a bitch Donnelly brought out last. Hood and gag. If we have to make an example of anyone, it will be him."

"Very good, sir."

"Then get it. We don't have much time."

* * *

Ashlyn entered the hangar bay and paused, looking

around. Ranged around the bay in various poses of relaxation were the Devil Dogs assigned to the lead elements of the landing. Not that it fooled her. She had been in this position too many times before. They were making sure their equipment and weapons were ready for the landing and they were thinking of home, of their loved ones and of who would be left alone if they didn't make it back. They covered their worry, even their fear, with bawdy jokes and an I-don't-give-a-damn attitude.

God, let them all come back from this mission.

Standing beside the lead attack shuttle were Admiral Collins, Captain Jareau and Talbot. They looked up as Ashlyn approached. Without a word, the Admiral motioned for her to join them. She nodded once and moved purposefully in their direction. Hopefully, they had an update on the latest intelligence from the surface.

"Are you ready, Angel?" Collins surprised her by using her call sign.

"Yes, sir. The Devil Dogs are ready to do whatever's necessary to retake the capital."

Even if it meant any or all of them wouldn't make it back.

"Then get your people in place. I'd say it is past time for us to take the fight directly to the enemy. We'll keep them off of your backs from the air."

"Thank you, Sir."

"Keep your comm open, Angel." For a moment, Collins let his gaze wander over the Marines. Then he nodded in satisfaction, obviously pleased with what he saw. "Master Guns, when you hit the ground, I want you to stick to your CO. She's a stubborn one and doesn't understand just how important she is to the rest of us." When Ash opened her mouth to protest, the Admiral shook his head, his expression firm. Then he motioned for her to walk with him a few steps away from the others. "Ash, you are not to take any unnecessary risks. I mean it. You need to make it back home for your son. Not to mention the fact that I do not, absolutely do not, want to have to tell your mother that anything happened to you. She'd have my head."

She couldn't help smiling because he was right. Her mother would try to take his head, or another part of his anatomy, if she thought he had not done everything possible to keep her safe.

"Not to mention the fact I received word from JAG that they would very much appreciate it if I could see to it that you were back on-planet in time for the trials of both Sorkowski and O'Brien."

Ash inhaled sharply. As she did, she felt a layer of tension falling away. The arrest of the two, as well as the others who had had been involved in the events leading up to what happened on Arterus, had helped convince her that things really had changed in the Corps and the military as a whole. But knowing that they would soon be facing trial and that she would have a chance to finally tell her side of the story and, hopefully, get justice for those who died as a result of greed and treasonous actions went a long way toward letting go the last of her doubts.

She wasn't there yet, but she was getting closer.

"When?" That was all she could say. She didn't seem able to form any other words just then.

"They are giving us three months to get things in hand here and then get you and your staff back home. So, Ash, think you can get things wrapped up here in time to make it to court?"

"Damned straight, Sir." She grinned, feeling better than she had in a long time. Then she sobered. As much as she relished the news, she couldn't let it distract her, not when they were about to put boots on the ground and – finally – take the fight to the enemy.

"Then let's get this show on the road." Collins extended his hand and she took it. Just then, they were two warriors about to head into battle. Mutual respect and the need to rely upon one another bound them together.

"Devil Dogs, you're the best we have. I'm counting on you to not only retake the capital and, with it, the planet. I'm counting on you to show the enemy just how foolish they were to think they could attack one of our allies and not face our wrath. Do the Corps, the Fleet and Fuercon proud."

"Oo-rah!"

"Let's do this by the numbers, boys and girls," Ashlyn took up. "Alpha Company will drop in as close to the administration buildings as possible. The LZ has been marked. Check your maps. Gamma Company, you will move toward the camp on the outer edge of the capital where the political prisoners are being held. Beta Company will join up with you there. Delta Company is being held in reserve." She paused and glanced at the Devil Dogs, the men and women who would follow her into Hell and back.

"I want you to know that I'm proud to say I am a Devil Dog and even more proud to serve with each and every one of you. Now, let's go kick those Callusian sons-of-bitches off this planet!"

"You heard the Colonel!" Talbot said, his voice carrying throughout the bay.

"Company commanders, get your people onboard the shuttles. We have ten minutes to launch!" With that, Ashlyn turned once more to Collins. "Sir."

"Good hunting, Colonel," he said, shaking her hand once again. "Give them hell, Devil Dogs!"

"Oo-rah!"

"Any questions?" Talbot asked and then glanced around, opening the discussion to the Marines standing nearby.

"Just one, Master Guns," one of the female Marines began,

quickly climbing to her feet and bracing to attention.

"Yes. Corporal Russell?" Ashlyn waited for the corporal to continue.

"Ma'am, what are your orders concerning prisoners? Do we leave them dirtside or bring them with us?"

"We'll figure that out after we retake the capital," she replied evenly. "Our priority is to get control of the capital, especially of its defense grid. That is first and foremost. However, don't take unnecessary risks and don't do anything foolish. You're all veterans. I trust you to act like it.

"I want you to remember one thing, Marines. We don't start trouble—"

"But we will, by God, finish it!" Talbot finished for her.

Ash nodded. Each of them would do whatever was necessary for the successful completion of their mission. She knew it just as she knew she would do whatever it took to get them all home safely. Then, catching a signal from Captain Jareau, she called the Devil Dogs to attention.

"Good hunting, Marines." Collins returned their salutes and then left the bay, Jareau on his heels.

"All right, boys and girls," Talbot said after Ash put them at their ease. "You heard the Old Lady. We've got a job to do. Finish your preflight checks and get onboard your assigned shuttles. Let's get this done!"

"Ooh-rah!"

* * *

Alec Sorkowski shuffled into the small, sterile-looking room and paused. As he did, the door slid shut behind him, bringing home yet again the dismal change in his circumstances. Mere weeks ago, he had lived in one of the most sought after residence buildings in the capital. His name may have been sullied by the charges that bitch Shaw had leveled against him, but he still had a comfortable life. He had been sure that between his connections and those of the people he had helped over the years, the charges would never amount to anything.

God, he'd been wrong. So very wrong.

Gone was his comfortable apartment and more money than he knew what to do with. Gone was the freedom to move when and where he wanted, a freedom he had taken for granted. Now he spent his days in a small cell in the detention block of the Security Building. Twice a day, he was escorted under armed guard to the gym where he was allowed half an hour to exercise. No one spoke to him. No one even looked at him if they didn't have to. When they did, they seemed to look right through him. It was as if they refused to admit he even existed.

Worse than the feeling of being reduced to nothing was the fear. He hadn't been there more than a week when the first threat was delivered. With his guards turning a blind eye, another prisoner had cornered him in the showers off the gym. His message had been short and brutal. If Sorkowski wanted to continue living, he was to keep his mouth shut. One hint that he was even considering cooperating with the authorities and he would die. But that would happen only after he'd seen proof that everyone he had ever cared about had died a slow, painful death. Then came a quick sample of what he could expect if he didn't do as instructed. He had lain on the floor of the showers, sobbing in pain, until the guards found him. But he'd kept his mouth shut. He'd kept it shut as he tried to find some way to get out of what looked like a no-win situation.

Now that fear had been brought home once again. Just that morning, his guards had taken almost sadistic pleasure in telling him what happened to O'Brien the previous evening in the showers. Other prisoners, or one of the guards, had jumped his former Marine CO. They had treated O'Brien to a beating – and worse – that would leave him in the medical ward for weeks. *If* he recovered and that was not guaranteed.

The unspoken message was simple. Sorkowski was to watch himself or he would soon be joining O'Brien.

Damn it. It was all that bitch's fault. If she had died on that mission on Arterus like she was supposed to, none of this would be happening. But no, she had survived and had even managed to find enough champions to clear her and the others to survive the mission of the charges he'd leveled against them. Now it was his life on the line and he could do nothing about it.

Nothing!

If only he had something the authorities and Fleet wanted. Well, he did but he had no way of offering it to them without that bitch Moreau finding out. In so many ways, she was worse than Shaw. While Shaw merely demanded that everyone stick to the rules the way she did, Moreau had no qualms killing to accomplish her goals.

So, even knowing what he did, he could not use it to barter for his freedom. He would no more risk the lives of his family than he would of himself. He either had to accept the fact he would never again see a day of freedom or he had to find a way to end his life.

Preferably in a manner a great deal less painful than it would be at the hands of one of Moreau's stooges.

He truly hated not being in control of his own life.

That thought focused Sorkowski's attention on the room's only other occupant. Seated at the small table in the center of the room was a short, graying man with dark eyes and a sharp nose. His representative. What a laugh. The man was nothing more than yet another link in the chain keeping him in line.

That had been made clear from the very beginning. Judah Petrovsky's sole purpose in representing him was to insure he pled guilty to the charges against him. No doubt he would put on a good show trying to build a defense for his client but it would all be a sham. Sorkowski knew the truth. The man was yet another of Moreau's tools to make sure he didn't try to make a deal with the prosecution.

"Sit, sit," Petrovsky said in a raspy voice, clearly annoyed he had been kept waiting.

"What do you want?" Sorkowski tried to hide his fear behind a veneer of apathy but the way Petrovsky sneered told him he failed.

"Shut your mouth and listen," the man ordered softly, his eyes glinting dangerously. "Your trial date has been set. It will begin in three months to give us time to prepare." Another sneer, one that told Sorkowski there would be no preparation. "You know what you're to do. Correct?"

"I do."

"And I assume you understand the message our friends sent this morning?" A slight smile, evil and predatory, lit the man's features.

"I do." Now he couldn't keep the fear from his voice. He had understood the message all too well and was still thanking all that was holy it had been O'Brien and not him.

"Excellent. We wouldn't want you doing anything foolish, would we?" As he spoke, Petrovsky slid a sheaf of papers across the table to his client. "Now, return to your cell and remember what you're supposed to do. Those pages are copies of the charging documents against you as well as the preliminary discovery motions. Do whatever you want with them."

Grinding his teeth in frustration, Sorkowski got to his feet and shuffled back to the door he'd entered through a few minutes earlier. It slid open and he moved through it. Despair warred with fury as he did. Why should he be the only one to pay? He wasn't the one who started it all. No. So why should he be the one to pay the ultimate price?

Knowing there would be no answer, he sighed heavily and followed the guard back to his cell. God what he wouldn't do to wake up in his own bed back and realize this had all been a very bad dream.

*   *   *

"Has there been any word?" Kannady asked as he crossed the room.

Evan Moreau forced herself to smile as he joined her. At last this time he hadn't been so foolish as to show up at her office unannounced and unexpected. Not that this was much better. She had just finished having drinks with a legitimate business associate when she saw Kannady enter the restaurant. She knew the moment he was certain she had seen him. His expression turned into a mirror of relief and he jerked his head in the direction of the back room. She'd given a minute shake of the head. Anger flared in his eyes but she wasn't going to call attention to either of them by jumping up just because he wanted it. He could wait until she judged it safe to excuse herself from her companion and join him.

Then the decision of when to move was taken out of her hands. Her companion thanked her and promised to have the contract changes to her office by close of business the next day. A moment later he was gone and, before she could react, Kannady was striding across the dining room in her direction.

It was only the knowledge that she was well-known for using this particular restaurant for business meetings that kept in her chair.

"We have really got to quit meeting like this, darling." She smiled and reached across the table to cup his cheek with her right hand. To anyone who might be paying attention to them, they would look like close friends or lovers meeting after a long day. At least she hoped so.

"You said you'd call me." His tone matched hers, light and teasing, but there was a dangerous glint in his eyes.

Well, she'd take care of that soon enough. She would not let him continue to put not only her mission but her life in jeopardy simply because he couldn't wait for an update.

"Darling, I told you I had meetings all day." She smiled

sweetly and nodded to the waiter who appeared at her elbow, a fresh bottle of wine in hand. He poured, set the bottle on the table and then moved on. "You risk much by coming here," she said softly once they were alone again. She may have been smiling but there was venom in her whispered words.

"You said you'd keep me informed," he countered just as softly.

She did a quick count to ten. Tempting as it was to deal with him right there, she couldn't. There were too many witnesses. Unfortunately.

"Petrovsky made sure he understands he has no choice but to sit back and face the charges against him." As he spoke, he quickly undressed. "From what Petrovsky said, our *friend* is so scared right now that there's no chance he will even think about trying to make a deal. He knows what will happen if he does."

"What about the others?"

"They are being taken care of. O'Brien was treated to a lesson last night to make sure Sorkowski understands exactly where he stands. The others will receive similar warnings. So quit worrying. I told you I would take care of everything. "

"And after the trial?"

"The word has already been passed to certain people, along with the proper payment, that our friends will no longer be of any use to us once their trials have concluded," she said. "I have no doubt it will look like the typical power play that happens so often when new cons arrive. It won't wash back on us."

"You had better be right."

The implied threat hung in the air.

"I always am." She let that sink in before continuing. "The plans are already in place. But we have to move carefully. You know that. We can't deal with any of them until we know they have said nothing to implicate us and until we have in our possession any records they might have kept. You know that."

"I do know and I apologize for doubting you."

She knew he didn't mean it. Not that she cared. Soon he would be no more of a concern than Sorkowski and the others.

CHAPTER TWELVE

"MA'AM, WE HAVE PERMISSION TO LAUNCH," THE SHUTTLE PILOT reported.

"Very good." Ashlyn nodded in satisfaction. "Relay the order. We launch in sequence. Let's do this by the numbers and bring everyone home safely."

"Sounds good to me, Ma'am."

"Donnelly." She turned to where the corporal sat next to Captain Nichols.

"Ma'am?"

"This is it." She moved to squat on the decksole in front of the younger man and pitched her voice so they wouldn't be overheard. "Ryan, you're a fine Marine and you've done an excellent job helping Captain Nichols put Delta Company's part of the op together. But we've come a long way to kick these bastards out of the system. I need to know that your head is in the game and not worrying about what we are going to find where your brother's concerned."

"I understand, Colonel, and believe me, the captain has already made it very clear that I'm to watch myself," he replied just as softly.

"Don't worry about him, Ma'am," Nichols said without looking up from the display he'd been studying on his datapad.

"He'll do his duty."

For a moment, Ash simply studied the two men. She still wondered if she had made the right decision in allowing Donnelly to come on the mission. Even though she had concerns, she wasn't willing to risk a bad mark in his jacket just because she didn't know how he would react. Besides, if the war lasted very long, there would be few of them who didn't know or weren't related to someone who had either been killed or captured by the Callusians. That was the way of war.

She gave them a nod before turning a look on Nichols that warned him his corporal had better not do anything foolish. Then she stood. It was time to get the mission underway and she couldn't do that as long as the shuttles were still docked in the landing bay.

"All right, boys and girls, this is it. Lock in, hold on and be ready to hit the ground with your feet moving and your weapons hot."

She banged her armored fist against the bulkhead to let the pilot know they were ready. Then she returned to her place near the cockpit and prepared for launch. Doubts were pushed back and she focused on what the next few hours – or days – would hold. The Devil Dogs were the best and if the Callusians were going to be pushed off planet, they would be the ones to do it.

Oo-rah!

*   *   *

"Hold him, damn you!" the guard growled angrily as the prisoner dug his heels in and once more pulled as hard as he could against the chains holding him.

Lieutenant Joss Donnelly growled angrily as the guards struggled to control him. When they appeared at the door to the cell he shared with two others from the *Tarrant*, he hadn't tried to resist. He had learned very quickly after his capture that disobedience was a sure way to find himself beaten into unconsciousness – but only after they made him watch as they tortured the others. So he had stood by, his gaze locked on a point in the wall well above their heads, as they locked the chains on his wrists. Then, with his arms extended from his sides, they had proceeded to beat him, leaving his ribs screaming in pain and his right eye threatening to swell shut.

It had surprised him to find himself being dragged into the open. It was the first time he had been the outside the cellblock since waking in the infirmary after the unprovoked attack on the *Tarrant*. His breath caught and he felt sure they were leading him to his execution. He had been expecting it. For weeks, ever since Fuercon had said it would no longer abide by a truce, the Callusians were not honoring, his captors had been threatening that he would die come morning. Well, it was morning and it seemed they were finally going to carry out their threat.

Then he saw other prisoners bound between stakes that appeared to have been hastily driven into the ground, almost as if they were a human wall to stand between their captors and – who? He recognized some of the prisoners. There were other survivors from the *Tarrant* as well as some of those who had served in governmental roles before the invasion. Behind them, clustered together, were others. The elderly and children as well as others who appeared to be more seriously injured than he. He couldn't tell if they were bound but they did appear to be too frightened to even think about fighting back.

"Get him in position!" a man yelled from somewhere to his right.

Donnelly once again dug in his heels, doing everything he could to slow his forward progress until he had a better idea about what was going on. The guards trying to move him into place didn't have the attitude of invincibility he had come to expect. Daring to look at them even as he tried pulling free of their control, he saw something he had not seen before. There was a desperation to them that went beyond the fact he was fighting back. Then, as the voice once again called out for them to get him secured, he knew something had happened. Something that might actually be for the good of the prisoners, if they could live long enough to find out what it was.

Something had happened and it had caught the Callusians by surprise. Could it be that Fuercon or its allies were finally making a move to try to retake the planet? If so, he had to do whatever it took to keep not only himself but also his fellow POWs alive. If that meant killing a few of the guards along the way, well he'd shed no tears over it. They deserved whatever happened to them after all they had done since the invasion.

But to do that, he had to break free of the guards trying to secure him to the posts.

"NO!" He threw himself forward.

His momentum pulled the last few links of the chain connected to his right wrist of the guard's grip. Reacting instantly, instinctively, Joss dove away from the other guard. As he rolled to his feet, he spun the chain with all his might at the guard still foolishly trying to hold him. Metal links smashed the guard's face with a sickening *thud*, shattering teeth and bone. With a howl of pain, the guard fell to his knees, hands flying to his face in a useless attempt to stem the flow of blood from his wounds.

Lt. Joss Donnelly, a navigation specialist who had never thought of himself as a warrior, wrapped the chains around his hands several times to give him better control over them. What a wonderful weapon the chains made. Then he turned, looking for the first guard. Unlike his fallen companion, that guard had shown his true colors and was sprinting away, yelling for help as he did. Deprived of his target, Joss turned again, only to find two other guards quickly dragging his first victim to safety.

He wouldn't have much time. He knew it. So he needed to

get as many of his fellow prisoners free of their bonds as he could before the guards regrouped and decided to try again.

* * *

"Damn it, are all your people incompetent?" Kasun demanded as he watched the prisoner hurrying toward the others. "Peltier, I suggest you deal with the situation right now or it will be both our heads on the block."

He didn't have time for this. It was only a matter of time before the Fuerconese landed troops. It surprised him that they hadn't already. He'd even begun thinking he might be able to get the prisoners in place to be used as bargaining chips. But no. He should have known it wouldn't be as easily done as he wanted. Not with those fools who reported to Peltier. Damn it, why hadn't he fought harder when High Command said it was pulling much of the occupation force from the system? At least then he might have had a chance to hold off the Fuerconese until reinforcements could arrive.

"Get the prisoners in place now or, by the gods, I will have you staked out down there with them!"

Damn it, was he the only one who understood just how serious their position happened to be?

"But –"

"Do I need to remind you what our superiors do to those who let hard won gains slip through their fingers?" Kason snapped, watching in growing concern as Joss Donnelly worked to free yet another POW.

Couldn't High Command have at least left me with a senior military officer who knew his ass from a hole in the ground?

"I suggest you get more guards down there and get the job done while there's still time. Then make sure our perimeter defenses are online. I swear if the Fuerconese get through, you will be in the leading element going out to engage them. Now get moving."

*   *   *

"C'mon," Joss urged, kneeling beside one of his fellow crewmembers from the *Tarrant*. "Get up, Bo. You've got to get up."

"Get back, LT. We've got him," Gunnery Sergeant Leroy Levitson said as he and Sergeant Karin Abramson dropped to their knees on either side of him.

For a moment Joss looked as if he might argue. Then his eyes locked on the far end of the compound. The heavy gate was slowly opening. That could mean only one thing. The guards were coming back. Time had run out and he had yet to form a plan of any sort that might keep his people and the other prisoners alive a little longer.

"Drag him back as far as you can and then get back here," he rasped and climbed to his feet. Bearing down against the pain from his injuries, he made his way as quickly as he could to where the rest of his people waited.

"Joss, are you all right?" Lieutenant Sharra Sinclair asked in concern.

"As all right as any of us are," he said. "Listen up, people. I think we all realize something's happened and it has the enemy running scared. My guess is they were going to try to use us to hold off an invasionary force. Whether it is the local Resistance or something else, I don't know. What I do know is we need to hold out until help gets here, no matter what quarter it comes from."

"What do you want us to do, LT?" Sergeant Ellen O'Donnell asked matter-of-factly.

"Those who don't have training in hand-to-hand, do what you can to free the others. As for the rest of us, there are no rules now. We're fighting not only for our own survival but for that of every person here. Don't hesitate to kill if you have to." He spoke firmly, hoping they were up to the task.

"One rule," Sinclair corrected from his side. "You're the

ranking officer now. So you stay with us and don't go off trying to win this thing on your own."

"Sharra –"

"No, LT. She's right," O'Donnell agreed and then nodded as the gate opened fully and guards began moving slowly in their direction.

He didn't say anything. Instead he looked at the guards and wondered how he was supposed to keep them away from the others. For one brief moment, he thought of his younger brother who had opted to join the Marines because he wanted to "take the fight to the enemy". Ryan would know what to do. He'd probably just smile and rush headlong toward the enemy, figuring the last thing they'd expect was a direct attack, especially from unarmed opponents.

"Just stay with me." That was the only warning he gave the others before racing forward. He'd probably die but if it kept the others alive until help came, it was worth it.

*   *   *

Kasun stared out the window, disbelief growing. The guards were acting as if they were the ones who were unarmed. Instead of rushing the prisoners, killing a few if necessary to get the others under control, they moved slowly, hesitantly into the area. Damn the cowards!

Without taking his eyes from the green, Kasun reached for his com-link. His fingers worked automatically to activate it. But the soft *beep* indicating an active signal never came. As Donnelly and the prisoners rushed toward the guards, the Occupation Governor looked at the link in concern as he once more tried unsuccessfully to activate it.

"Peltier, try your 'link," he said, fear rising. "Tell your people to move in. They are to do whatever it takes to regain control of the compound."

"Nothing!" Peltier said a moment later, his own fear evident.

Turning from the window, Kasun hurried across the office to his desk. His fingers danced across the virtual keyboard as he typed. Command sequence after command sequence failed. No one responded to his calls for support. Swallowing hard, he tried to activate the link to the spaceport. Silence. Fear erupted and sweat pricked out on his upper lip. Something was very definitely wrong and he had a feeling their time had run out.

But he couldn't give up. Not yet. Not without proof.

Dear God, what was going on?

"We need to get to the bunker," he said, gathering up the datachips and looking around to make sure he was leaving nothing behind of any import. "Get word to your people that the POWs and other prisoners are not to be allowed to escape. Lock down the compound and make sure they are where we can still use them when the time comes."

"See to it, Kerrigan," Peltier ordered the guard standing on the other side of the open door.

"Send someone to Comms and try to reach Parnian. See if he can send us help from the spaceport."

As he spoke, Kasun reminded himself not to panic. He had to maintain at least the illusion that he was still in control. But it was hard. So very hard. Especially when he wanted nothing more than to hide until it was safe for him to come out and find a way off this hellhole of a planet.

* * *

"Sir, we've got a visual," Captain Jareau reported.

"Put it up on the secondary screens," Collins ordered.

An audible gasp filled the flag bridge as the image appeared on the displays before them. It looked like a primitive war was going on and the survivors from the *Tarrant* were right in the middle of it. Worse, there were too few of them, even with the help they were receiving from the other prisoners, to hold out for long against the armed guards. But at least they were holding their own for the moment. Hopefully, the Devil Dogs could reach them before all was lost.

"Comms, signal Colonel Shaw. Tell her to go to Code Red. I repeat. Code Red. They are to drop and secure the area now," Collins said coldly.

"Signal away, Sir."

"Hang on, everyone. We're coming. Hang on just a little while longer."

*   *   *

"Fall back!" Joss yelled as the guards withdrew to regroup. "Damn it, fall back!"

Slowly, those of his people still on their feet gathered around him. Even as they did, he shook his head in disbelief. With the guards armed, they might have well been outnumbered more than three to one. But they had held their own, finding makeshift weapons and recovering the weapons from the guards who fell. Somehow, they not only lived but, with the exception of Bo Geist who lay at the far end of the arena where they had taken him before the fight began, they were relatively unscathed.Well, not exactly. They were battered and beaten but they hadn't broken. True, Sharra Sinclair remained on her feet through sheer stubbornness and several others were little better. Fortunately for all of them, the guards were not working as a cohesive unit. That lack of coordination made it easy to exploit weaknesses in their attack. Even so, Joss knew that if he didn't find a way to win soon, all the prisoners would die.

But he was damned if they would go down cowering in fear.

Cursing silently, he let his eyes roam the area before him. His gaze swept over the guards who were gathering to attack again. There was something different about them this time. Where they had been cautious before, now they appeared almost hesitant. There was a sense that they were waiting for someone to give an order, any order, but none came. It didn't make any sense. The guards might be outnumbered – and he wasn't sure they were – but they most definitely weren't outgunned. The POWs had only managed to get their hands on a few of the weapons dropped when guards fell during the initial encounter.

Joss looked around, searching for anything that might explain why the guards had yet to press their advantage again. He scanned the area, frowning. Then he turned his attention back to the guards. Some wore light armor. Others were in their daily uniforms. But none of them wore the insignia of a senior officer. He wasn't even sure there were any senior non-coms among them. If that was the case – and he had no idea why there would be no one with any real authority present – then it would explain why none of them seemed to know exactly what they were to do.

"Where are all the officers?" O'Donnell asked softly from his side.

"More importantly, where is that bastard Peltier and why isn't he here?" Joss wanted to know. "He wouldn't miss a chance to hurt any of us. So where is he?"

"Sir, it looks like they've decided to try again," Levitson reported softly.

Frowning, Joss looked in the direction of the guards. Levitson was right. They were coming again, but even more slowly than before. Perhaps the sight of their fallen companions was enough to make them remember just how deadly people could be when they knew they had nothing to lose. Now it was his turn to make sure the POWs exercised enough caution to keep the guards off of them and yet hold out long enough to find out what in the hell was going on.

Even as the question formed, he knew the answer. It would mean some of his people, military and civilian alike, might die but it would keep more of them alive. They had to continue to take the fight directly to the guards. Without someone willing to give orders, the guards would not work as a single unit. He had already seen that. Now he had to press that advantage and try to drive the guards out of the compound long enough that the prisoners could secure the gate against them.

"Close up our ranks. We need to push them back, out of the gate. If we can secure it against them, maybe we can hold out until we know what's going on.

"Levitson, get yourself some people and move to the right flank. Keep low as we try to push the guards back. Watch for my signal. If necessary, I'll call you into the fight. I'm hoping I won't have to. If that's the case, as soon as we get the guards beyond the gate, I want you and your people to get it shut. I don't care what you have to do. Just do it."

"Understood, Sir." The man turned and scanned the faces of those closest to him. It didn't take him long to choose half a dozen.

Joss watched as they moved slowly to the back of the group. Nodding in approval, he waited another moment and then focused on the rest of those still able to fight. "Let's do this. Let's take the fight to them."

He lifted his right fist and focused on the slowly advancing guards. He wanted them to get a little closer before ordering the attack. Just a little bit more. Let them think the POWs had finally started having second thoughts.

"Come on," he whispered, every muscle and nerve tense. "Come on. . . NOW!"

A battle cry rose from the throats of those behind him and filled the air. He almost laughed as the guards faltered, fear washing across the expressions of many of them as the poorly armed but very determined POWs suddenly rushed in their direction.

CHAPTER THIRTEEN

BRIGADIER GENERAL ELIZABETH SHAW STARED OUT THE WINDOW behind her desk. Below her, visible if she increased the magnification, the members of FirstDiv, Second Batt were doing PT. The division was on standby, waiting to learn where FleetCom decided it was most needed. While most of her attention had been on making sure the division was ready to move out, one part of her remained focused on the Devil Dogs. Unless something unexpected happened, they should now be trying to drive the Callusians from Cassius Prime.

"Are you all right?"

Elizabeth turned at the sound of Helen Okafor's voice. The woman stood just inside the door. Her expression reflected her concern. Then, before Elizabeth could respond, the Commandant of the Marine Corps stepped further into the office and the door slid shut behind her.

"Just having a mother moment." Elizabeth smiled slightly and motioned for Okafor to take the desk chair. It didn't surprise her when Okafor shook her head before dropping onto one of the chairs in front of the desk.

"I know. I feel that way whenever I think about Jarrod," Okafor said, referring to her son who commanded a cruiser in Third Fleet. "But you know Ash isn't going to do anything foolish. Nothing is going to keep her from attending Sorkowski's and O'Brien's courts-martial."

Elizabeth nodded. "Any word on O'Brien?"

When she had first learned of how the former Marine CO had been attacked, the only thing that had surprised her was that she wasn't surprised. Then relief that Ashlyn was off-planet filled her. That meant her daughter couldn't be blamed for the attack on the man. Not that it had stopped some members of the media from speculating about it.

"The doctors say he'll be able to stand trial, assuming he doesn't have another *accident*." Okafor's expression turned grim.

"Good. Death is too easy an escape for that bastard."

"Agreed." Okafor paused and Elizabeth wondered what was on her mind. "Liz, I had a visit from Rico Santiago earlier."

Elizabeth dropped onto her chair, not sure if she wanted to know what FleetCom's Intelligence Chief had to say.

"It seems he is looking into what happened and has been comparing notes with JAG."

"And?"

"He's convinced that what happened to O'Brien was meant as a message to not only him but to the others arrested with him, especially Sorkowski."

"But that doesn't make sense."

Not unless there were others involved they didn't know about yet.

"Unless we've missed something," Okafor said.

Elizabeth blew out a breath, not sure what to think. She had always felt there was more to what happened to Ash and her people than they knew. Over the last few months, she'd also found herself wondering if there wasn't more to the Callusians resuming hostilities than they thought. Could the two somehow be connected?

"What do you want me to do?"

"Meet with Santiago and compare notes. I know you've been looking into what happened as well."

"Understood."

"Good." Okafor stood and quickly motioned for Elizabeth to stay where she was. "Keep me informed."

With that, she was gone, leaving Elizabeth wondering when things would return to normal – if they ever did.

* * *

Kasun cursed loudly as an attack shuttle opened fire on the shuttles resting with cold engines at the landing field. They went up in a ball of flame no one could miss. Then that precision targeting turned to his groundside defenses. Yet through it all there was no demand for surrender, no contact whatsoever.

"Who are they?" he demanded helplessly.

"Does it matter?" Peltier countered, bracing himself with a hand on the wall as an explosion rocked the building. "We're dead no matter who they are."

Kasun knew the guard captain was right. Even if the invaders should somehow decide to break off the attack, the POWs were still there. He knew they wouldn't hesitate to kill him if they managed to get their hands on him. He had to prevent that. But how? He had lost any advantage he had when the prisoners decided to fight back.

"Captain, have your people make sure the POWs are locked down. Barricade the gates and the underground access. We can't worry about them and these damned invaders as well," he snapped. "Make sure everyone's armed, support staff as well as your people. Then get back here. Hopefully by then someone will figure out we need help."

Assuming they aren't in the same position we are.

* * *

"LT!" O'Donnell yelled from across the arena.

Hearing the disbelief in the woman's voice, Joss quickly

turned in her direction. As he did, the unmistakable roar of an attack shuttle streaking across the sky filled the air. It was followed almost instantly by the sounds of several explosions. A huge fireball shot across the sky only to disappear in the distance.

"Get under cover!" Joss ordered. "Run!"

Joss moved as quickly as he could toward the meager shelter offered by the walls of the buildings. The POWs might not be able to get inside but at least they could stick close to the structures as the fighting raged around them.

Without pausing, Joss grabbed O'Donnell as she stumbled and dragged her forward. As he did, he thanked a God he wasn't sure he still believed in. At least so far they still lived. Hopefully, that wasn't about to change.

Another series of explosions rocked the compound. Joss stumbled, pain tearing up his left leg. Before he could fall, O'Donnell steadied him. Then they slid the last few feet to where the others waited in the shadows of the administration building.

"What's going on?" one of the politicians who had been captured during the initial invasion wanted to know.

"Someone's decided they hate Kasun as much as we do," Joss replied as he looked around to make sure everyone had found cover. "Sharra?"

The sight of the bloody makeshift bandages at shoulder and abdomen worried Joss. Somehow, he had to get medical help for the woman, and for the other injured, as quickly as possible. But how, when he didn't know what was going on outside the arena?

"I've been better, Joss," the blonde replied.

"You just sit still and try to rest."

"The LT's right, Sharra," O'Donnell said gently as she knelt at Joss's side. "I'll sit with her. The Gunny thinks he's found something to get those chains off you." She nodded at the chains still hanging from each of Joss's wrists.

For a moment, he hesitated. Then he nodded. Like it or not, he was needed elsewhere.

"All right. I'll be back."

*　*　*

Kasun stared at the scene below and shook his head. He didn't feel anything. No longer did his brain register shock or fear. Why should it? He was a dead man and he knew it. It was only a question of when he would die and by whose hand.

He released the breath he had been holding. There were no words to describe the carnage below. Marines wearing midnight black battle armor relieved only by the insignia of those thrice damned Fueronese Devil Dogs swept across the grounds. They killed anyone and anything that appeared to pose a threat. Now they were bearing down on the administration building.

Time was up. If he didn't try to get to the bunker now, he would never have the chance.

Turning, he took two steps and then stopped as the sounds of fighting in the outer office reached him. A moment later, the office door blew open with a deafening blast. The force of the explosion knocked him back several steps and he fell to his knees. If possible, he would have tunneled out of the office.

Instead, before he could look to see where Peltier was, pain exploded in his ribs. The heavy boot connected once and then again and he sprawled on the floor. Tears burned his eyes and he gasped for breath. Looking up, he found himself staring down the barrels of four battle rifles and he once again cursed High Command for stripping away most of his defenses.

Gods above and below, he didn't want to die like this.

*　*　*

"Loco, secure these pieces of scum," Ashlyn ordered as she removed her battle helmet. She tossed it onto the nearby desk before activating her comm. "Sir, Admin's now under our control. Squads One through Four are continuing to sweep the other parts of the outer area. As soon as the area's secure, we'll move to the inner compound."

"Excellent, Angel," Admiral Collins replied. "As soon as you have the building secured, move on to the grounds. There are injured out there who need our help."

"Understood, Sir," Ash responded and glanced out the door as the sounds of several people approaching reached her. A moment later, she nodded in satisfaction as Corporal Donnelly and Captain Nichols appeared. Both looked ready for anything and Ashlyn found herself pitying the two men now cuffed and kneeling on the floor a few feet away.

"Report," she said simply.

"This floor is secured, Ma'am. Teams are moving on to their next targets."

Ashlyn nodded. Then she once again turned her attention to the two prisoners. Her upper lip curled back as she recognized the older man. They had lucked out and found one of their primary targets without really trying. All she had to do was make sure the man told her everything she wanted to know.

"Name?" she snapped as she stood over him. When he remained silent, even refusing to meet her eyes, she nodded to Talbot who signaled for two of their team to move behind the prisoners. "Your name," she repeated as one of the Marines forced the man's head back by the simple means of grabbing a handful of hair and pulling.

"K-Kasun," he stammered.

"Rank and assignment?" she asked even though she knew the answer.

"A-anton Kasun. Occupational Governor."

"Well, Occupational Governor Kasun, I am Lt. Colonel Ashlyn Shaw, First Battalion, First Division, Fuerconese Marine Corps. It is with extreme pleasure that I inform you that we are now in control of this planet."

"No!"

The gasp was torn from Kasun as he stared at Ashlyn in disbelief. She simply returned his stare, giving him time to accept the fact that they really were there and not haring off to the Nystrom System.

"Yes," she countered coldly. "I really don't care whether we keep you alive or not. That's up to you. Give us the information we want and you'll live. Refuse and I'll leave you here to explain to your superiors what happened and how you managed to lose an entire system. I'm quite sure they won't be as understanding as I am."

Both Kasun and Peltier blanched at her words. Nothing could be truer. They were dead men. The Callusians didn't suffer losses well. And this was, in so many ways, worse than a loss in battle. The Cassius System was supposed to be their advanced base of operations for when they launched the final attack on Fuercon.

"What do you want?"

"It's really very simple. Give us the computer access codes and the locations of every POW on planet as well as those shipped out," Ashlyn said. Her voice was clam, but the way her hand rested on the pulsar at her hip spoke volumes about what would happen if he failed to comply.

"I can't!"

"You can or you die. It's that simple," she countered coldly. Then, before Kasun could say anything else, she turned her attention to the second prisoner and an unholy delight appeared in her eyes.

"This one?" she asked Talbot, her voice dripping with cold contempt.

"Name's Peltier, Ma'am. The security chief," the Marine replied with disdain.

"How appropriate that we have the two of them," she

mused, a sardonic smile touching her lips. "Let me make it easier for the two of you to come to the right decisions. The corporal here – " She waved her hand and Ryan Donnelly stepped forward. – "has a very personal matter he'd like to *discuss* with you. But he's a Marine. He'll hold back if ordered," Ash continued coldly. "What he would dearly love is to take apart, piece by piece, anyone who's hurt his brother and I have a feeling he wouldn't mind one bit starting with the two of you. Isn't that correct, Corporal?"

"It is, Ma'am," Donnelly growled, pinning the two with the hard, hot gaze of pure hatred.

"Now, he's been told he can't do as he wants. However, I have no compunction about reversing that order." Ashlyn's voice was almost casual now and all the more fearsome because of it. "But before I ask for your *assistance* again, let me tell you something else that might help you make up your minds.

"Every Marine present, every Marine who has taken part in this mission, has one order. We are to take back the system. If some of us die to do so, that's part of being a Devil Dog. That means we will do whatever it takes – whatever – to accomplish the mission and return home with our people.

"So, Occupational Governor Kasun, what will it be? Are you going to answer my questions or do I turn you over to Corporal Donnelly and his friends?"

The resulting babble from both of the prisoners came even quicker than Ashlyn had dared hope.

* * *

"Sir, we just received confirmation from Captain Monroe that Gamma Company has secured the port. Beta Company is now moving on to the outer defense complex. Enemy resistance has been minimal, all things considered," Captain Jareau reported, satisfaction clear in her voice.

"Excellent, Jules."

Collins forced himself to relax. The news was good. Hopefully, once they had the chance to examine the data banks and other records, they would have a better idea about what the Callusian battle plan might be. He would welcome anything FleetCom could use to bring this latest war to a quick and decisive end.

But none of that eased his concern over what was happening at the administration complex. The fighting there had been much more intense than elsewhere. He hadn't factored in the knowledge that the Blood repaid failure or defeat with death and not just the deaths of those directly involved. No, whole families would be killed unless the evidence showed their loved ones died a "righteous" death fighting the enemy.

At least the injuries to the Devil Dogs hadn't been serious – so far. There really was something to be said for superior training and equipment. But that didn't make those injuries any easier to accept.

Worse, they had yet to reach the POWs. At least the visual feeds no longer showed the prisoners fighting the guards. But the way they appeared to be bunkering down didn't particularly reassure him either. He couldn't tell who was in charge of the prisoners any more than he knew if any of the *Tarrant*'s crew still lived.

Damn but he wanted to be dirt-side!

"Sir." Captain Jareau's voice interrupted his reverie. "Captain Monroe requests that we send some computer techs as well as a spook or two down. She seems to think there is more to the data they are recovering than appears at first glance."

Maybe they were about to get lucky after all. "I believe Commander Hickson has a team standing by to begin a complete download of the data banks. Get them on their way. Then let Captain Monroe know."

"Aye, sir."

"Ben, get me Colonel Shaw on the comm."

"Aye, Sir," Lt. Commander Levy replied. "You have an open channel to the Colonel, Sir," he reported a few moments later and Collins nodded his appreciation.

"Angel, talk to me," he said simply.

"Sir, we have secured the administrative buildings. I thought you might like to know that we have the so-called occupational governor and security chief among our prisoners," Ashlyn reported. She paused and Collins heard the tell-tale murmur of someone reporting to her. "Admiral, we will be moving on to secure the outer area where the prisoners are next. There is one problem, the main gate leading to the area where they are has been barricaded on both sides,"

Collins nodded to Levy and waited. A moment later, the holo screen image shifted and split. One half continued to display the system, pinpointing where all their ships were. The other showed what Collins assumed was the gate Ashlyn referred to. Machinery, furniture and debris had been piled high before the heavy gates.

"Ashlyn." Now that he knew her position was secure, he switched away from her call sign. "I want that compound secured ASAP. Use one of the shuttle's tractor beams to move what you can't by hand," he ordered firmly.

"Ash, we can't go in with guns blazing. These are our allies and they've been terrorized enough. Put your head together with your people and decide the best way to proceed. But hurry."

"Leave it to us. Shaw clear."

Breathing deeply, Collins leaned back and closed his eyes. This had to be the most nerve-wracking mission he had ever been on.

* * *

"You heard the Admiral. Any ideas?" Ashlyn asked as she

turned to Talbot and several others.

For a long moment, no one spoke. Instead, they looked at the debris piled before the gate. Already every Marine not on prisoner watch or sentry duty was tearing into it, tossing aside what they could. But it wouldn't be enough and it certainly wasn't quick enough.

Not by a long shot.

"Angel, I think he had the right idea but we can do better. Use two of the shuttles you've kept in the air. Their tractors should make short work of all that." Talbot waved his hand at the pile.

"As for the rest of it, I recommend Corporal Donnelly and Captain Nichols go in first once we've cleared the gate. You can send a squad in with them."

"Agreed, but with a couple of modifications. First, I'm going in with them. The POWs need to see a figurehead and, like it or not, that's me. Second, we go in with weapons holstered."

"Angel!' Talbot looked at her as if she had sprouted horns or another head. "No way. We don't know what the situation beyond that wall is."

"The shuttles will be covering us," she reminded him. "But the Admiral's right. We have to do whatever we can to reassure those poor bastards inside. Going in with guns drawn and in full battle armor won't do that."

For a moment Talbot looked like he was going to argue. Then he nodded once, decisively. Relieved, Ash gave him a quick smile. "Now let's get to work."

CHAPTER FOURTEEN

"SIR, IT SOUNDS LIKE THEY'RE WORKING ON THE BARRICADE outside the gate," a grizzled man reported as he slid to a halt before him.

For a moment, Joss studied him, trying to recall his name. But he couldn't. Kasun and his goons had done their best to keep him segregated from most of the other POWs.

That was why he had been so surprised when so many of the POWs had been willing to follow his lead. They didn't know him. Nor did they know the other survivors from the *Tarrant*. But they had willingly listened to what he had to say and they had been willing to make a stand against the guards. Was it possible that they might actually manage to hold out long enough for help to get to them?

In fact, there had only been one point of contention among the POWs. Joss had insisted that any Callusians the POWs came across not be killed out of hand. If they resisted or tried to harm a prisoner, they deserved whatever they got. But if they surrendered, they were to be secured and stripped but nothing more. Some of the POWs had protested, wanting the opportunity to give the guards a taste of what they had been forced to endure. But Joss had stood firm, reminding them that they were not like the Callusians. They were not animals.

They would do this his way or they could join those waiting out the fight in the shadows of the building.

Now Joss and the other survivors from the *Tarrant*, those still on their feet, wore the captured gun-belts. He had even, over the objections of O'Donnell and Levitson, armed some of the other POWs, reminding the two that they were all in this together.

"Thank you." He paused, looking at the man in the hope he would supply his name.

"Greeley, Sir. Sergeant Jonathan Greeley. I was part of the Marine contingent assigned to the Fuerconese embassy before the invasion," he said.

"Are there any others from your billet, Sergeant?"

"Yes, Sir. Right now they are seeing to the injured."

"Very good, Sergeant. Hopefully, we're about to get out of here. In the meantime, I'd like you to help set up our defenses. We still don't know who's out there or what's going on."

"Understood, LT. With your permission?"

"Go," he said simply before turning to O'Donnell. "Any word from the medics?"

Medics!

That was a laugh. So far they had found only three POWs with any real medical training and that training had, sadly, been long ago. But that was better than nothing. He had to remember that.

"We've lost two civilians from their injuries," the blonde reported grimly. "As for our people, most are walking wounded. Bo and Sharra are both unconscious, which is probably for the best. The medics don't have anything to give them for the pain."

"I know."

He ran a hand over his face, wincing in pain as he rubbed against the cut over his right eye. Now that all they could do was sit and wait, every injury he had suffered since the guards first came for him that morning seemed to scream in pain. Only determination kept him on his feet and he knew that if something didn't happen soon he would have to get some rest. But he couldn't. Not yet at any rate. Not until he knew for sure what was going on.

"Ellen, we can't sit here forever." He turned and moved away from listening ears. "We're going to have to make a move if something doesn't happen soon. If we don't, we run the risk of losing more of the injured."

"Aye," the blonde said grimly. They had watched one of their own die a slow, horrible death at Kasun's hands just so the *governor* could show them how helpless they were. "But you need to rest before we make our move."

"We all do, but I don't think we'll have that luxury."

Before he could continue, a shout from outside interrupted. Cursing softly, Joss started forward at a slow, limping run. Before he could take more than a few steps, Sergeant Greeley was there, pointing skyward. Hovering high above them was an attack shuttle. Shielding his eyes against the sun, Joss watched, unaware that he was holding his breath until his lungs began to burn. Forcing them to remember the mechanics of drawing in fresh oxygen, he waited, wondering what they were about to face.

"This is Colonel Ashlyn Shaw, Fuerconese Marine Corps. The Devil Dogs, as part of a taskforce sent by FleetCom, has taken control of the capital. The invaders have either been captured or killed. The area is secure and we want to make entrance into the compound. However, we will not do so until you are ready. Shaw clear."

For a moment, Joss stared at the shuttle in disbelief. Relief filled him to know help had finally arrived. But then there were the doubts. Could he really trust a disembodied voice to be what it said it was?

What if this was another of Kasun's tricks? If it was, the

moment he allowed these so-called Marines into the compound, he would sign everyone's death warrants. Even so, did he dare not risk it? They couldn't hold out forever. Didn't he have to take the chance?

It all came down to one thing: did he trust his gut or not?

"LT?" O'Donnell prompted softly, her own disbelief clearly written on her face.

"We have to risk it," he said. "I want you, Gunny and Karin to make sure everyone holds position. We'll let them come in but not without keeping our eyes and ears open. If this is a trap, they'll pay for it."

"Right away." O'Donnell flashed a quick salute and then took off, calling to their fellow crewmembers as she did.

"Sergeant Greeley!" he called. He waited until the Marine slid to a stop in front of him. "Is there anyone you can vouch for who can hold military discipline?" he asked.

"Yes, Sir."

"Good. Take them and set up a defense in front of the injured. I don't want anyone but our people getting to them without my permission."

The man gave a quick nod and then ran off to do as Joss said. Satisfied, Joss once more turned his attention to the shuttle high above his head. Now all he had to do was figure out how to let them know they had permission to enter. Unlike the shuttle, he didn't have any communication equipment. But he did have the barricade on this side of the gate. The shuttle would be able to pick up on their activity if they started tearing it down. That ought to be enough to let them know that they had their invitation.

"Lt. O'Donnell!" he yelled as he started across the compound in the direction of the gate. "I want a work crew to start breaking down the barricade. Let's give them the invitation they asked for."

*　　*　　*

"There it is, Ma'am!"

Corporal O'Donnell's relief mixed with excitement and apprehension as the image transmitted from the shuttle showed the first POWs beginning to tear down their barricade. At his side, Ashlyn nodded slightly. She would never admit it but she had worried they wouldn't believe help had finally arrived. If they hadn't, there would have been no other choice but to force their way in. But this was much better. So very much better.

"Yep, kid. So far so good."

But what would they find beyond the gates? The images from the shuttle were too far away for them to pick out individual features. All she could tell was that some of the POWs, all too few of them, wore what looked like Fuerconese naval uniforms.

Worse, what if they managed to get inside the compound only to learn their people had already been moved off planet?

She couldn't worry about that now. First things first. Clear the barricade on their side of the gate. Then get inside and get the injured medical treatment. Once that was done, she could begin the process of learning who from the *Tarrant* had survived the attack. She knew first-hand that the survivors would need to be debriefed, but only after she made sure they understood they were about to go home.

"All right, Corporal. Let's get our people ready. I want everyone in place and ready to move as soon as that barricade is down."

"Understood, Ma'am."

Eagerly, the young man raced off to spread the word. God help them all if, after all this, he discovered that his brother wasn't among the POWs.

*   *   *

"That's it," O'Donnell commented from Joss's side as the last of the debris comprising the barricade was hauled away.

"Everyone, take your positions!" Joss ordered in return, face grim as he refused to let himself hope. Not yet. "Hold your positions until I say different. I'm hoping this is exactly what it looks like but I don't want anyone taking unnecessary chances."

As he spoke, he realized that those from the *Tarrant* who were still ambulatory were quickly, silently taking up protective positions around him. How easily they fell back onto military protocol. Nothing Kasun had done to them had stripped that dedication and sense of duty from them. Now he prayed he wasn't leading them into another trap.

Slowly, agonizingly slowly, the gate began moving. Joss's hand found the pulsar at his hip and his fingers curled around the grip. If this was a trick of some sort, he would die before returning to Kasun's tender mercies. He would not be a prisoner again.

"You're to stay behind us, Joss," O'Donnell said softly, firmly without taking her eyes from the gate. "I promised Sharra I'd protect you and I'm not about to break that promise."

"You may have to," was all he said.

After what seemed an eternity, the gates finally opened. At first nothing happened. Even so, the evidence of the firefight that had taken place outside the walls was there for all to see. Vehicles looked like they had been picked up and tossed about by giants. Scorch marks covered the buildings beyond. Windows had shattered, covering the area with shards of neo-glass. Someone or something had taken a definite dislike to Kasun and his crew and that alone made them worth listening to.

Then, moving slowly into the breach left when the gate opened, came a squad of Marines. Joss watched warily as they neared. All wore the midnight black armor of the Fuerconese Marine Corps. If that wasn't enough to reassure him, the sight of the Devil Dog insignia each of the Marines wore was. Not even the Callusians would dare take up the Devil Dog's markings and not fear reprisal.

Still, he held everyone where they were and watched as the Marines continued to slowly approach. None of them wore battle helmets. More surprising, their weapons were holstered or slung across their backs. Only those sporting the markings of medical personnel carried anything in their hands and they carried multiple medical kits.

Without a word, Joss pushed through his pack of guard dogs. As he did, O'Donnell hissed a warning. Joss merely lifted a hand, signaling for her to hold her post. If anyone was going to risk himself by meeting these newcomers it would be him. Besides, if this was a trap, Joss planned on taking as many of them with him as he could before they took him down.

"Lieutenant Donnelly, Taskforce 119 and FirstBatt are now on station," a woman said as she stepped forward and snapped to attention. "We may be late, LT, but we are here and I promise you, those bastards responsible for destroying the *Tarrant* and invading the system will pay."

Unable to believe his eyes any more than he had his ears earlier, Joss could only shake his head. Then, scanning the faces of the Marines waiting for him to give them permission to see to the wounded, he knew it was no trick. They were the Devil Dog and the Callusians had been defeated. Then the cheers of the POWs filled the air and he broke out of his reverie.

"Lieutenant, I know you must have a number of questions. I'll answer all of them. I promise. But I recommend you let my people tend to your wounded first," she continued, moving forward, hand extended.

Even as the Marine spoke, Joss's eyes fixed on the Marine standing just behind her. Of all the things he might have expected, this was the very last one.

"Ryan?"

CHAPTER FIFTEEN

RYAN DONNELLY ROCKED FROM TOE TO HEEL, FIGHTING THE EVER increasing urge to rush through the gate come what may. The gate was moving so slowly, too slowly. He wanted – no, he needed – to find out what awaited them inside. Not just for himself but for his parents and the families of the others from the *Tarrant_*who waited to find out if their loved ones had survived the ambush.

But, no matter how badly he wanted to rush ahead, he couldn't. Colonel Shaw was right about needing to do all they could to reassure the POWs. A battle-ready Marine racing through the still opening gates would do anything but reassure them. So all he could do was wait, throttle down her anxiety and wait.

That didn't mean he had to like it though.

Finally, after what seemed an eternity, the gate finished its slow trek. Colonel Shaw nodded once and softly reminded them to stay wary but to make no sudden moves. Then she started toward the opening, moving with a careful ease they all tried to imitate.

Eyes carefully scanning the area as they entered the POW compound, Ryan stayed close to Shaw. Then he saw the small knot of people to their right. Despite their bedraggled, battered appearances, there was no doubting their military bearing. Then they parted, obviously reluctantly, and a man about his height limped forward.

"Joss," he whispered.

Moving toward them, limping heavily, was the one person he had prayed they'd find. Joss might be hurt, he might look like he'd been through hell the last few months, but he was alive. Just then, nothing else mattered.

"Hold position, Corporal," Shaw said softly when he took a step forward.

He nodded, internally raging against the order. But she was right. They needed to be sure no surprises awaited them. At least there were others with them who could do so because he couldn't take his eyes off his brother. Relief vied with worry as he watched Joss continue his slow trek in their direction.

The right side of Joss' face was swollen and bruised. That eye was swollen shut. Blood streaked his face and his shipboard uniform was tattered and worn.

But it was the almost animalistic wariness reflected in the one dark eye not swollen shut that worried Ryan. What had those bastards done to his brother?

Time stood still for Ryan as he stared at his older brother in disbelief. Metal bands with several links of chain hanging from them were locked about Joss's wrists. He stood before them, his expression wary. None of the instant humor and warmth Ryan remembered so well was there.

Dear God, what had those bastards done to him?

Slowly, one heartbeat at a time, Ryan forced himself not to turn and go in search of any of the guards who might have been responsible for the injuries his brother bore. The sole part of his brain that still functioned reminded him that she couldn't kill Kasun, the security chief or any of their prisoners out of hand. But, dear God, he wanted to. He wanted it so badly she could taste it. No one treated his brother that way without paying a high price for it. But he could do nothing about – yet.

Breathing deeply, mouth clamped tight to keep from cursing aloud, he looked to Shaw for guidance. He knew the Colonel would know how to deal with the situation. Besides, he had a feeling Shaw wouldn't let the injuries Joss and the others had suffered go unpunished.

Until then, all he could do was keep his emotions under control. But it was so very hard. He hadn't felt such depths of anger since the attack on Fuercon. That day, he had been forced to admit Fuercon wasn't as safe from he had always believed. The enemy had brought the fight home, at least for a short time. That had shattered the peace of mind of the entire planet and it had proven just how unprepared they had been for a direct attack.

But this was different. It was personal and he would make sure those responsible for the attack on the *Tarrant* paid

"Colonel?" Anger roughened his voice.

"Easy, Ryan," she soothed. "Let's keep it chilled."

He nodded. She was right, not that it made waiting any easier.

"Lieutenant Donnelly, Taskforce 119 and FirstBatt are now on station," the colonel said as she stepped forward and snapped to attention. "We may be late, LT, but we are here and I promise you, those bastards responsible for destroying the *Tarrant* and invading the system will pay."

From where he stood, Ryan watched as his brother considered what Shaw said. For a moment, Joss didn't seem to react. Then he looked at Ryan and the younger O'Donnell stood rooted in place. Would his brother accept that they were there to help or had the Callusians managed to break him?

"Ryan?"

Disbelief filled Joss' voice. Then he stepped forward, one hand reaching out for his brother. Ryan didn't wait for Shaw.

He stepped around her, closing the distance between him and his brother.

"Mom wanted to know why you missed Sunday dinner," he choked. His eyes burned and he fought the urge to grab his brother up in a hug.

"You can tell her I had something unexpected come up." Joss' smile might not have reached his eyes but at least he'd tried. That had to count for something.

Didn't it?

* * *

It was a dream. It had to be. There could be no other explanation. When the *Tarrant* was attacked, he'd known they would all die. But Julia Sykes had proven one last time why she was such a respected ship's commander. As she ordered most of the crew to abandon ship, she had all major systems slaved to her console on the bridge. Once that had been done, she'd ordered the bridge crew to get to the escape pods. They all knew it was a fool's errand and none of them had wanted to abandon their CO. But Sykes simply looked at them, told them it had been a pleasure to serve with each of them and then told them to get the hell off her ship. She needed them to get word back to Fuercon about what happened. It was their duty just as it was hers to buy them as much time as she could.

Now, unbelievably, it seemed like at least the few who still survived would be able to not only get her message home but make sure FleetCom knew of her sacrifice.

Please, God, let this be real.

Painfully, hesitantly because it could all be a fragile dream, he stepped forward. Stopping several feet away from the woman who had identified herself as Colonel Shaw, he did his best to brace to attention. Head held high, body as erect as possible after the abuse it had suffered, he drew the tattered shreds of his dignity and pride close around him. No matter why they were there, no matter what the ultimate cost, he would do nothing to bring shame on the memory of Lt. Commander Sykes. He owed her that much and so much more.

"Lt. Joshua Donnelly, Colonel."

"At ease, LT." She smiled and reached out to shake his hand. "I know this is a lot to take in right now but we're here to take you and your people home."

"Thank you, Ma'am. There are survivors from the *Tarrant* as well as members of the embassy staff here along with prisoners the Callusians took when they invaded."

"I understand, LT, and we'll take care of it." She turned and motioned to the others of her party to move forward. "I'd appreciate it if you would tell your people to stand down so we can check them and do what we can to make them comfortable until we can get everyone re-settled."

He nodded and motioned to O'Donnell. She nodded in understanding and then sent others to relay his orders. As they did, he turned his attention back to the Marines.

"Now, LT, I'd appreciate it if you'd take a few minutes to reassure your brother that you're all right. Once you have, the medics will take a look at you. Then you and I need to have a talk."

"Yes, Ma'am." Now he turned to his brother. "What the hell are you doing here, Ryan?"

"I think I'm saving your ass, big brother." Ryan grinned and, for the first time since waking in the infirmary, Joss felt himself smiling in return.

"Donnelly, report back to me in ten," the woman said before moving off.

Joss suddenly found himself engulfed in a bear hug. His brother held him close. Then, a few moments later, he released him and stepped back. His eyes shone with unshed tears and Joss knew his looked the same. It was all almost too much to take in.

"Damn, big brother, I've seen you looking better."

"I don't know, kid. I think I look pretty good considering the alternative."

Just then, he would take battered and bruised over blown to bits any day of the week.

"So do I, big brother. So do I."

They walked slowly in the direction of the other POWs. As they did, Joss watched as medics and Marines moved carefully among the wounded. Even though he couldn't hear what was being said, he had a pretty good idea just from the body language of the Marines and the expressions on the faces of the POWs. Reassurances and promises that things were going to be better.

God, he prayed it was all true.

"Joss, look at me," Ryan said softly.

He did as his brother said.

"Joss, you're going home. I promise. But I'll warn you right now, Mom's going to make you wish you were back here the way she'll hover over you." Joss grinned. He couldn't help it. Their mother was a hoverer. She wouldn't give him a chance to breathe in her attempt to make sure he was all right.

And that sounded very, very good just then.

"I need to talk to the others, Ryan. They need to know that this isn't some trick."

"I understand. Let's go. Then you're going to let the medics take a look at you."

He nodded. Maybe by then his brain would have caught up with everything that had happened.

*　*　*

The moment Donnelly brothers moved off, Ashlyn turned, her expression cold and hard. In the time she had been dirt-side, he had seen enough to know her worst fears were true. The Callusians had done their best to break their prisoners. It showed in their eyes and in the way they hunched their shoulders. Haunted eyes peered out at her from sunken

232

features. Everywhere she looked, a POW showed all the signs of physical torture. Worse, their eyes spoke volumes about the mental and emotional tortures they had endured. Clearly, the taskforce had come none too soon.

"What can you tell me, Luce?" she asked as Ortega joined her.

"That I want to kill those mother-fuckers," her XO growled.

Worried, Ashlyn turned to study her. Ortega's jaw was clinched so tightly it was a miracle she hadn't ground her teeth to dust. Her right eye twitched madly. Far worse was the hatred smoldering in her eyes. Ashlyn breathed deeply and then nodded for her to continue.

"Ash, these poor bastards were nothing more than *things* to be used, abused and killed at the whim of Kasun and the guards." She stopped and visibly struggled to get control of her emotions. "Ash, from what we're hearing, they used some of the POWs, male and female, as sex slaves. Others were forced to take part in *medical research*. That doesn't even touch on the pure torture all had to endure."

"Make sure your people document it all for me, Luce. We'll begin the debriefings as the POWs are processed by the medics." Ashlyn frowned and closed her eyes to shut out the sights before her. Unfortunately, it didn't help. Nothing short of vengeance for those poor souls would and she knew it.

"Put a detail to work processing the POWs. Separate our people from the natives. Until we can transport our folks off-planet, they'll have to remain here. But move them onto the attack shuttles. We'll house the other POWs in the administration buildings until we can return them to their homes. Right now, however, our first order of business has to be getting them cleaned, fed and treated."

"Understood, Ash."

"I want to meet with you, Talbot and Adamson in three

hours. I'd like preliminary numbers on the POWs as well as our prisoners at that time. Then I need to meet with company commanders. Colonel Johnson will be sending down reinforcements shortly."

"Yes, Ma'am. I'll get right on it." For a moment Ortega studied the scene as the Devil Dogs continued to move among the POWs, doing their best to reassure them. "Ma'am, if I may, I recommend Corporal Donnelly stay close to his brother, at least for the moment."

"Agreed. I'll leave it to you to make sure both he and Captain Nichols know." A sigh, heavy and heartfelt, escaped Ashlyn's lips. "We've a great deal to do and no time to waste. Sooner or later the Callusians will send a ship – or more – in-system to find out what's happened. I'd like to have local defenses shored up and be well away from here by then."

"You know the Devil Dogs will get it done, Ash," Ortega said.

"Most definitely. It's what we do," Ash replied and then watched as Ortega hurried off. Then she keyed on her comm. It was time to report in.

CHAPTER SIXTEEN

GODS BE DAMNED, HOW DID THIS HAPPEN?

Anton Kasun, once Occupational Governor of the Cassius System, sat on the narrow cot and dropped his head into his hands. As he did, the terrible irony of it all hit him like a rock. He now occupied the same cell that son-of-a-bitch Donnelly had. And, like Donnelly on most occasions, he now wore nothing but his skivvies as he shivered in the cold and damp.

Could this be a prelude to something more, another reminder of how he had failed? He couldn't be sure, not now. Not after the impossible had already happened.

How the hell had those Fuerconese bastards managed to retake the system without High Command at least having some warning about what they were about to do?

"On your feet, scum," a rough, brutally cold voice ordered from the cell door.

Heart jumping, a moan forcing its way out of tightly clamped lips, Kasun forced himself not to start nervously. But the sound of a heavy boot on the cell floor broke through the tattered vestiges of self-control. Trying not to tremble, Kasun shoved to his feet, cursing this sudden reversal of roles.

Without a word, the Marine grabbed Kasun and threw him against the far wall. Before the former *governor* could catch his breath, his arms were painfully twisted behind him and secured. Then he was propelled out of the cell, surrounded by four battle armored Marines who looked as if they would like nothing more than to erase him from existence in the most painful manner possible.

Shuffling along between the Marines, Kasun shook his head in disbelief. Each cell in the block was occupied by his people, one per cell. Like him, they had been stripped down to their underwear. Some, like Peltier, showed signs of having been on the losing end of a very brutal beating. Worse, they all had the air of hopelessness he was beginning to know all too well.

A few minutes later, he was convinced that his worst nightmares had suddenly come to life. The Marines paused before a simple, ordinary looking door on the lowest level of the cell block. It was a door Kasun knew all too well. Without a word, one of the Marines activated the controls and the door slid open, revealing the small room every prisoner wanted to avoid.

"No!"

Frantically, uselessly, he tried to dig his bare heels into the cold stone of the floor. Scrabbling for any traction to keep from being forced inside, he fought against the hands holding him. He knew what could happen in that room, what had happened there. He wouldn't let them put him in. He wouldn't.

But there was little he could do about it. With a look of disgust, the first Marine, aided by the strength given him by his powered battle armor, simply grabbed the struggling man by the scruff of the neck and tossed him inside. At his command, the others quickly carried Kasun to the metal chair bolted to the floor at the end of the room's small table. Ankles, wrists, waist and neck were quickly encircled by powered metal bands, securing him to the chair.

Helpless, so scared he was hyperventilating, Kasun waited.

Why couldn't this be a nightmare he would soon awaken from?

* * *

Joss lay still, assessing how he felt. He ached, not that that was anything new. There had hardly been a day since awakening in the infirmary when he hadn't hurt somewhere. But there was something different this time. The aches didn't seem as bad and there wasn't a damp chill in the air.

For one moment, he fought for control as he realized he was not in his cell. Then, before the fear could take over, memory of the events of the previous day washed over him. If it hadn't all been some sort of dream, he was free. And not just him. All the POWs, those from the *Tarrant* as well as those taken when Cassius Prime fell. They were safe and free and the Callusians who had imprisoned them were now the ones sitting in the cells, wondering what was going to happen next.

Carefully, Joss sat up and swung his legs over the edge of the bunk. As he looked around, he smiled in relief. It hadn't been a dream. He really was onboard one of the attack shuttles from Taskforce 119. More importantly, the other bunks in the cabin were occupied by the other survivors from the *Tarrant*, at least those who weren't in need of constant medical supervision.

Before he could get to his feet, Joss smiled slightly to see Ashlyn Shaw moving all but silently in his direction. She had shed her battle armor but still carried her battle pack and weapons. Then, seeing him sitting up, the Colonel smiled and hurried forward.

"Shh."

She held a finger to her lips and motioned to where O'Donnell and Levitson slept in the nearest bunks. Nodding, Joss carefully stood, wincing slightly as his injured knee screamed in pain. That had been just one of a number of injuries the medics had been unable to do much for with the relatively primitive facilities of the compound. But they would soon be able to transfer to the *Cassin Young* and other ships of taskforce. Then all of the former POWs would be able to get the treatment they needed.

Without another word, Shaw led Joss through to the next cabin. As he stepped through the hatch, Joss felt his eyes go wide at the sight that greeted him. Laid out on several makeshift tables was more food than he had seen at one time since his last leave. More enticing than all the food were the steaming pots of coffee and tea that invited him to all but dive in. Not quite sure what he should do, he looked to the Colonel for guidance. A smile that held an understanding he didn't understand, she reached for a mug and poured a cup of coffee. Taking that as his cue, Joss did the same. Then he brought the mug to his lips, inhaling the rich aroma before carefully sipping.

"The medics have left some very explicit orders for you, Donnelly" she began, motioning him to one of the benches against the bulkhead. "You are to shower and change. Then you are to eat your fill. Once you have, Admiral Collins wants to meet with you."

"But—"

Part of him wanted to do exactly as Shaw said. But another part rebelled. He was an officer of the Fuerconese Navy. That meant his duty was to give the Admiral his briefing first, before seeing to his own needs.

"Donnelly – Joss, more than anyone else here, I know what you're feeling right now," Shaw said and a cloud seemed to pass over her expression. Then it was gone. "Believe me, the Admiral knows the medic's orders and agrees. It's out of your hands. So eat your fill and then we'll get you into some clean clothes."

"Colonel."

"Look at it this way. You want to make sure your people from the *Tarrant* are all right. You want to deal with Kasun and his people, to let them see that they didn't break you and the others. And you want to reassure your brother that you're all right. Does that sound about right?"

A nod was all he could manage.

"Then do as the medics want. The sight of you, the filth of this place washed off and dressed in a clean uniform, will do more to reassure your people and your brother than anything else you could do or say. As for Kasun and the others, well, seeing you in a clean uniform and back among your own will have more of an impact on them than you going in looking bedraggled and hungry."

She was right. That didn't make it any easier though. Still, he would be better prepared for what he needed to do after eating.

"All right," he agreed. "But I'm not sure there's enough coffee on this shuttle to make up for all of it I've missed since the *Tarrant* was attacked."

Laughing, Shaw reached out and snagged one of the carafes and topped off his mug. Then, leaning back, she took a moment to study him.

"You'll do, Donnelly. You'll do." She lifted her mug in salute. "And I promise, there is more than enough coffee for all of you. If not, I'll make sure we scrounge some up for you. Now you'd best eat something before the medics come in and have both our heads."

Half an hour later, dressed in a fresh uniform, Joss watched as the lift doors slid open. He waited as first Colonel Shaw and then Captain Ortega stepped into the corridor. Then, as the next highest ranking officer, he followed. Close on his heels were Master Gunnery Sergeant Talbot and two Marine ratings.

Memory of the corridor filled him and his breath caught in his throat. He breathed deeply, fighting for calm. He knew this corridor well, too well. Nothing good ever happened down here. At least this time he wasn't in chains. It wasn't his nightmare he was walking into.

He hoped.

* * *

Hearing the door to the room slide open, Collins turned. His expression lit at the sight before him. Ashlyn Shaw and the other Devil Dogs looked ready to handle anything that might happen. They were the muscle. The sword to strike down anyone or anything foolish enough to try to attack. If all went right over the next hour or so, all they would have to do is stand there and put the fear of God in the former Occupation Governor. If something happened, well, he knew enough to keep out of the way as they handled it.

But it was the sight of Lt. Joss Donnelly that reassured him. Six hours of sleep, as well as food, a shower, change of clothes and medical treatment had eased some of the doubt and distrust from his expression. It would take time for him to get over all that had happened but he would. At least Collins hoped he would.

"What do you think, Lieutenant?" he asked, motioning to the screen in front of him.

Donnelly moved to stand beside him, his attention fully focused on the image he indicated. A low growl, no other word could really describe the sound, escaped his lips and he nodded in satisfaction. For not the first time, Collins wondered exactly what Kasun and those under his command had done to the POWs. But this was neither the time nor the place to go into it.

"It's fitting, Sir." Joss said softly. "He would have us taken in there to be *questioned*. But, as you can see, it is really more for his own amusement."

Joss nodded to the various instruments that hung on the wall behind Kasun's chair. As he did, it was Collins who all but growled in anger. Joss had just confirmed his fears. Now he wanted nothing more than to use some of those same instruments on the man responsible for the injury and deaths of so many others. But he couldn't, no matter how badly he wanted to. But he could do something else, something he felt sure would scare Kasun as much.

"Are you ready to face him, Lieutenant?"

"Yes, Sir."

For a long moment, Collins studied the younger man. The last thing he could afford was for Joss to do something foolish. Then he nodded in satisfaction. He saw Joss' anger, even his thirst for vengeance. But he also saw young man's control, a control that was almost as scary as his need for revenge because of how it had been forged.

"Then let's go."

With that he led Joss out of the room, Ashlyn and the other Devil Dogs on their heels. As they entered the interrogation room, Collins had to fight to hold back a laugh of satisfaction. Almost against his will, Kasun had turned his head to see who had entered. The fear that leapt onto his expression had been priceless, especially as the man's eyes locked on Joss. Then Kasun began struggling helplessly against the metal bands securing him to the chair, all but keening in panic as he realized just how helpless his situation was.

While Collins moved to sit at the opposite end of the table, Joss walked to stand behind his former captor. Collins eyed him warily, not sure what the lieutenant had in mind. Then, as he gave an almost imperceptible signal to Ashlyn to stand ready, he began to relax. Instead of acting, Joss simply stood there, his eyes never leaving the top of the former governor's head. That was enough. Sweat pricked out on Kasun's face and he turned pleading eyes to the Admiral.

"K-keep him away from me!"

"Quiet!" Collins snapped in return. Kasun flinched, biting his lip to keep as if to keep from saying anything else.

"Lieutenant Donnelly is here at my request not only to represent the POWs but to also make sure you tell us the truth.

"Now, you were told yesterday that the only way to insure we didn't leave you here to face your own people was to give us the access codes to the computers. That meant all the computers. It seems you failed to do that. I'm going to give you ten seconds to comply."

"All right," Kasun sobbed, rattling off a series of commands one of the Marines took note of.

"Now, are there any POWs, either Cassian or Fuerconese, on planet housed anywhere besides here?"

"No!"

"He lies, Sir," Joss said simply, coldly.

"I said, no lies." Collins pinned the man with a steely look.

Before he could continue, Collins sucked in a breath in fear. Joss had leaned over Kasun, his hands sliding down the man's shoulders and across his chest. Then he put his mouth next to the man's ear and whispered something that drained all the color from his face. A thin line of spittle dribbled from one corner of Kasun's mouth and his eyes all but rolled back in their sockets. Joss whispered something else and then straightened, leaving his hands on the man's shoulders.

What happened then was something Collins would never forget. Kasun began speaking so rapidly he had to tell him to slow down. The former governor listed several other locations, remote sites, where POWs who had been selected to be sent off-planet as slaves were taken to be *trained*. Once he was done, Kasun collapsed against his bonds, sobbing uncontrollably.

"You bastard," Joss said softly, venom all but dripping from her voice. "If anyone else has died because of you, I will make sure your worst nightmares come true."

Listening to him, Collins swallowed hard. The hatred in Joss' voice spoke volumes. Whatever had happened since the destruction of the *Tarrant* had left a mark on the young man, one that would be a long time in healing.

"Captain, let's leave it now to Colonel Shaw and her people. They'll keep us informed of the status in the search for the other locations," Collins suggested as Joss moved almost reluctantly away from Kasun.

"Sir, I'd like to accompany them," Joss said. "Please."

"No, Lieutenant. I need you to remain here."

"Admiral, you don't understand. I *need* to do this."

"Joss," Ashlyn began, taking a step toward him.

Collins watched as Joss turned to her. For a moment, rebellion filled the lieutenant's eyes. Then he inhaled deeply and nodded once. At the same time, he stepped away from Kasun. The moment he did, Talbot motioned for the two ratings to take the lieutenant's place.

"Yes, ma'am?"

'Joss, I've been where you are. I've been a prisoner, completely at another's mercy, unable to help myself much less those I was responsible for. God knows how much I've wanted to be able to get vengeance on those responsible for what happened to me and to them."

Collins waited, wondering how Joss would react. When he didn't say anything, Ashlyn continued.

"Right now, you need to stand down. It is my job to make sure those responsible for what happened to the *Tarrant* and to the Cassians are taken into custody. Believe me, FleetCom will take care of them." Now she reached out and lightly rested her right hand on his arm. "LT, what's going to happen isn't your kind of mission. I'm sorry but you would be a distraction and a liability. I can't let you go with us."

"Colonel Shaw is right, Donnelly," Collins said. "But, so you know what's happening, we'll make sure you're tied into the battle-net. That way you can monitor the mission. Will that be satisfactory?"

"Just find them and then take us home," he said softly. "Please."

"Lieutenant, nothing would give me greater pleasure," Collins assured him. "Colonel, will you see to it that he's tied into the 'net?"

"Of course, Sir."

"Very well. We will let you continue the interrogation, Colonel. Keep me informed if the governor has anything else of import to say."

"Roger that, Sir." She paused and looked at Donnelly. "With your permission, Admiral, I'll leave Captain Ortega to conduct the interrogation while I get the rest of Alpha Company ready to follow up on the information he gave us about the other POWs."

"Very good, Colonel. See to it." He nodded and started out of the room. At the door he stopped and turned back. "Donnelly, you're with me."

It was better to remove the lieutenant from the temptation to do something foolish than to leave him there.

CHAPTER SEVENTEEN

DAMN THEM ALL TO HELL AND BACK AGAIN!

Evan Moreau angrily paced up and down the length of her office. She desperately wanted to throw back her head and scream in frustration. That bitch Ashlyn Shaw and her supporters had done it to her again. Despite everything she had done to find out what FleetCom and the government had planned, they had managed to send a mission to the Cassius System without word of it leaking until it was too late. Now, not only had FleetCom sent ships in an attempt to break the interdiction around the system, they had managed to liberate the system and retake Cassius Prime. Worse, the Devil Dogs, under Shaw's leadership, had played a major role in it all.

That was bad enough. Worse was the fact that her employer would not take kindly to finding out that her government sources had apparently dried up. If she could no longer pass along information about what Harper and his allies planned before they managed to put it into action, she lost much of her value to those who currently employed her. Worse, if they decided to make an example of those they held responsible for the loss of the Cassius System, she knew her life would be forfeit.

Damn it!

But they hadn't beaten her. Not yet. She still had sources she could squeeze. Better yet, she had people she could offer up to her employers in her stead, starting with that idiot Kannady. All she had to do was stay one step ahead of everyone. She'd made a living doing just that for years and she wasn't about to stumble now.

First things first. She would make sure those arrested in connection to the false charges against Shaw received another *reminder* about what would happen if they even thought about cooperating with the authorities. O'Brien was still confined to the medical ward. So he was out of reach. Too many questions would be asked if anything else happened to Sorkowski. But there were others who could be used.

Yes, that would work and it would satisfy her employers that she had at least that part of her assignment under control. As for the rest of it, she'd simply be proactive. She'd send a report tonight to her handler outlining how one of her political contacts had betrayed her by giving her bad information. It would mean sacrificing that contact, so she needed to be careful about who she named. Not that it really mattered as long as it bought her time to cover her own tracks.

She poured and drink and stared at the amber liquid in her glass. How had things gone so wrong so quickly? It was rare when she was caught this much off-guard. She had to find her center again and do so quickly. Either that or she had to go off-world. If she didn't, she had a feeling her days were numbered.

The only problem was she didn't know by whom.

*　*　*

"Donnelly, I need a moment of your time," Admiral Collins said as he entered prefab that served as field hospital until they could transport the POWs shipboard.

Three days had passed since Task Force 119 retook Cassius Prime. Since then, the Devil Dogs has been scouring the Capital, looking for any of the invaders that had managed to slip away in the confusion of the initial attack. Now, as they were slowly returning the POWs to their families and helping the surviving members of the government figure out just where the System stood, Collins knew it was time to start thinking about sending the survivors from the *Tarrant* home.

The one truly negative note from the last three days came from Ashlyn Shaw. She had led Alpha Company as they attempted to locate the remote compounds Kasun told them about. Unfortunately, when the Callusian overseers learned they were surrounded, they had killed their prisoners and then themselves. Forty seven POWs, half a dozen of them from the *Tarrant*, had died and Collins would never forgive himself for not getting to them sooner.

Now, standing in the field hospital, Collins frowned and shook his head in resignation. Medical teams from every ship in the taskforce had been working around the clock to treat the POWs, civilian and military alike. Even so, too many of them were so badly injured they might not recover.

They had learned from Kasun's records that close to three dozen crewmembers from the *Tarrant* had been picked up after they'd abandoned ship. Most of the rest of the crew had died when the Callusian ships had simply destroyed their escape pods. Of those three dozen, only a dozen still survived. But they had fared better than the embassy staff had. The Callusians had killed most of the Marines assigned to guard Fuercon's embassy. Only four Marines still lived and the civilian staff hadn't fared much better.

"Yes, Sir?" Ryan Donnelly asked as he braced to attention.

Collins put him at his ease before continuing. "How's your brother?"

"Sir?" His brow furrowed in question.

"Son, I know you've been spending as much time as you can with your brother. Colonel Shaw has been keeping me informed. What I need to know is how your brother is and if he's said anything about what happened to him and his shipmates that I need to know?"

"Honestly, sir?"

Collins nodded and waited for the young man to continue.

"I'd gladly give up my career, even my life, to kill Kasun, Peltier and all the others for what they've done to him," Donnelly said.

"I happen to agree. But that's the last thing we can do, no matter how badly we want to. Not yet at any rate."

"I can't say I like it, Sir, but I do understand."

"Frankly, Donnelly, I don't agree either but we have no other choice right now. If we do anything else, we will prove ourselves no better than the Callusians." He pinned the young man with a firm look and held his gaze until he nodded reluctantly.

"Now" Collins continued. "I really do need you to answer my question."

For a long moment, Donnelly said nothing. Then he blew out a breath. "Sir, I think Joss is damned lucky to be alive. He tried to argue when Lt. Commander Sykes ordered the bridge crew to abandon ship. It's a miracle his escape pod wasn't one of those destroyed by the enemy and it's a miracle those sadistic bastards didn't kill him later. It's going to take him time to get over what happened, but he will."

"I happen to agree," Collins said. "But has he told you anything you think I need to know."

"No, Sir. To be honest, he hasn't said much of anything about what happened to him. He asks about his people, even the civilian POWs, but that's about it. As I said, it is going to take time for him to get over what happened."

Collins frowned. He understood. He had seen too many of their people after they'd spent time as *guests* of the Callusians. The enemy had turned torture, mental and physical, into an art form. No one who spent more than a very short time in their custody emerged unscathed. Not that it helped the taskforce just then. They needed to know if the Callusians were going to be sending more ships to the system anytime soon. Until reinforcements arrived from Fuercon and their allies, they risked losing the system again if the enemy sent a large enough force.

"All right. Get back to your brother. Let me know if he says anything that might help us know when, or even if, the enemy is scheduled to send supplies or reinforcements."

With that, Collins turned and left. Striding across the compound, two Marines at his back, he sent word for Captain Jareau to set up a briefing with the taskforce's senior officers.

*　*　*

Kasun paced the short length of the cell and cursed long and hard. He still didn't understand how everything had gone so bad so quickly. When he had accepted the position of Occupation Governor, his superiors had assured him of the system's security. Those fools on Fuercon wouldn't try to retake the system. Not now. Not after so much time had passed. There was no way, those same superiors told him, that the system would ever come under attack. It was, in short, the closest assignment to perfection possible.

All he had to do was run system efficiently, providing the manpower and other material needed. The powers-that-be really didn't care what he did with the POWs as long as he continued to supply *workers* when needed. He had done all that and more. But it hadn't been enough to keep those Fuerconese bastards from invading.

And he knew exactly who the High Council would blame. He would be the one they'd point to, saying he should have had better defensive systems and procedures. But what could they expect? They had taken away most of his ships and troops. He'd had to make do with systems damaged in the invasion and not yet fully repaired and troops no other commander would take.

None of what happened was his fault. If anyone was to blame, it was the High Council. They should have anticipated what Fuercon did. What good was this new partner in the war if they didn't get the information needed to anticipate an attack by Fuercon or its allies?

He was damned if he was going to take the fall for their mistakes.

* * *

"Ten-hut!"

The dozen men and women sitting at the conference table quickly climbed to their feet. Before they could brace to attention, Collins waved them back to their seats. He was tired and there was just too much to do to worry about protocol just then. Even so, they waited for him to be seated before returning to their chairs.

"Thank you, Conrad. As long as we have coffee, I think we're fine. I'll send for you if I need you." He waited until his steward left the room before continuing. "All right, everyone. You know the task ahead of us. We are to hold the System until reinforcements arrive. The good news is, that should happen within the week. Word from FleetCom is that Second Fleet will be arriving in the next five to seven days. Once it arrives, we will hand over command and control and return home."

He nodded to see the relieved looks almost everyone at the table wore. Everyone had been working long hours, often pushing themselves and those under their commands to exhaustion, to make sure the capital as well as the system was safe.

"However, before we start relaxing too much, let me remind you that we don't know when, or if, the enemy will be returning to the system. The records we've recovered give no indication about patrol or delivery schedules and that worries me. Captain Jareau?"

"Thank you, Sir." His executive officer activated the holo screen over the table. A moment later, the system map appeared. "This is a real-time representation of the System. The green dots are our ships. The blue are the defense platforms and the red are mine fields. The yellow dots represent planned minefields. The green dots are sensor arrays.

"Thanks to Chief Murozovski's crews, the defense platforms are fully operational. The security codes have been changed so the enemy will not be able to easily hack into them should they return."

"Excellent, Jules. Thank you." Collins nodded in appreciation. "Colonel Shaw?"

"The defense station has been cleared. After the Devil Dogs made the initial breach, Colonel Johnson's troops held it while they did search and rescue. They found no Cassians onboard. Records indicate the few staffing the station at the time of the invasion were killed in the initial attempt to take over the station. Since it is basically fully automated, the Callusians kept only a skeleton crew onboard.

"We are still working to make sure there are no pockets of enemy resistance anywhere in the capital or any of the major cities. It is slow going but the Resistance has been a great deal of help. The good news is, the Callusians pulled out most of their troops before we arrived. The bad news is we don't know why and we don't have an accurate count of how many they left behind. My professional opinion is that we make sure the major cities are cleared and then leave it to the locals to check the outer areas."

"I happen to agree with you, Colonel. There is one thing to remember, it won't be our decision in the long run. By the time FleetCom decides, Second Fleet will be on station and we will be on our way home."

"Sounds good to me, Sir." Ashlyn grinned slightly and he

understood. How could he not when part of his last briefing package from Fuercon had included a reminder from her mother that Ashlyn needed to be home in time to participate in the courts martial of O'Brien and Sorkowski.

Now Collins turned his attention to Joss Donnelly. The lieutenant sat near the far end of the table, looking slightly discomfited to be included in the briefing. "If you're up to it, Lt. Donnelly, I think it is time for us to hear what you can tell us about what happened to the *Tarrant* and after you and your crewmates abandoned ship."

"Yes, Sir."

Donnelly sat up a little straighter and his expression turned serious. Seeing the difficulty he appeared to be having, Collins decided to help out. "Lieutenant," he began quietly, almost gently. "Start with that last day on the *Tarrant*. What happened?"

Donnelly nodded once again and closed his eyes. A moment later, he opened them and reached for his mug. He sipped and then began. "Sir, we were on a standard courier mission. We had dispatches from home for the embassy. It had been an easy trip, nothing out of the ordinary happening. Because of that, Commander Sykes didn't have extra crew on duty."

Donnelly paused and swallowed. The pain of what happened was written on his face. "As we crossed over into the system, we prepared to squawk our ID. Then scanners picked up a reading that didn't make any sense. Commander Sykes was notified. It didn't take long to figure out what was happening. The commander ordered our course altered and we did our best to stay out of sensor range as she began collecting data to send back to FleetCom."

"Did you have any confirmation at the time of who the invaders were?" Captain Jareau asked.

"Negative. The invader's ships weren't squawking IDs and

the configurations didn't match anything we had in our databases." He paused and it looked like he was trying to remember something. "No, that's not completely correct. CIC made a possible ID but I never heard what it was. When they relayed it to the commander, she said they had to be wrong. That there was no way they would be taking part in something like this."

"You're sure she didn't say anything that could help us ID the ships?" Collins asked.

"I don't remember, Sir. Everything was happening so fast by then. We'd been spotted and LACs as well as several cruisers were closing on us. Commander Sykes ordered all but a skeleton crew to get to the escape pods. She waited for them to launch and then altered our course again in an attempt to draw the enemy ships away from the pods. But it wasn't enough. The LACs opened fired and picked the pods off one by one. Then they turned their attention to the *Tarrant*.

"The commander kept gathering data and preparing it for transmission home. Once she had, she ordered us to slave our consoles to hers. When we had, she ordered us to abandon ship. She knew the *Tarrant* was doomed. But she was going to do whatever it took to make sure FleetCom knew what was going on.

"Admiral, none of us wanted to leave her but she insisted. She told us we had a duty to get away and make sure FleetCom knew what had happened. It was up to us to make sure the sacrifices of our crewmates was remembered and honored. Then she told us to get the hell off her bridge." He drew a ragged breath and Collins felt for him. He'd never had to abandon ship before and especially not do so and leave behind someone he respected and liked as much as Donnelly clearly had Sykes.

"None of us blames any of you for what happened, Lieutenant," he assured the younger man. "You did not only what your CO ordered but what was necessary. Remember that."

"I'll try, Sir."

He went on to describe his anger as he watched the *Tarrant* destroyed in a hail of missiles. He still didn't know how his escape pod survived when so many others were destroyed. It was towed onto one of the Callusian ships and he was pulled out. Before he could react, he'd been beaten unconscious. The next thing he knew, he was in the infirmary dirtside and was one of only the too few survivors from the *Tarrant*.

"Lieutenant, did you ever see anyone who didn't seem to belong with the invaders?" Ashlyn asked. Before anyone else could say anything, she continued. "I'm not talking one of the prisoners. I mean someone who appeared to be working with the invaders, perhaps in a consultation role or something." Now she paused, frustration reflected in her eyes. "What you told us about the CIC report to your commander and then her response to it worries me. It also tends to lend confirmation to something I've been wondering about. Is it possible the Callusians have found themselves an ally, someone we don't know about?"

Collins looked at her in surprise. Then he shook his head. She was right. If there was a third party they didn't know about, a lot of what had happened the last few months made sense. God, could there be someone out there acting behind the scenes, possibly even directing the actions of the Callusians?

If there was, they were screwed, at least as long as they didn't know who it was.

Damn it all to hell and back again.

"No. Once I was on-planet, I never saw anyone but the Callusians or other POWs. Sorry, Ma'am."

"Don't apologize, Lieutenant. You've helped us more than

you know," Collins told him. "Are there any other questions for the lieutenant?" He glanced around the table, waiting to make sure no one spoke. "Very well, Lieutenant. You are dismissed."

"Thank you, Sir." He stood and braced to attention before leaving the room.

"Thoughts?" Collins asked once the door slid shut behind Donnelly.

"We need to finish going through the data we've recovered, Sir," Jareau said thoughtfully. "And we need to have another go at the senior POWs, especially the *governor*." She almost spat the word out.

"I agree with her, Sir," Ashlyn said and the others nodded in agreement.

"Very well. Jules, I leave that part up to you. Everyone else, get me your reports and recommendations by morning. I wish I could tell you to stand down from alert status but I can't. Not yet and certainly not after what Donnelly had to say. You can share our concerns with your senior staff but no one else. At least not until we know more."

He stood and waited for the others to follow suit. Once they had, he dismissed them. Watching as they left the room, he wondered how what had started out as a rather straightforward mission had gotten so complicated.

CHAPTER EIGHTEEN

"WHO THE HELL YOU THINK YOU ARE?" HE DEMANDED, SLAMMING his bottle of beer onto the table.

The sound of glass striking the table's surface cut through the noise of the nearby conversations. Voices hushed and heads turned in their direction to see what was going on. Even as they did, Evan Moreau cursed silently. She knew she should have chosen a more secure location for this meeting but time had been of the essence, especially since Kannady had insisted they meet somewhere public. The seedy tavern was far off the beaten path of the politically active and the media hounds that it might as well not exist. But that didn't rule out the underbelly of society and Moreau knew it. In fact, she counted on it. That seedy element would have a role to play in the night's agenda that her companion had no idea about and she planned to keep it that way.

"Keep your voice down!" she snapped as several heads turned in their direction continued to watch and wait for what was to come next. There were too many people around, too many ears to overhear what he might say. Did he always have to act such a fool? "You should know by now not to question me. So quit acting the fool and start thinking of how to turn the situation to our advantage."

"Our advantage!" Outrage warred with disbelief as he looked at her. "There is no advantage to this situation."

Sighing heavily, fighting to keep her calm, she reached out and tapped his hand with one expertly manicured fingernail. When he turned bleak eyes on her, she gave him a quelling look.

"There is always an advantage to be found if you look hard enough," she corrected softly, willing him to believe it.

"But—"

"No buts, Kannady. Think about it. Your stocks are going to rise now that we are at war. The news that we have moved to retake the Cassius System from the Callusians will ease some of the fears investors have had recently. This is a win-win situation for you – as long as you keep your head and don't blow it."

She spoke firmly, doing her best to make him understand that this was certainly not the time to try to strike at their common enemy. How in the world had he lasted so long in the business world without understanding its basic working of politics? Pure, dumb luck didn't seem to be answer enough.

"Right now, Harper's popularity is higher that it's been since he was elected as president." She continued softly, leaning into him so no one beyond the table could hear her. "He responded quickly and decisively to the attack on Ahlstrom's Landing. He sent the taskforce to the Cassius System and retook it from the Callusians. He even gave the public the hero they wanted in the form of that bitch Shaw. But his star will fall. Just give it time."

"Dammit, I know that!" he exploded. "What you don't seem to understand is that time is the one thing neither of us has."

"There you are wrong. We have all the time in the world, as long as we keep our heads," she said simply and he stared at her in disbelief. "Your constant need for reassurance, your panicked responses to news items is a threat to all of us, not just you and not just me. Our *friends* do not like the attention your actions could call to their work."

"We have to back off for a while before the authorities figure out what's happening!"

"I'll tell you what. If you want to call off our arrangement, fine. Just don't think about marching yourself down and telling the authorities what we've been up to. That's the sort of thing that will sign your own warrant of imprisonment but that of the rest of your family as well."

"You bitch!" he rasped, eyes hard with hate.

"You knew that going into all this," she countered. "Now put your emotions behind you and do what needs to be done. And don't contact me again. I'll let you know when – and if – we need to meet."

With that, she climbed to her feet and all but glided across the room and outside. If she had to stay one more minute in his presence, she would kill him. Not that she had to. That was already taken care of.

As she stepped outside, she nodded to a man all but hidden in the shadows. He nodded in return and slipped away. Grinning, relieved to know at least one problem was about to disappear, she continued down the street. She'd go home and wash off the stink of this place. Then she might just go out to celebrate.

Things were starting to look up again.

* * *

Kasun jerked awake as a hand closed about his throat and roughly hauled him to his feet. Gurgling as he tried to breathe, his hands clawed frantically at the fingers crushing his larynx. Despite it all, he struggled futilely against the merciless grasp. Then, as he felt himself losing consciousness, he was flying through the air. He smashed into the far wall, breath exploding from his lungs. Without realizing it, he slid down the wall to the floor as if he didn't have a bone in his body.

Then the hand closed about his arm, hauling him upright once more. Cold, hard eyes that he knew would haunt his nightmares for the rest of his life locked on his. Hatred deeper than any he had ever known stared out at him and he knew in that moment what it was like to look Death in the face.

"No!" he screamed, insides turning to water. "Please. What do you want?" Tears filled his eyes and he pulled helplessly against that implacable grip. Even with the benefit of her battle armor, how could she be so strong?

"You have one chance only to tell me what I want or you're dead and no one here will do a thing to stop me," the woman rasped, nodding to the half dozen Marines standing behind her.

The sight of them scared Kasun almost as much as the woman did. They looked at him with impassive eyes, cold and dead. Even as Shaw lifted him so his toes barely touched the ground, they simply stood there, for all the world as if they were simply watching her toy with an annoying pest before killing it.

"What? Tell me what you want to know," he pleaded.

"There are other databanks. Where? And where are the backups?"

For a moment he stared at her in disbelief. Then he swallowed hard to see the way her muscles gathered once more to toss him about like so much unwanted baggage. His one moment of triumph, the one thing he knew could keep him alive once High Command learned he had lost the system, fled. Somehow she had found out about those damned data chips he had recovered from the office safe before the first wave of Marines landed. But how?

Peltier.

That spineless weasel had told them. There was no other explanation. Damn that traitor. He'd pay. If it was the last thing Kasun did, he'd make Peltier pay.

But now he had to figure out what to do. If he gave them the data chips, he signed his death warrant with High Command. But he if didn't, he had no doubts Shaw would kill him right there. It was a no-win situation.

But what choice did he really have? At least he bought himself some time if he gave them what they were looking for. Of course, he didn't have to give them all the 'chips. There was no way Peltier knew how many there were, much less what they contained. Give them something and buy some time to figure out what his next move should be.

"You have five seconds," Shaw told him.

"All right!" he sobbed. "They're in the anteroom of my office. There's a safe hidden in a false bottom of the safe on the eastern wall."

"How do we access it?"

"I'm the only one who can."

"Don't take me for a fool, Kasun," she said almost conversationally as she shoved him toward the Marines. One of them caught and held him in a grasp that made hers feel like a lover's embrace.

"Let me put it to you in a way even you can't ignore." She moved to stand before him, holding his face so he couldn't look away, her fingers bruising the soft flesh of his cheeks. "Each of these Marines fought in the last war. They lost friends, family and brothers-in-arms. They would dearly love to do to you what you and your people did to our fellow Marines. So either tell me exactly how to access the contents of that safe without damaging them in any way or I'll turn you over to them. It won't take them long to start taking you apart, piece by very little piece.

"You can't! The Accords!"

"Accords!" the Marine holding him bellowed, spinning him around like a rag doll so they stood face-to-face. "We'll respect the Accords exactly as much as you did."

Gorge rose like lava flowing over the dome of an active volcano. He had finally met someone more coldly cruel than him. No doubt these Marines would willingly, even gladly kill him if he didn't tell them what they wanted to know. Gods above and below, protect him.

"All right!" he all but screamed and the information they wanted spewed from his mouth almost without bidding.

Hopefully it was enough to keep them from hurting him any further.

"Master Guns, I leave him to you and your people. Find out if there's any other information he has that we need," Shaw said coldly before turning to leave.

"No!" Kasun screamed as the Marines closed in around him.

* * *

Ashlyn entered her quarters and shut the door behind her. As she did, she cursed long and hard. Everything she had done before as a Marine had fallen squarely within the boundaries of the Accords. There had been times when she'd been tempted to cross the line but she never had. Until today.

Today she broke the oaths she had taken as a Marine and as an officer to uphold the laws of Fuercon and to abide by the Accords that governed how war was conducted. Not that the Callusians had ever felt constrained to follow the Accords. But they weren't the Callusians. They were better and that meant they had to obey the rules.

But things had changed for her as she listened to Joss Donnelly recall what had happened onboard the *Tarrant*. A sense of urgency had filled her. From the moment she first realized the capital was under attack and she had to do whatever was necessary to protect Miranda Tremayne, she had known there was something different to what was happening. It was as though the Callusians had changed the rules without telling the other players.

Well, two could play that game. If breaking the rules was what it took to protect her homeworld, she would.

And it had been worth it. When she had finally located the cache of datachips, she'd known they were important. Why else would Kasun have hidden them of all the 'chips he possessed? The only problem was she didn't know what they contained. She had logged them in and then turned them over to the computer techs.

A soft beep announced someone outside her door. She breathed deeply and prepared herself. Then she pressed the control panel next to her bed. As the door slid open, she stood, ready to be taken into custody – again.

"You can quit looking like you are about to meet the executioner, Ashlyn," Collins said as he stepped inside and the door closed behind him. "No one is reporting what you did but you owe Talbot and the others a big thank you. They saved your ass back there. Apparently you were big and bad enough to scare the hell out of that bastard Kasun. He is still babbling his head off."

She exhaled a long, shaky breath. Knees weak, she sank onto the edge of the bed. Then, remembering that she might be in her quarters but that a senior officer was present, she pushed back to her feet and braced to attention.

"But don't relax yet. I know why you acted as you did. Hell, girl, I'd have done it myself. However, that was your one pass. And, to make sure you don't do anything else as foolish as that, you are to report back to the ship. You can coordinate with Colonel Johnson the relief of the Devil Dogs by his troops. I don't want to see your ass dirtside again without my direct permission. Understood?"

"Sir, yes, Sir!"

"Good." Now his expression softened. "Ash, I do understand and, to be honest, preliminary reports sound like you hit the goldmine. But I will not have you risking your career again. Pack your kit and report to the shuttle. You have an hour."

"Thank you, Sir."

The moment he left the room, she collapsed onto the bed. Then, realizing that Collins has given her a reprieve, she stood. There was a lot to do, starting with briefing her staff, before reporting to the shuttle.

CHAPTER NINETEEN

ALEXANDER WATCHMAN STORMED INTO THE CONFERENCE ROOM and threw the hard copy report onto the table. Its pages went flying, scattering much as those unfortunate souls present wished they could. The Intelligence Tsar in this mood was never something anyone wanted to see much less be close to. Too often people died and each of the four present enjoyed living too much to sit still and let that happen.

But what could they do?

"Sit," he growled, waving for them to resume their places. As he did, he dropped onto his own chair at the head of the table. Almost instantly, a page appeared and poured him a cup of tea before quickly leaving the room.

"Now," Watchman continued coldly. "Would someone care to tell me what the hell happened?"

From his place down the table, Admiral Boniface swallowed almost audibly. If anyone was likely to be blamed for what happened, it was him and everyone present knew it. After all, he had been the one to send that fool Kasun out to the Cassius System as Occupation Governor. He had been the one to convince the others that it was safe to rely upon the Callusians to hold the system without additional reinforcements.

"Sir, our reports are still preliminary at best," he began, glancing down at his data pad. "It is going to take time to get a more complete picture of what happened."

"I know that," Watchman drawled coldly. "What I want to know is how did those Fuerconese bastards manage to not only plan but execute an operation against our assets in the Cassius System without us finding out?"

"We just don't know," Boniface said and Federov nodded in agreement from across the table. "Everything pointed to the fact that they weren't going to make a move against the system. They had waited so long. Then, when word of the attack on the Nystrom System reached them, they reacted immediately. All our analysts said that was a clear sign they had written off the Cassius System.

"Obviously, we were wrong. My guess is that President Harper or someone from FleetCom went looking through their intelligence reports and realized our *allies* had withdrawn a number of their ships from the system. If the Callusians had done as we instructed and left their forces intact, none of this would have happened."

"Federov?" Watchman turned a dark look on the man, his upper lip curling slightly to see how the younger man blanched slightly before speaking.

"The Admiral's correct as far as my sources have been able to determine. We know now that FleetCom has been in a major buildup since Harper took office. It could be that they delayed going to the Cassius System until they had more hulls available.

"All right. I don't like it but everything the two of you say makes sense. However, there is one aspect of the operation that clearly failed us." Watchman paused again, this time looking at the ceiling thoughtfully. "Our operative on Fuercon should have known about the operation and should have warned us. She did not. So the question becomes did she miss something or has she turned on us? The next question is even more important. Is it possible the Fuerconese could have recovered anything from Cassius Prime that could point to our involvement in the war?"

"Doubtful on both counts," Boniface replied. "Our operative has never failed us before and has never shown any indication that she might betray us. She, more than most, knows the penalty for that. After all, she is who we usually send to exact punishment from those who fail to do what they promise. I think it is simply a case of her having to build a new network within FleetCom after the changes following the election."

"And Cassius Prime?"

"Again, doubtful. Our so-called allies know the price of letting the Fuerconese know of our involvement before we are ready."

"But we can't be sure," Federov put in, ignoring the glare Boniface turned on him. "Sir, we have to face facts. The Callusians may be useful at the moment but they are also a time bomb ticking down toward detonation. We can't rely upon them to do as we say. Their egos and their damned sense of superiority mean they aren't going to be in any mood to do as we say unless we use a very big stick to enforce them. And as for Moreau, I think it's time we consider that she has outlived her usefulness."

"Very well. Contact the cadre on Fuercon. Inform them that they are to do two things as soon as the taskforce returns. They are to determine what, if anything, was discovered on Cassius Prime. If there is anything that ties the Callusians to us, it has to be destroyed or new evidence planted that will make the incriminating evidence appear to be something it isn't. I don't give a damn how they do it. Just get it done.

"Secondly, they are to make sure any prisoners brought back from the Cassius System are silenced before they can talk.

Once that is done, they are to deal with Moreau. When they do, they need to make sure they retrieve any records she has kept of her work for us."

"Yes, sir," the two men answered in unison.

"Federov, I want to meet with the Callusian representative on-planet. It's time that he make it very clear to his superiors that they have to play this by our rules or we will make sure Fuercon destroys them."

"Sir, I'm not sure there's a way in Hell we can do that," the man said softly.

"Well I am and that's all that really matters, isn't it?"

"Yes, Sir." He swallowed hard.

"Then see to it, both of you. I want reports from you by mid-day tomorrow."

They both scrabbled to their feet, relived to be getting out of the room alive. Now, if they could just make sure they stayed that way. . . .

*　*　*

The sound of ice cubes clinking against the crystal high ball glass broke the silence of the apartment. Smiling in satisfaction, Evan Moreau refilled her glass. She deserved the extra drink. Everything had gone exactly according to plan. It couldn't have been better had she done it herself.

Well, that wasn't exactly true. If she had done it herself, she would have had the satisfaction of seeing the fear in Kannady's eyes just before he died. But it had been too dangerous for her to do it. Besides, this way she had an alibi on the off-chance the authorities did come to question her. After all, who would believe she snuck off to kill someone when she had the Assistant Attorney General in her bed?

It had been a stroke of luck she'd run into him at the restaurant. Not only did he give her an alibi should she need one but he was more than passable as a lover. What better way to celebrate taking care of a problem than with a good meal, even better whiskey and some satisfying lovemaking?

Now she had to make sure her employers didn't blame her for what happened. That ought to be easy enough. In a few days, the assassin she'd hired would turn up dead, killed in an apparent argument over a debt. She'd make sure there was enough evidence found on him to tie him to Kannady's murder. Then she could concentrate on the real task at hand – keeping Watchman and his people thinking she was an asset.

Smiling slightly, confident that she could pull it off long enough to get safely away, she poured a second glass of whiskey. She did, after all, have a lover waiting for her. She might as well make sure he enjoyed himself enough that he would have no trouble remembering where he was should she need him to confirm her alibi. Morning would be soon enough to worry about the rest of it.

First things first, she reminded herself. *You've waited this long. A little longer won't hurt.*

* * *

Lucinda Ortega stepped inside the gym deep in Marine territory onboard the *Cassin Young* and paused. As she did, a smile of approval touched her lips. No matter what the time, the gym was always in use. Even so, there seemed to be more Marines taking advantage of the gym than usual. Nor was there any mistaking the sense of approval and watchfulness that filled the air. No matter what they were doing, whether working with free weights or sparring with a partner, each Marine stood ready to act if anyone or anything should bother one of their own.

Understanding, Ortega scanned the faces of those present and then nodded in satisfaction. Across the gym was the object of her search. Dressed in a traditional gi, Ashlyn worked her way through a series of progressively more difficult katas. Her dark hair was pulled back in a single braid. Perspiration glistened on her face and stained the top of her gi. Her face was a mask of determination as she moved, her body obeying her mind's demand for precision in execution.

Since her return from Tarsus, Ashlyn had spent as much time in the gym as she could. Ortega knew it was partly a stress reliever for her friend. She suspected another part of it was the need Ash had to never feel helpless again. Whatever the case, in the months since she had been freed, she had put on much of the weight she had lost. Even better was the improved muscle tone she sported. But best of all was seeing her confidence return.

"Very nice," Ortega commented in approval and stepped up to the mat as Ash finished the last kata and began a series of stretches to let her muscles cool down without stiffening.

"Thanks," she replied with a grin.

With that, Ash once more turned her attention to her stretches. At the same time, Talbot stepped forward, stopping next to Ortega. Together they watched as Ash finished her stretches. As they did, Ortega wondered if Talbot had been as worried about their CO and friend as she had. Something had happened on Cassius Prime and she had a feeling it was something bad. Why else would Ashlyn have suddenly been sent back to the ship? But no one, not Ashlyn and not Talbot, who was with her almost every moment she was awake, would tell Ortega what happened.

A few minutes later, Ash left the mat, accepting a towel from Talbot and using it to scrub the perspiration from her face. Ortega chuckled softly when Ashlyn tossed the towel at the man. Talbot snorted in response and snatched the towel in midair just before it connected with his face. Ash laughed gaily before turning her attention to Ortega.

"You here for a workout, Luce?"

"I thought I might get in a quick swim," she admitted and then shrugged, coming to a quick decision. "But the main reason I'm here is to find you. I was hoping you'd join me for dinner in my quarters tonight."

"Sure. Give me a few minutes to shower and change. Grab your swim if you want."

"Naw. It really was just an excuse." She grinned as Ash shook her head, a smile playing at the corners of the Colonel's mouth as she recognized the truth in what her friend said.

Ashlyn nodded and moved quickly in the direction of the adjoining locker room. Ortega watched closely, approving of what she saw. A nod here, an encouraging smile there, a touch and a laugh where needed. Yes, Ashlyn had come a long way since her return from Tarsus. But she wasn't back to normal. Not yet and Ortega wondered what she could do to help before her friend imploded.

"Ma'am?" Talbot prompted.

"You have the night off, Kevin," she said. "I've had a chance to review the security arrangements for our arrival home. I downloaded them to your terminal. I'd like you to review them and have your comments and recommendations to me by twenty hundred hours."

"Yes, Ma'am."

"In the meantime." Now she smiled and clapped a friendly hand on the woman's shoulder. "You know, Loco, it would help if you told me what happened just before Angel got herself sent back to the ship."

"I know, Ma'am, but it's not my story to tell." Talbot spoke softly, concern reflected in his eyes. "Talk to the Colonel. She needs to be the one to tell you."

"I know." But the question was, would she? "Go on, Loco. I'll see what I can do about getting her to tell me."

"Tell you what?" Ash asked as she rejoined them, surprising them both by how quickly she had reappeared.

"It can wait," Ortega replied with what she hoped was an easy grin. "If you're ready, let's get out of here. I want to kick back and relax for a while."

CHAPTER TWENTY

SAFELY TUCKED AWAY FROM THE PRYING EYES OF THE MEDIA, A small group waited in a private landing bay near the main government complex. Four people, two men and two women, huddled close together, speaking in hushed voices. Nearby stood a Marine security detail.

"Five minutes, Ma'am," one of the Marines reported softly and General Okafor nodded in response.

"Thank you, Captain Andrews." She turned to her companion as Andrews stepped back. "Is everything ready?"

"It is," Elizabeth assured her. "The cars are waiting and the media hasn't found out what's happening."

"Excellent."

She studied the others for a moment and smiled slightly. There would be time later to brief the press. That would come after she'd had a chance to debrief her officers and report first to SecDef and then to the President. But today was for something else. Today she would make sure everyone had come through the mission without any lasting scars, mental or physical.

To her relief, the mission had gone much better than she'd hoped. All the care they had taken to make sure no one leaked their plans had paid off. No one, not the media and not the enemy, realized what Taskforce 119 was about to do. With all that could have gone wrong, it was amazing nothing had. She could have been meeting the caskets of her people instead of being here to welcome them home. She would take that any day over the alternative.

Besides, I wouldn't take this away from Liz and Abe if my life depended on it.

She knew how hard it had been on them to watch Ashlyn shipping out so soon after finally getting her home from Tarsus. If there had been anyone else she could have sent on the mission, she would have. But Ash was the best and, now that they were at war again, they needed the best.

A few minutes later, a muted chiming signaled the approach of an incoming shuttle. Everyone gathered watched expectantly as the pilot expertly maneuvered the craft into the bay and to a gentle landing. Instantly, the docking bay crew rushed forward to assist with the shutdown.

As they waited, Elizabeth slid her hand into her husband's. Abe pulled her close, his arms going gently around her. He held her against him in a protective embrace.

Together they watched as the shuttle hatch slid open. A few minutes later, Admiral Collins emerged from the shuttle. He walked down the ramp. Then he turned and watched as the rest of his party appeared.

"Thank God," Elizabeth said softly as her daughter appeared.

"I told you she'd make it home." Okafor grinned and then watched as the remaining passengers disembarked."

* * *

As the shuttle came to a gentle landing, the four Marines comprising the security complement quickly assumed their stations. Two took up places by the forward hatch while the other two moved to the rear of the shuttle. At the same time, the pilot initiated systems shutdown. As he did, the co-pilot confirmed the departure of the second shuttle for the clinic. Admiral Collins nodded in response and climbed to his feet.

From where she sat, Ashlyn breathed deeply, stomach churning and heart pounding. The fear she had held at bay since first boarding the shuttle burst forth with terrifying strength. Collins may have looked the other way when she violated the Accords but that didn't mean everyone else would. She'd already seen how the military courts could be manipulated and she knew she still had enemies in the Corps. When she stepped off the shuttle would she be met by her family or by MPs there to arrest her?

Swallowing hard, she forced herself to remain calm. If the MPs were there, she would deal with. Not that she'd have much choice in the matter. She'd known when she assaulted Kasun what the risks were. But, if it meant finding something to help end the war just one day sooner, it was worth it, even if it meant a return to the Tarsus military prison.

And, from what little they had been told in the Admiral's briefings, it had been worth it. Much of the data still had to be deciphered. But, what they had deciphered pointed to another party working with the Callusians. If true, that would explain why the *Tarrant* hadn't been able to initially identify the ships attacking it. It would also explain the differences, slight though they might be, in the Callusian tactics this time. Now, if they could only find something to prove – or disprove – it all, it would have been worth it.

No, if true, she wanted to know who the secret partner was. Until then, Fuercon was in danger.

"Are you ready, Ash?" Collins asked as she forced herself to her feet.

"Honestly?" she asked with a smile as shaky as her knees felt. He nodded, an understanding gleam in his eyes. "I'm terrified and you know why."

"Ash." He stepped closer, pitching his voice for her ears

only. "There's nothing to be afraid of. I promise."

"I hope you're right," she said just as softly, not fully convinced.

Collins gave her hand a reassuring squeeze before moving toward the forward hatch.

As she waited for permission to disembark, Ash breathed deeply, striving for calm. Talbot stood just behind her. When she glanced back at him, he smiled and leaned close to whisper something in her ear. A soft chuckle escaped her lips as he reminded her once again that this was her time, her chance to thumb her nose at all those who had betrayed her. After all, they must be choking on fear to know that she'd made it back in time for their trials. Lips twitching in an attempt not to smile, she softly thanked him. Then, reaching for her slim briefcase, she squared her shoulders and prepared to meet her fate.

Suddenly, the hatch slid open with a muted *swoosh*. With one last glance around the cabin, Collins stepped out. Swallowing hard, reminding herself she was next to disembark, Ashlyn moved toward the hatch, Talbot close behind.

This was it. Was she going to get to go home or would she find herself on her way back to Tarsus?

As she stepped into the waiting area, a wave of emotions crashed over her and she stopped short. Tears burned her eyes relief filled her. No MPs waited to arrest her. No representative from JAG was there to question her. Instead of stony faces of men and women who wanted her head, her parents stood there, waiting for her to join them. With them were General Okafor and a member of her staff. Maybe Collins had been right. Maybe she was being given a pass this time.

She stepped forward, winking at her parents as she moved to stand in front of Okafor. As she braced to attention, she knew she was a very lucky woman. She was home and soon she would be reunited with her son. Before long the war would intrude and she'd have to ship out again. But, for now, she would enjoy what she had.

"General, FirstDiv reporting in," she said and snapped a crisp salute. "It is my honor to report the successful completion of our mission," she added with a slight smile.

"Welcome home, Colonel." Okafor extended her hand in greeting.

"Thank you, Ma'am. It's good to be here."

"Ashlyn, you did good." Okafor's approval meant a great deal. "Your orders now are to go home and spend some time with your son. No working and no worrying about the Devil Dogs. I've already issued orders that they have leave today and tomorrow. You can have your final debrief after that."

"Thank you, Ma'am."

"Don't thank me yet. As CO, you aren't getting as much time off. I want to see you in my office tomorrow for your after action report."

"Yes, Ma'am," Ashlyn said, once again worried that her actions were going to come back to haunt her. "When do you want to meet?"

"0900. We won't be able to keep the lid on the media much longer than that I'm afraid," Okafor replied seriously. "As soon as they know the taskforce has returned, they are going to be clamoring for interviews."

"That's above my pay-grade, Ma'am."

"Only if I say so, Colonel," Okafor countered with a grin.

"Whatever you say, Ma'am." Ashlyn braced to attention once more.

"Until tomorrow, Colonel," Okafor said. Then she turned and left the waiting area, her Marine escort following close behind.

As they left, Ashlyn turned to face her parents. The strain of her being off on a mission showed on their faces. She didn't remember seeing it before when she would return home. But then, those times had been before her stint on Tarsus. Those two years, and the events leading up to them, had taken a toll on all of them. Hopefully, with the court martial of Sorkowski, O'Brien and the others, they could start getting past that horrible time.

At least she hoped so.

Before Ash could take more than one hesitant step forward, her mother all but flew across the room in her direction. Ashlyn stood rooted in place and opened her arms. A moment later, she found herself folded into her mother's welcoming embrace as tears flowed unchecked down her cheeks.

Then her father was there. They stood in a tight knot, arms around each other, doing their best to reassure themselves it wasn't a dream. Ashlyn buried her face against her father's chest, breathing deeply the same evergreen scent she remembered from childhood. That, almost as much as her mother's tears of joy, finally convinced her she wasn't going to be talking to the MPs anytime soon.

"Mama, Daddy," she whispered in joy as she freed a hand to scrub away her tears. "I'm home."

"You are, baby. You really are," Abe said as he grinned down at her.

"And we're going to coddle you and spoil you for the next few days," her mother added, eyes shining brightly with tears as yet unshed.

"I just want to go home, Mama. That's all."

"And that's exactly where we're headed," Elizabeth assured her. "Transportation's waiting."

"Thank you." She smiled and said a quick prayer of thanks. Another mission successfully completed and another homecoming. "Is Jake there?"

"Of course, dearest," Elizabeth assured her, sliding an arm

about her waist. "He wanted to come but your father and I thought it would be better if he waited there for us."

"Besides, he said he had something he needed to finish before you got home," her father added.

Grinning, looking forward to being able to hold her son again, Ashlyn let her parents lead her away. As she did, she knew there was nothing better than coming home.

*　　*　　*

"Are you sure?" President Derek Harper restlessly paced the length of his office, his expression troubled.

"Everything is preliminary yet, Mr. President, but I am confident the computer techs have interpreted the data correctly," Rico Santiago said. He stood before the President's desk, closely tracking the man's movements as he paced.

"Helen?"

"You know my thoughts on the matter, sir. I've said from the moment the capital was attacked that there was more to what happened than we thought. If the techs are right about the data, this proves it."

Harper returned to his desk. Instead of sitting, he leaned against it. For a moment, he didn't say anything. Instead, he stared at something none of the others could see. Then he nodded, his mind apparently made up.

"All right. Let's get all the people on this that we need. I want that data deciphered ASAP. In the meantime, Rico, find out what you can about our so-called friends. Start with their embassy staff. History has taught us nothing if not that you intelligence folks like to use diplomatic postings as cover for intelligence work."

"Right away, sir."

"Helen, I know you had planned on sending the Devil Dogs out after they had some time to recover from the mission. However, until we have finished going over the data, I want them held here. Those bastards have already attacked us once.

If they try again, I want our best Marines here to hold them off."

"Yes, sir."

"As soon as you have more information for us, Rico, we'll put together a plan of attack. I'll pull in the rest of the command staff when we do. Until then, keep this between the three of us."

"Mr. President, what about Colonel Shaw and Admiral Collins? I have no doubt they share our concerns and have possibly shared them with their staffs." Okafor's concern was clear.

"I will have a chat with the admiral tomorrow. We're playing a round of golf. I'll leave it to you to make sure Shaw understands my instructions about the matter." Now he took his place behind the desk. For the first time since they had entered the office, some of his worry appeared to have eased. "Now get out of here before someone starts asking why I'm meeting with the two of you."

Okafor and Santiago saluted and left the office. As they did, Harper leaned back and sighed. If their suspicions were correct, things were going to get a lot worse before they got better.

*　　*　　*

I don't think I can stand much more of this, Ashlyn said to herself and slipped outside.

As she stepped into the dark stillness of the night, she sighed in relief. This day, wonderful as it had been, had also been difficult to endure. She understood her family was glad she was home. Hell, she was glad to be home. But all the togetherness had been too much. She needed time to decompress after the mission, to accept all she had done and why she had done it.

At least she hadn't lost the ability to slip her parents' loving but all too often unwanted supervision. A faint smile touched her lips at the memory of other times she had snuck out to meet friends. All her life her parents had protected her, had her guarded simply because of who they were. Wanting a "normal" life, she had perfected ways to sneak away from the house so she could enjoy some adolescent foolishness without some overzealous adult trying to stop her.

What did surprise her, however, was the fact she had managed to slip away from her son. Since her return from Tarsus, Jake had made it his job to act as her escort and body guard whenever she was home. So how had she managed to get away from him tonight? Not that it really mattered. All that did was that she was finally alone.

Breathing deeply, Ashlyn closed her eyes and simply let her other senses register her surroundings. How wonderful it was to feel the soft breeze against her cheeks, to smell the slightly salty fragrance of the sea just beyond the ridge to the north. She could stand there forever, simply treasuring these simple pleasures.

A soft footstep behind her broke her reverie. She tensed, prepared to react to an attack should it come. Then she forced herself to relax, reminding herself she was home now and not on the front line. She was safe. She needed to remember that.

Turning, Ashlyn smiled to see her mother moving almost silently in her direction. As she did, she chuckled softly. She hadn't been as good at slipping out as she thought. Not that it mattered. All that did in that moment was the love and concern reflected in her mother's eyes and the love she felt blossoming almost painfully in her chest.

"Are you all right?" Elizabeth asked softly as she reached for her daughter's hands.

"I am. I just needed a few moments."

"I know it's been a little overwhelming, darling. I'm sorry. It's just that we're so glad you're home."

"And I'm glad to be here, Mama," Ash assured her. "But

you're right. It is overwhelming. As much as I love all of you and am glad to be home, I need time to decompress after the mission. I hope you understand."

"Of course I do, Ash. We all do."

Ash smiled slightly and let her mother pull her close. As Elizabeth's arms wrapped around her, she did her best to push aside the worry that had nagged at her since finding the data chips. Fuercon had been betrayed by an ally. She knew it. She could feel it in her bones. But was there enough on those chips to convince FleetCom, much less the politicians who set policy?

More importantly, would they understand the data before it was too late?

"Come on, Mama. Isn't it about time for dessert?"

She linked her arm through her mother's and led her inside. She wasn't going to find the answers to her questions tonight. So she might as well enjoy being home with her family. There would be plenty of time later to figure out what the next step should be.

At least she hoped there would be.

AUTHOR'S NOTE

VENGEANCE FROM ASHES, THE FIRST BOOK IN THIS SERIES, WAS A book that was a long time in the works. The germs of the story were planted years ago, when I found a battered copy of Heinlein's *Starship Troopers* in a closet at my grandmother's. Another foray into that same closet, which looked like it was where my grandmother stored all the books and records my father and his five siblings had left at the family homestead, yielded more books by Heinlein, early copies of *If* and more. I read the stories, dreamed of spaceships and adventures and I was hooked.

Vengeance turned into a book I had to write. It had several other iterations. But the basic premise has always been the same – duty and honor and family. Family doesn't necessarily begin and end with your blood relations. It can also be those men and women who are your brothers-at-arms.

Duty from Ashes builds upon those themes. There is, deep inside most of us, a strength to do what needs to be done. It isn't always for ourselves. More often than not, it is for others. That strength can lead to self-sacrifice or to glory, often when glory isn't sought

Duty is the second of a three book story arc. There will probably be more books in this universe, possibly centering on

Lt. Joss Donnelly. But the first three books will center on Ashlyn and her fight to do her duty as well as her need to get vengeance – and justice -- for the wrongs done to her people.

IF YOU ENJOYED *DUTY FROM ASHES*, CHECK OUT THESE TITLES BY THE AUTHOR:

VENGEANCE FROM ASHES
(Book 1 of *Honor and Duty*)

First, they took away her command. Then they took away her freedom. But they couldn't take away her duty and honor. Now they want her back.

Captain Ashlyn Shaw has survived two years in a brutal military prison. Now those who betrayed her are offering the chance for freedom. All she has to do is trust them not to betray her and her people again. If she can do that, and if she can survive the war that looms on the horizon, she can reclaim her life and get the vengeance she's dreamed of for so long.

But only if she can forget the betrayal and do her duty.

Check out these titles written as Amanda S. Green:

NOCTURNAL ORIGINS (*Nocturnal Lives*, Book 1)

Some things can never be forgotten, no matter how hard you try.

Detective Sergeant Mackenzie Santos knows that bitter lesson all too well. The day she died changed her life and her perception of the world forever. It doesn't matter that everyone, even her doctors, believe a miracle occurred when she awoke in the hospital morgue. Mac knows better. It hadn't been a miracle, at least not a holy one. As far as she's concerned, that's the day the dogs of Hell came for her.

Investigating one of the most horrendous murders in recent Dallas history, Mac also has to break in a new partner and deal with nosy reporters who follow her every move and who publish confidential details of the investigation without a qualm.

Complicating matters even more, Mac learns the truth about her family and herself, a truth that forces her to deal with the monster within, as well as those on the outside. But none of this matters as much as discovering the identity of the murderer before he can kill again.

NOCTURNAL SERENADE (*Nocturnal Lives*, Books 2)

Lt. Mackenzie Santos of the Dallas Police Department learns there are worst things than finding out you come from a long line of shapeshifters. At least that's what she keeps telling herself. It's not that she resents suddenly discovering she can turn into a jaguar. Nor is it really the fact that no one warned her what might happen to her one day. Although, come to think of it, her mother does have a lot of explaining to do when – and if – Mac ever talks to her again. No, the real problem is how to keep the existence of shapeshifters hidden from the normals, especially when just one piece of forensic evidence in the hands of the wrong technician could lead to their discovery.

Add in blackmail, a long overdue talk with her grandmother about their heritage and an attack on her mother and Mac's life is about to get a lot more complicated. What she wouldn't give for a run-of-the-mill murder to investigate. THAT would be a nice change of pace.

NOCTURNAL INTERLUDE (*Nocturnal Lives*, Book 3)

Lt. Mackenzie Santos swears she will never take another vacation again as long as she lives. The moment she returns home, two federal agents are there to take her into custody. Then she finds out her partner, Sgt. Patricia Collins, as well as several others are missing. Several of the missing have connections to law enforcement. All are connected to Mac through one important and very secret fact -- they are all shapeshifters. Has someone finally discovered that the myths and bad Hollywood movies are actually based on fact or is there something else, something more insidious at work?

Mac finds herself in a race against time not only to save her partner and the others but to discover who was behind their disappearances. As she does, she finds herself dealing with Internal Affairs, dirty cops, the Feds and a possible conspiracy within the shapeshifter community that could not only bring their existence to light but cause a civil war between shifters.

NOCTURNAL HAUNTS (novella)
(Part of the *Nocturnal Lives* series)

Mackenzie Santos has seen just about everything in more than ten years as a cop. The last few months have certainly shown her more than she'd ever expected. When she's called out to a crime scene and has to face the possibility that there are even more monsters walking the Earth than she knew, she finds herself longing for the days before she started turning furry with the full moon.

SWORD OF ARELION
(*Sword of the Gods*, Book 1)

War is coming. The peace and security of the Ardean Imperium is threatened from within and without. The members of the Order of Arelion are sworn to protect the Imperium and enforce the Codes. But the enemy operates in the shadows, corrupting where it can and killing when that fails.

Fallon Mevarel, knight of the Order of Arelion, carried information vital to prevent civil war from breaking out. Cait was nothing, or so she had been told. She was property, to be used and abused until her owner tired of her. What neither Cait nor Fallon knew was that the gods had plans for her, plans that required Fallon to delay his mission.

Plans within plans, plots put in motion long ago, all converge on Cait. She may be destined for greatness, but only if she can stay alive long enough.

Check out these titles written as Ellie Ferguson:

HUNTED

When Meg Finley's parents died, the authorities classified it as a double suicide. Alone, hurting and suddenly the object of the clan's alpha's desire, her life was a nightmare. He didn't care that she was grieving any more than he cared that she was only fifteen. So she'd run and she'd been running ever since. But now, years later, her luck's run out. The alpha's trackers have found her and they're under orders to bring her back, no matter what. Without warning, Meg finds herself in a game of cat and mouse with the trackers in a downtown Dallas parking garage. She's learned a lot over the years but, without help, it might not be enough to escape a fate she knows will be worse than death. What she didn't expect was that help would come from the local clan leader. But would he turn out to be her savior or something else, something much more dangerous?

HUNTER'S DUTY

Maggie Thrasher is looking for a man, not to love but to kill. Duty to her pride and loyalty to her family demands it. Joshua Volk has betrayed pride, pack and clan. All he cares about is destroying the old ways and killing anyone, normal or shape-changer, who gets in his way. Jim Kincade is dedicated to two things: upholding the law and protecting the pride from discovery. When Jim is called to the scene of a possible murder, the last thing he expects is to discover the alleged killer is a tracker from another pride. Now he's faced with a woman who is most definitely more than she appears. Complicating matters even more, there's something about her that calls to him and his leopard is determined to claim her for his own. Joshua Volk is looking for revenge. Maggie killed one of his own. His vengeance will bring Maggie's worst nightmares to life. Is the passion between Maggie and Jim enough to defeat Volk's plans or will Maggie's determination to fulfill her duty to her pride be the death of them both?

HUNTER'S HOME

They say you can never go home. That's something CJ Reamer has long believed. So, when her father suddenly appears on her doorstep, demanding she return home to Montana to "do her duty", she has other plans. Montana hasn't been home for a long time, almost as long as Benjamin Franklin Reamer quit being her father. Dallas is now her home and it's where her heart is. The only problem is her father doesn't like taking "no" for an answer.

When her lover and mate is shot and she learns those responsible come from her birth pride and clan, CJ has no choice but to return to the home she left so long ago. At least she won't be going alone. Clan alphas Matt and Finn Kincade aren't about to take any risks where their friend is concerned. Nor is her mate, Rafe Walkinghorse, going to let her go without him.

Going home means digging up painful memories and family secrets. But will it also mean death – or worse – for CJ and her friends?

WEDDING BELL BLUES

Weddings always bring out the worst in people. Or at least that's the way it seems to Jessica Jones as her younger sister's wedding day approaches. It is bad enough Jessie has to wear a bridesmaid dress that looks like it was designed by a color blind Harlequin. Then there's the best man who is all hands and no manners. Now add in a murder and Jessie's former lover – former because she caught him doing the horizontal tango on their kitchen table with her also-former best friend. It really is almost more than a girl should be expected to handle. . . .

Look for *Honor from Ashes* coming Fall 2015!

www.ingramcontent.com/pod-product-compliance
Lightning Source LLC
Chambersburg PA
CBHW030028180626
46810CB00001B/260